Bitterly, Connecticut, has been a haven for a woman shattered by painful memories—until a handsome stranger appears and threatens to awaken the ghosts of her past...

For the last eleven years, Savannah Callowell has led a peaceful existence in Bitterly. As the owner of an old farm, she's mostly kept to herself, not daring to let anyone get too close. None of her neighbors know that she's haunted by tragedy, and she's done everything possible to escape her ghosts. She thinks she's succeeding, until her new foreman shows up—and he's far from being the college kid she was expecting...

A worldly former professor, Adelmo Gallegos has his own reasons for wanting to hide out on Savvy's farm, and he isn't about to share them with anyone, not even his enticing new boss. Still, Ade can't help himself, the more time he spends with Savannah, the more he longs to lure her out of her protective shell. But how can he convince her that opening her heart is the only way to heal? Especially since he too has secrets he's unwilling to share? Only when the past catches up with them may they be able to free themselves of it...

I0665196

Books by Terri-Lynne DeFino

Seeking Carolina
Dreaming August
Waking Savannah

Published by Kensington Publishing Corporation

Waking Savannah

Terri-Lynne DeFino

LYRICAL PRESS
Kensington Publishing Corp.
www.kensingtonbooks.com

Lyrical Press books are published by
Kensington Publishing Corp. 119 West 40th Street New York, NY 10018

First Electronic Edition: October 2016
eISBN-13: 978-1-60183-522-2
eISBN-10: 1-60183-522-1

First Print Edition: October 2016
ISBN-13: 978-1-60183-523-9
ISBN-10: 11-60183-523-X

To Eric Reynolds, who believed in me first

Acknowledgements

Here, in the third Bitterly Suite book, my sixth published novel, I feel that I've thanked everyone who needs thanking, multiple times. Instead of all those involved in the creation of this book, from writing peers to friends to the staff at Lyrical and Kensington, I'm going to give this space to the ones who shaped the me I've become—my family.

Mom and Dad, thank you for the love that continues to grow and evolve from day one to day forever.

Michael, Mark, Karen, thanks for all the mischief we got into, from dressing Mark in drag to decorating grandma whenever she fell asleep, to Gingey-films at Christmas. With you, I'm always a kid.

Jamie, Scott, Christofer and Grace, thank you for never being embarrassed to hug me in public, for the pride you instill, and the pride you have. Thank you for being the ridiculously cool kids who became truly extraordinary adults. (And by cool, I mean super-geektastic.)

As always, the last thanks goes to my Frankie D, for all the stories I share on Facebook, all the silliness and love and faith, you are my everything.

Chapter 1

memories of other days

I didn't like fireworks when I was a squirt. That boom. Ugh. It made my stomach swish. Having to sit through them ruined the Independence Day picnics for me. I always wished Mom and Pop would let me go home instead of making me stay. Though, really, our house was too close to town for it to have made a difference.

I can't count the Independence Days that've come and gone since then. Time doesn't pass the same way it used to. One minute it's high summer and the fireworks are booming, the next, I'm leaving pebbles in a shoe by the light of the full Hunter's Moon. Maybe that's why I'm still here in this Nowheresville of Nowheresvilles having conversations with myself as if someone's listening. As if I'm telling a story.

* * * *

Thunder rumbled in the blue, July sky. Savannah Callowell understood New England storms well enough to know when the mountains would guide the black clouds beyond Bitterly, and when they'd let them in. Today felt like a welcome mat set out for the electric boom.

She stepped into the yard, shielding her eyes from the sunshine. The Fourth of July town picnic had, once again, been a raging success. In all the years since she moved up from Georgia, there had not been a single rainout. The produce was gone down to the last potato. The few soaps and jellies left were mostly back on the shelves in the farmstand store. Lambs in their pens, chickens in their coop, Savvy's was as restored as it could be until the next harvest came in.

"Good morning, boss." Benny picked her way across the yard, her eight-month old daughter in a baby sling strapped to her chest. Ever since her own life had gone from miserable apathy to marital bliss, Benedetta Grady-Hendricks-Greene had been on a mission to rid the world of unhappiness. Darling Benny. She had no clue, and Savannah wanted to keep it that way.

"Did you get a good rest yesterday?" Benny asked, hefting her baby higher and adjusting the sling.

"I did, thanks." Savannah rubbed at her forehead. July 5th's typical banger of a headache had dulled back to the familiar throb. "Has Dan recovered from the tug-o-war?"

Benny rolled her eyes, added in a dramatic sigh. "My husband seems to think he's still twenty. He'll survive. Probably just a pulled muscle in his shoulder."

"So, what brings you here this morning? You have the next two weeks off."

"I was hoping you had some of that liniment Darla and Sandra make. Dan isn't just delusional, he's stubborn. He won't go to the doctor about his shoulder even though he groaned all night long. As if Irene doesn't keep me awake enough."

Savannah laughed. "I think there might be some left. Come on in."

They went into the farmstand store. Savannah flipped on the lights. Rummaging in the lone box as yet unpacked, she called, "Why don't you make us a cup of tea?"

Savannah only pretended to look for the liniment until she heard Benny clattering around in the office. This time of year left her feeling fragile, and unable to cope with the cheerful chattering her friend was famous for, the chattering that usually brought an affectionate smile to Savannah's lips. Watching Benny's transformation the year prior, from grieving widow to wife and mother, had been magical. For a time, Savannah thought, maybe, her joy would rub off. Honor. Determination. The ferocity that took her from temperate Georgia to finicky Connecticut. Such things gave her purpose, but they were not joy.

Tube of liniment in hand, she joined Benny in the air-conditioned office. Her friend was just pouring hot water from the kettle, and Savannah's frazzled nerves became somewhat less so. She handed over the tube in exchange for a steaming mug. Snuggled against Benny's bounteous chest, Irene slumbered as deeply as only a healthy, happy baby could. Savannah remembered the feel of soft, sweet breath on her neck, in her nostrils. She remembered the heft of not one but two contented little bundles on her chest. She remembered.

Blowing across the top of her mug, fragrant steam carried unwanted thoughts away. "Mmm. Is this the chocolate mint?"

"My favorite." Benny wrinkled her nose. "Dan nearly murdered me when he found out I planted a patch out back."

Savannah's muscles bunched. "Don't say murder. I bet he wasn't even really angry. You're so dramatic."

"True. But it did take over, and started threatening his precious lilies. I should have known better. Mint is so aggressive."

"Did you…" Savannah sipped down the lingering jitters along with the tea. "Did you sow them directly? The mint?"

"What do you mean?"

"Are they in the ground? Or in pots?"

"Ground."

Savannah took another soothing sip. Talking about plants carried her further from that word, from the past. "There's only one way to keep mint from spreading. If you don't want to container-garden, you have to dig up that whole patch and replant a few bunches in those clay chimney flues sunk in the ground. That'll contain the root system. As long as you clip them before they flower and fall, your mint will behave."

"Oh, really? That's so cool. How'd you figure that out?"

"I didn't. Until coming to Connecticut, I never even planted a flower in a pot on my porch. Edgardo and Raul taught me everything I know."

"That's crazy." Benny tugged at a lock of long, dark hair caught in the shoulder strap of the baby sling. Cursing under her breath, she unslung her infant. "I finally got my hair to grow past my chin and I want to hack it all off again, but I refuse to do the new-mom-pixie-cut thing."

Benny set Irene down on the cot in the office. After all the years they'd been friends and coworkers, she still didn't seem to get that there was a reason Savannah gave all her workers two weeks off after Independence Day. Before last year, when Benny came awake again after too many years grieving, her oblivion was understandable. Now, her oblivion felt a little forced. A lot forced. Savannah wouldn't rise to the bait. Not even if Benny asked her outright why she became a hermit for two weeks every July.

"Did Edgardo and Raul get off all right this morning?" Benny sipped, looking at Savannah over the rim of her mug.

"As far as I know. They left on time, at least. I heard them at around three this morning."

"It's so strange to me, them living apart from their families most of the year."

"They must be used to it." Savannah sipped. "They've been working for me for eleven years, and I'm not their first American gig. They're here to plant the first seeds in March and stay until the last of October's pumpkins are cut. At least they go home for these two weeks. I force them to."

"We're lucky to have them." Benny leaned in, whispering, "They've got to be getting old though, don't you think?"

"They can't hear you, Benny."

She slouched back in her chair. "You never know who's listening."

"Well, the pictures tacked to the wall in the double-wide never change. Children? Grandchildren? I have no idea. Maybe both."

"Grandchildren? You think? But they don't have a gray hair between them."

"No, but their faces are lined like roadmaps."

"And yet they don't seem old." Benny harrumphed. "Why do men age so much better than women? Not fair. Not fair at all."

Savannah relaxed despite herself, as the minutes ticked into a chatty hour. Benny laughed easily, drew the same out in her. Even the throbbing in Savannah's head eased. Irene stirred, and then she whimpered. Benny sat on the edge of the cot and nursed her happy again. The back of her tiny blonde head, thick with curls like her daddy's, made Savannah want to twirl her fingers in the swirl at her crown. Baby hair, like baby breath, was the sweetest of things she could imagine.

"Savvy? Yoo-hoo, earth to Savannah." Benny was no longer sitting on the cot but wrapping her baby into the folds and twists of her sling.

"Sorry, my mind wandered."

"Your headache okay?"

"My—oh, yes." Savannah touched her head. "It's fine. What were you saying?"

"I was just saying that I'd better get this little biscuit to her grandma and grandpa's so I can get ready for my big date. It might take a little while to squeeze myself into the dress I bought. Svelte, I have never been. What was I thinking, buying something so tight?"

"Big date?"

Benny leaned in and kissed Savannah's cheek. "You really are still tired," she said. "It's Dan and my anniversary, remember? You were my maid of honor."

"Oh…oh! Benny, I'm so sorry." Savannah hugged her tight. "Happy Anniversary, sugar. May this be the first of many happy years to come."

"If the rest are only a quarter as happy, I'll count myself lucky. Thanks, Savvy."

Savannah walked Benny outside. It still surprised her to see her friend climb into the hybrid car Dan surprised her with on her birthday, rather than onto the scooter she had always ridden. Strapping the baby into her car-seat, Benny said, "We leave for Bar Harbor tomorrow. You sure you have enough help while I'm gone?"

"Don't start that again." Savannah laughed. "There is almost nothing to do but watch the vegetables grow. Besides, I have enough kids available to fetch and carry for me if I need them. Go. Have fun camping. I'm green with envy. Bar Harbor is one of my favorite places on the planet."

"Thanks for the recommendation." Benny tossed the baby wrap into the car and opened her arms to Savannah. "I'll see you in a couple of weeks."

"Bring me back some seashells."

Waving her friend away until her car was a red speck in the sunshine, Savannah's mind raced with all there actually was to do on the farm despite her assurances to the contrary. Watering and staking, feeding, weeding, pest-detecting and eradicating. There were secondary crops to start and seedlings to tend. And the lambs...the spring lambs were nearly ready to go, whether to slaughter or sale. Picking which ones would go where was a task she hated, and one she wouldn't foist onto someone else, not even the brothers Gallegos, for whom such a task wasn't so heartrending.

Savannah Callowell would dive headlong into all these tasks that were better than being idle this time of year, better than having to be with anyone she loved. The high school students who changed by the year were all she could handle.

Heading back to her office, the lists and the planning and the ordering of her present filled her thoughts to capacity. Savannah watched her feet instead of the sky now black and roiling and rumbling thunder, just as she predicted.

Chapter 2

whilom happiness

July rolled along, and with it came the sort of heat wave Savannah would barely have noticed in Georgia, but one that flattened Bitterly, Connecticut like a soggy pancake. The air conditioner in her office whirred nonstop. She had taken to sleeping there rather than in her un-air-conditioned house. In all the years she lived in the north, she had never needed one.

Edgardo and Raul would be back in two days. Savannah had exhausted every effort to find a window unit for their doublewide. Though the men would put up craggy hands and, in a combination of English and Spanish, assure her it wasn't necessary, she wanted one for them. She wanted them to know she regarded them as more than men who worked her farm. They were like beloved uncles in this town of more acquaintances than friends.

Delivering the window fans she had managed to find at the local thrift store to their home, the unmistakable sound of masculine voices in the kitchen halted her. She paused. Spanish. Definitely the rural variety she had come to recognize, and not the one she learned in college. Savannah relaxed and set the fans onto the floor.

"Edgardo? Raul?"

The voices abruptly halted. They whispered. Edgardo, the elder and taller brother, hurried out of the kitchen, followed quickly by Raul.

"You're back early," she said.

Edgardo shuffled from foot to foot. "Only two days. We talk, okay?"

"Sure. Of course. We can go to my office if it's too hot…"

The brothers laughed. "Not hot," Raul said. "Is cool, no? Like Alaska."

Savannah laughed with them. Sarcasm or comparison to Ecuador, she couldn't tell which. Still shuffling foot to foot, casting glances at one another, the men fell silent once more.

"Okay, guys. What's up? Just tell me."

Raul nodded, urged his brother to speak with a gesture, and stepped back. Edgardo placed a work-roughened hand gently to Savannah's shoulder. "We work many years, good years. Now is time we go home. Stay home."

Savannah only looked at that hand on her shoulder. Dark on dark, yet not at all the same. She studied the contrast while her brain tried to process what he'd just said. Leave Bitterly? Leave her? This sudden loss trembled through her, ice down her sweating back.

Her slow fingers grasped for his. "I...I don't know what to say."

"Is *sorpresa, si?* Forgive for that. *La jefa*, she say is time. I am no young. She is right. Is time."

Savannah searched his dear, lined face. Had Benny known something she didn't? Guessed something she'd been too preoccupied to even consider? Breaking the unspoken rule between them, she hugged Edgardo tight. The man fidgeted, but held her in return.

"*Lo siento*, Savvy."

"Don't be sorry," she managed to say. "I'm just going to miss you, is all."

"We stay the season," Raul said. "Teach *mi sobrino* what he do."

Sobrino?

When the men spoke to one another, it was full of the rural lilts and slang she recognized but couldn't decipher. When they spoke to her, they stuck mostly to English peppered with the Spanish she knew. And Savannah knew that word.

"Your nephew?" She looked from man to man. "You brought your nephew here to take your place?"

"My son." Edgardo patted his chest proudly. "Adelmo. College boy, *si?* He study many years. He come here, work *para ti*. Learn. Next season, he be ready."

"Good boy," Raul added. "Very good. You like him."

Trading two seasoned foremen for a college kid made her uneasy. Savvy's had a good reputation as a farm that, while not certified organic, was close to it, all thanks to the experience of the two men smiling and nodding uncomfortably before her. "Well," she sighed, "where is he?"

"Not here," Edgardo told her. "Two days, he come. Five o'clock airplane. Okay?"

"Okay. Yes, good. Thank you, gentlemen."

She took a deep breath, let it go along with the dread. They were leaving her. Edgardo and Raul, who had worked the farm as long as she had, were going home as they always did in October, and wouldn't come back. Ever. In their place, a boy without their experience, a boy she had no attachment to, but would, in time, because no matter how hard she tried not to care, Savannah Callowell usually did.

"I brought you window fans." She turned abruptly and headed to where she left them. "There isn't an air conditioner to be had in all of Connecticut or Massachusetts. If it gets too hot, you can sleep in the office…"

* * * *

The dark crescent that always preceded a full-blown headache appeared in her periphery. Savannah padded to her bathroom and grabbed the bottle of pills Margit had prescribed for her. Of all those she left behind in Georgia, her friend and doctor was the only one she kept in touch with, under sworn promise not to tell anyone where she was. Ever.

Through Margit, Savannah got her medication and any pertinent news of home. Her adoptive sisters and brother, old friends and ancient Auntie Bea had not changed, as far as she could tell. Keeping in touch made it easier for Savannah to stay away, to pretend doing so somehow helped.

Swallowing down the pills, she closed her eyes against that crescent harbinger. The medication never averted the headache, but it did help. She jiggled the bottle. Only six left, and it wasn't even August yet. Savannah put it back in the medicine cabinet, fished the cellphone from the pocket of her tattered robe, and punched up Margit.

"Hello?"

"Hey, Margit." Savannah cleared the gravel from her voice. "It's me. Savvy."

"I can read my caller ID." The sweet, rich voice on the other end laughed. "Out of meds?"

"Almost. Can you call it in?"

"It's been over a year since I've seen you, Savvy. You know I can't prescribe these meds without seeing you annually. Come home."

Savannah pressed fingertips to her eyelids, rubbing at them until sparkles appeared.

"Savvy? You still there?"

She let go a sigh. "Yes."

"Well?"

"I am home. Can you meet me in New York again?"

"No."

Savannah let her hand fall. "What?"

"No, I won't meet you in New York, but I'll tell you what I will do."

"Okay, what?"

"I'm coming to see you. I want to see the farm. And the childbirth clinic."

"I…"

"You what? Don't think it's a good idea? Too bad. It's that or you can find another neurologist to prescribe your meds for you. I can have all your records—"

"No. Sorry. Of course I want you to come. I'd love to see you."

"Oh, you are such a liar." Margit laughed again, this time a little sadly. "But I'll pretend I don't know I'm unwelcome and come anyway. How's next week look for you?"

"Fine. It's fine. Just let me know your flight plans. And I have to warn you, I have a houseguest staying the summer. You'll have to sleep in my room with me."

"Like when we were in college. Does this mean we get to stay up all night talking about boys and smoking pot?"

"Margit."

"Fine, fine. We won't talk about boys. We'll talk about men. I'll email you later. Do you have enough pills to last until then?"

"It's debatable. You know how much worse they get this time of year."

"I'll try calling in an emergency prescription after we hang up. Same pharmacy?"

Savannah hung up her phone, slid it back into the pocket of her robe, barely remembered contributing to the idle chatter after Margit agreed to try. Leaning close to the mirror, she pulled at the corners of her eyes, but the lines around them reappeared the moment she let go. Women in her family were famously unwrinkled well into their cronehoods. She, only just tipped into her forties, had enough to make up for all of them. She blamed the sun, but it was the headaches aging her.

Turning away from the mirror, Savannah shucked off her tattered robe. It puddled on the floor. She stepped into the shower and let the cold water shock her out of thoughts she didn't want to have. Instead, she thought about Margit's visit, about Edgardo and Raul leaving, about the heat and the farm and the college boy about to become her new foreman. Anything but the thoughts etching lines into the corners of her eyes.

* * * *

Town has changed so much, and not at all. It's swell hanging around after the big picnic, scrabbling around like a rat in the garbage left behind, but it ends up making me sad. Just like scaring people, especially the teenagers, ends up making me sad. They remind me of all I didn't get to be.

I've met others like me, here in Nowheresville. I try to talk to them so I don't have to talk to myself, but aside from the old lady who never leaves the cemetery, they don't stick around long. Strange, I haven't noticed her in a while either. I think. There's that time thing, you know. I wonder where she got to. Maybe she finally let go of whatever was keeping her here. I know I should too.

It's just not fair. He gypped me out of my life, now he's gypping me out of my afterlife. But I'm just so scared. What if what's waiting beyond Nowheresville is way worse? What if what's waiting is him?

Chapter 3

my musing gaze

Though Edgardo assured her his son would be very comfortable bunking with him and Raul, she didn't want Adelmo to start his new life on a couch in a double-wide trailer barely big enough for two. Her home, though modest, had an unused bedroom she utilized as a catchall for anything she didn't feel like putting away. The treadmill, currently a place to hang clothes, and the filing cabinet, full of outdated seed catalogs, were things she'd meant to get rid of long ago, anyway. Clearing out the house was a relief, as was fitting it with a futon, second-hand dresser, cable, and even a mini-fridge for the young man to stash beer and ice cream in.

The Berkshire Mountains were already absorbing the heat wave, leaving behind the breezy days and cool nights she had grown to love during her years in Bitterly. As she transformed her spare room for Edgardo's son, her misgivings about a college student replacing her seasoned foremen began to dissipate. She trusted their judgment. Implicitly. If they said he was the right person for the job that was good enough for her.

"Ade stay when we go," Edgardo said as they stood in the doorway of the renovated room. "He write his paper before spring."

Paper? For grad school, she guessed. Adelmo—Ade to his father and uncle—would move into the trailer come their October departure. Edgardo's discomfort over his son living in the house with Savannah was as endearing as it was antiquated. Did he fear she would fall prey to his son's wiles? Or that he would fall prey to hers?

I would have daughters nearly his age, she wanted to tell him. But Savannah Callowell didn't have daughters. Not anymore. Not in a very long time. Ade was, nevertheless, perfectly safe.

Savannah got on the scooter Benny gave her after Irene was born, and headed to the thrift shop just outside of town proper. Though she'd be in East Perry on Wednesday, getting to one of the big stores before or after her volunteer shift at the childbirth clinic never happened. It would be too late anyway. Adelmo was to arrive sometime on Tuesday. For his sake, and his father's, she would have the window shades up and functioning before then.

Benny had given her a helmet along with the scooter, making her promise to wear it. A promise Savannah did not keep. There was no helmet law in Connecticut. As a doctor who worked her stint in the ER, she knew all too well what could happen to a head sans helmet. Idiotic as it was, the helmet sat, dusty and unused, in the top of Savannah's hall closet. Riding the quiet lanes along the river, she thought nothing of idiocy or nephews or foremen leaving, only of the summer warmth that would all too soon become autumn's brisk chill. Savannah reveled in the sensations of sunshine on her skin and wind in her hair, and the sound of insects buzzing in tandem with her scooter's engine.

Pulling into the lot at the thrift store that had once been a bank, she noticed a car with New Jersey plates. She glided into a spot, switched off her engine and headed hopefully inside. The steady stream of chatter started a smile that the clipped, red head turned grand. Savannah snuck up behind her, putting a finger to her lips so the clerk wouldn't tell, and tapped the young woman on the shoulder.

"Savvy!" Charlotte McCallan threw long arms around her before Savannah could see her face properly. She had been one of the first high school students hired on the farm all those years ago. Charlotte's unfailing energy made her a quick favorite with Edgardo and Raul. Her willingness to do those tasks the other high school kids balked at—like cleaning the lamb pens—earned Savannah's respect. It was Charlotte's genuine kindness and incomparable hutzpah that made Savannah love her like she loved few others in Bitterly. But Charlotte didn't live in Bitterly anymore.

"You cut your hair again." Savannah tugged at a spikey lock. "Too hot?"

"Yes and no." Charlotte fingered the hair near her ear. "I donated it. Matt was so pissed."

Matt. The boyfriend. Savannah quelled the instinct to grimace. She had only met the man once, after all. "Why was he angry?"

"He likes long hair." Charlotte shrugged. "He said the donation isn't a donation, really, because the organization that gets the hair sells the wigs they make."

"Some organizations do, true."

"Not the one I donated to. I checked it out first." Charlotte nudged Savannah in the side, winking dramatically. "A bunch of little kids are running around with my red hair on their heads and I didn't even have to give birth to them. Sometimes Matt forgets I have a brain."

"You do have a college degree."

Charlotte shrugged. "Culinary school."

Holding her tongue became nearly impossible. Savannah knew all about men like Matt. How long before his failed attempts to chip away at Charlotte's self-esteem turned physical? Savannah's hand went automatically to her ribs, to that phantom ache always reminding her. She pretended to scratch an itch. "How long are you here for?"

"I was trying to get here for the picnic, but things get crazy in Cape May on the Fourth. Matt's minding the bakery so I can stay a few days, but I really have to get back for the weekend. Will you come to Dad and Johanna's for a barbeque on Friday? Nina and Gunner will be there with Tabitha."

"Tabitha?"

Charlotte shoved her playfully. "The mysterious Tabitha they brought home from Greece. How could you possibly forget that juicy bit of gossip?"

Savannah remembered, vaguely, hearing about the orphan Nina and Gunner Coco-Allen brought home from their curiosity-seeking voyage around the world. "I don't do gossip, sugar. You know that."

"Well, you'll meet her anyway. Will you come?"

"Only if I can bring something."

"Watermelon and tomato salad?" Charlotte crinkled her nose. "No one makes it like you do."

"Absolutely."

"Fantastic." The young woman threw her arms about Savannah again, rocking her back and forth. "I'm so excited. Now I have to go home and tell Dad and Johanna they're throwing me a barbeque on Friday."

"Charlotte!"

Dancing off, Charlotte laughed. "I'm kidding. Be there at six."

Waving, shaking her head, Savannah let it go. Charlotte was a force to be reckoned with, and there was no thwarting her. She pushed away thoughts of Matt and his undermining ways and instead ticked through the ingredients for the salad she had become famous for after Benny posted it on the *Savvy Gardening* site. Tomatoes still green before the picnic would be the perfect ripeness come Friday. She just needed to buy a watermelon.

She searched for window shades, found a pair that matched, and a third that matched well enough for a young man's room. Adelmo probably wouldn't even notice. Savannah laughed softly under her breath. Despite his father's uneasiness, he probably wouldn't use them at all. The more she prepared for his arrival, the more she liked the idea of having him around. Edgardo and Raul taught her everything she knew. Now she would have the next generation to teach in turn. Though they never said his degree had been in agriculture of any kind, Savannah couldn't imagine him earning one in another field and still consenting to take his father's place.

Savannah halted in her tracks, nearly dropping the shades in the process. In all the years Edgardo and Raul worked her farm, she had filed the appropriate applications, gained the proper visas and never had a problem with immigration.

She had not done so for Adelmo.

Heat rushed to her cheeks. Would the boy be there on a work visa? An education visa? Her heart stuttered. Illegally? Her foremen's announcement, coming when it did, had been a shock, one that clouded this very important detail. She purchased the shades without even haggling about the price, dumped them in the milk crate carrier that was bungee-corded to her scooter and headed for home.

* * * *

I always liked that redheaded panic. I knew her name once. I've forgotten now. Memories are hard to hold on to, in my state. I think they're for the living. Makes things easier. Anyway, I put pebbles in the panic's shoes once. In all the years I've been doing it, she was the only one I let give them to someone else. Honestly, I couldn't have done anything about it anyway. She made the switch and called her little sister to the porch without ever giving me the chance. I couldn't let her get away with it, of course, and ended up scaring her a little later that night when she was out with her friends. Just for fun, really. A tap. Or two. She probably doesn't remember anymore. I usually remember all my little tricks. Maybe dead-girl memory is just selective.

But the Negro lady? I don't know her, really. I've seen her, of course. She's hard to miss, considering, you know, she's not white. Maybe there are more in Bitterly these days. That'd be peachy, wouldn't it? Still, I thought I kind of knew everyone in Bitterly. Once, everyone knew me. Then everyone knew of me. Now, well...anyway...

They didn't even know I was there, sitting on the rock jutting out of the river. Though I guess I should be used to that by now. There aren't many who can feel me near, let alone see me. Not unless I want them to. A fleeting glimpse works best. Scares the bejesus out of people. I know it's kind of mean, but it's a little something I feel entitled to.

The water is shallow here, not like that other rock where he tossed me all wrapped up in a carpet I can still smell sometimes, though don't ask me how. Maybe it's just the shadow of the dust and my own blood in my nose. And the water. So cold. I don't go to that rock, even if all the kids dare one another to swim there like it's a rite of passage or something. It makes me angry, them making a game out of what happened to me. Sometimes angry enough that the traffic lights in town don't work for a week.

It's funny, not in a ha-ha way, but in a strange way, how I was drawn to the Negro lady today. At first, it was the panic who caught my attention, but then I saw her, and noticed that angry thing hovering nearby. And then I noticed those two little girls standing between it and her. Once I saw them, I couldn't not see them anymore. I'm not sure if they noticed me. I really don't know how it all works. And now I'm curious. That's something I haven't been in, well, however long it's been. I know, I know. Curiosity killed the cat, but I'm already dead, so...

* * * *

"No worries, no worries." Edgardo had laughed when Savannah expressed her concern. "Ade have papers. All legal. No worries."

"But I didn't fill out any—"

"He have papers from university," Raul assured her, winking. "Is good, promise."

Savannah had left the men in their trailer and went to the computer in her office. She clicked through all the sites she could find about education visas. Despite the myriad of possibilities rattling about in her mind, Savannah let it go. She hoped Adelmo spoke better English than his father and uncle, hoped he would have an adequate explanation for her. The last thing she wanted was trouble with immigration. Savannah Callowell had crusaded for more than her share of injustices in her forty-two years. After she bought Larson's and changed the name to Savvy's, she decided that the illegal farm workers issue was not one she had the stamina to maintain. She found Egdardo and Raul through serendipitous, though proper, channels, and hired local kids for the summer months. Adelmo's legal status, or lack thereof, had the potential to change the easy balance on her farm. It made Savannah exceedingly nervous. And headachy.

She took one of the few remaining pills, hoping the rest would last until Margit arrived. The pharmacy had rejected the emergency prescription, citing the rules and regulations regarding certain medications. No paper script, no fill. Simple and uncompassionate as that. She tried not to worry, tried to sleep. Adelmo would arrive Tuesday afternoon. Tomorrow. Everything would be fine.

It was the time of year, the shock of losing her foremen and friends, the farm's constant busyness. Savannah's thoughts churned, keeping her from sleep. She tried warm milk, then reading the dull book for the library book club that month. Not even that made her yawn. No matter how hard she tried to deny what she needed, Savannah knew. She didn't want to, never wanted to, but she was desperate enough, at last, to do it.

Getting out of bed, she steeled her nerves. Her head pounded harder with each step. A buzzing between her ears whined but she continued to the cedar chest under the windows. And she took out a box.

The Box.

That's all it was. A box with a few priceless things in it. Mementos that still smelled of them. Items they had touched. Loved. She was Pandora letting the forbidden fly out, including hope. Because there was no hope. Her girls were dead. And she was alive when she wasn't supposed to be. Only these things remained. To make her cry. To soothe her. To rebuild the faltering will demanding she honor their lives with her own lived well. To let her, at last, sleep to the creaks and groans of the old house still settling into itself.

Chapter 4

in the twilight

Adelmo Gallegos shifted in the too small, economy seat. Going home to the farm in Ecuador had been a mistake. It took two days of flights, layovers, and interminable hours in a car, buses, and trains to get back to the States. Having money for a nonstop would have helped. Marginally. After his years in academia, he didn't have much of that left, only enough to see him through his placement in Connecticut, maybe enough to buy a used car to get around. He would not be earning a regular salary until Taytay and Tío went home, and even then it would be next spring, after the planting began. At present, he would earn an hourly wage.

Hourly. After all his schooling. All his experience. All the sacrifices he made and the hard work he put in. He was to be an hourly worker. What had it all been for? How had it happened? Two months ago, he'd been in Boston, sad and excited during the commencement exercises. Life was finally going to begin. Rather, it was finally going to be the life he'd envisioned for himself. Instead, he ended up humiliated, disenfranchised, and on his way home to *la jefa*, who had held him close before smacking him in the head and telling him it was time he settled down and started providing grandchildren.

Were it not for Taytay, he might never have left Ecuador again. Things had a way of working out for him, and though the position in Bitterly, Connecticut wasn't what he'd had in mind all these years of working his way to a goal, it was better than going home. It was a new start, if humble. At present, Ade wasn't entirely opposed to humble.

Leaning back against the headrest, his empty belly lurching as the plane began its descent, Ade wished he was the weeping kind. It would have felt good to cry. But he was not. He was a man, and men did not cry where he came from.

The seatbelt sign dinged. The captain's voice came out of the air.

"Ah, we're beginning our descent into Bradley Airport. Clear sailing. Buckle up."

Those awake obliged. Those not were awakened so they could. A layover in Miami, another in Washington, DC, the interminable and exhausting hours traveling made him long for the days he didn't have to find the least expensive flight. Flying coach was bad enough, but layovers? Just punishment, he supposed, for being a fool.

* * * *

Savannah woke, curled up at the foot of her bed like a kitten. In each hand, a crocheted baby bootie. One yellow. One green. Savannah had made them herself after she discovered she was carrying twins, but didn't wish to learn their sexes until Doc came home. His specials training was almost finished. He'd be assigned, and they would move. After that, if they decided to, they would ask at the next ultrasound if they were having boys, girls, or one of each.

Savannah kissed one bootie, then the other, and tucked them back into the Box alongside the other things. She didn't give in to the impulse to take out something else—the ribbons, pink and green—search the contents for her lost babies—Sally's hair had been dark and dense. Ginger's, lighter and sleek. The things inside were just that—things.

But she did feel better. Despite the bugaboo of approaching the Box, it never failed to ease the prickling sensation under her skin and diminish the headache, once she held it in her hands. No matter how often her practical, clinical side told her it contained only links to memories, she felt them so keenly once she opened it. It was as if the contents were a conduit of some kind, able to channel only the good of what they had been, and nothing of the horror of their deaths.

Tucking it back into the trunk, Savannah let go a long exhale. What made her hide it away and resist its pull when it was the only thing that helped, she couldn't say. Perhaps it made her feel weak, or imbalanced. She was a doctor, for goodness sake, not a bog witch. Whatever psychosomatic illusion—delusion—worked on simpler minds had no relevance in her own life. She closed the lid of the trunk, chastised her night of weakness, and left her bedroom as the headache began to bloom all over again.

Savannah looked out the kitchen window. The old tank of a pick-up Edgardo and Raul drove around the farm wasn't parked outside. Had they left already? Savannah checked the clock. Eight-thirty, and far too early to head out to the airport for a five o'clock arrival. Turning from the window, she saw the truck kicking up plumes of dirt out of the corner of her eye. She grabbed her mug of coffee and stepped out onto the tiny back porch.

Gravel crunched. The trunk squeaked to a brake-weary stop. Three heads were visible in the windshield, not two. Savannah sipped her coffee. She had assumed Adelmo's flight was arriving at five in the afternoon, not in the morning. She was glad she'd already hung the shades. Waiting, sipping the strong coffee, she watched the men descend from the truck. Edgardo from the passenger's seat. Raul from the driver's. And Adelmo.

Like his father and uncle, he was lean and not overly tall. From where she stood, Savannah could make out the same aquiline nose and deep-set eyes of his father, but where Edgardo's features were broad and big and sturdy, the lines of Adelmo's face were finer. Like both men, he had the jet-black hair of his people, but his skin was, while not light, more fair. Unlike both men, there was no question about his age. Adelmo was definitely not a college kid.

"*Buenos días*, Savvy." Raul waved over his head as she came slowly down the steps. "Come. Meet Ade."

Savannah's stomach clenched. She tried to pretend she wasn't caught completely off guard, and failed. Edgardo and Raul exchanged glances.

"Savannah Callowell," Edgardo said. "My son. Adelmo. *Ade, esto aquí tu jefa*, Savvy."

"I am very pleased to meet you, Ms. Callowell."

The rich, accented voice matched his appearance perfectly. Confident. Old-world aristocratic. He was at least as old as she, herself. Looking at him now, close enough to see the creases in the corners of his eyes, and that they were not brown, but forest green, Savannah found him rather peculiar looking in a handsome sort of way. No wonder his father had been uncomfortable, having the man stay in her home.

"Savannah, please," she managed to say. "Savvy, once you feel more comfortable."

"Then you must call me Adelmo, Ade when you are more comfortable."

His smile was ill-behaved, and the kind of perfect only lots of money or really good genetics could provide. Charisma oozed from him like sweat. A darted glance to Edgardo, still fidgeting uneasily beside his son, and Savannah came to the conclusion that this man had to look more like his mother. Either that or Edgardo's life had been far harder than she ever imagined.

"Is something wrong?"

Savannah quelled the school-girl urge to laugh. "You aren't who I expected."

"No? Who did you expect?"

"A boy straight out of college."

Adelmo turned to his father, spoke in rapid rural Spanish. The three men laughed. Edgardo, at least, had the decency to look abashed, but Raul thumped his nephew on the back, again speaking that rural tongue.

"What's so funny?"

"My uncle made a joke about my advanced age and…stamina. I promise you, I am not that old, and I might not be able to keep up with my father, but I will perform as needed."

"How old are you?" It came out so quickly. Savannah's cheeks burned. "Sorry. It's just your father and uncle look…it's none of my business."

"Of course it is. I am an employee. Forty, as of last winter. I have been living and working in the United States for many years. I understand you have some concern about the legality of my being here. Rest assured, there is no problem. I can provide you with the proper paperwork if—"

"No need," she said. "I'm certain they're all in order."

"Still, it would make you feel better to have the papers. I will see to it."

"All right, thanks."

He bowed his head. When he looked up again, there were those good genetics curled into a grin that made Savannah fidget just a little bit.

"I imagine we have many things to talk about, Savannah." *Sah-vah-nah* he'd said, the lilt and tone of his voice like a song she'd never heard before. "And this is not the best place."

"We could go to my office."

"I have been traveling for days," he said. "I'm exhausted and not at my best. Dinner this evening would be preferable. Would you do me the honor? We can consider it my official interview, in light of the fact you took me on at my father's word and he neglected to mention a few things."

"That might not be appropriate. Dinner, I mean."

"I am to live in your home until my father and uncle leave in the autumn, but having dinner together is inappropriate?"

Again, the burn in her cheeks. Backing out of the arrangement felt ludicrous. Just because he was a man and not a boy? It was the twenty-first century, and a male housemate was no longer scandalous. *Well fiddle-dee-dee, what is wrong with you, sugarbeet?* Savannah took in a slow, steadying breath. "True enough. All right, Adelmo. Dinner tonight. But it's on me."

"Absolutely not."

"Then we go Dutch."

"You have a Dutch restaurant in town? Intriguing."

"No, I meant…you're teasing me."

"I am. Forgive me. I am, however, an old-fashioned gentleman. It must be my advanced age."

"I'm older than you are."

His smile momentarily faltered. "*Lo siento.* I meant no offense."

"None taken."

"Please, it would give me pleasure to buy you dinner, at least to make up for not being what you expected, and to thank you for the honor of living in your house, and working your farm."

He was, indeed, nothing she'd been expecting. Working her farm was no honor to this man who was obviously not a farmhand. What the hell was he doing here? In Bitterly, Connecticut? Working her little farm when he looked like he would be more comfortable in a boardroom, or a classroom?

"All right then." Savannah set her coffee cup onto the steps. "I wouldn't want to dishonor such chivalry."

"Excellent. As I do not know the area, perhaps you would choose the location."

"Sure. Seven o'clock good?"

"Seven is perfect." He turned to his father and uncle, dispelling their confused expressions with indecipherably rapid words. Raul grinned and thumped his nephew's back again. Edgardo's eyes darted from his son to Savannah, but he said nothing.

"I'll show Adelmo to his room," she told the other two men. "I made you fried chicken and potato salad for lunch. There's plenty for everyone. See you at noon?"

The two older men ambled to their trailer. Edgardo turned back once, but continued on. If Savannah knew them, they'd be out in the fields within the hour. She turned to Adelmo.

"If you would be more comfortable staying with your father and uncle, I understand. I was expecting a kid young enough to be my son."

"And you set up a room for me, like a good mother."

Savannah pretended she didn't notice the way his voice deepened. "You might find it a bit juvenile."

"I am certain it is fine." He followed her up the porch steps. "And if you are still willing to allow me in your house, given my advanced age, I would much prefer it to my father's couch. Thank you."

Savannah led Adelmo through the large farm kitchen and into the parlor. "You're welcome to use any part of the house," she said. "The fireplace is working, but the flue is a little tricky." She moved to the steps bisecting the Cape Cod, pointed to the family room on the other side. "There's a TV in your room, but if you want to hang out down here, feel free. And borrow whatever books you want from the shelves. I just ask that you don't break the spines. I'm kind of persnickety about that."

"Persnickety." He laughed, a low sound like a drum. "I like that word."

"You've never heard it before?"

"I have, but not the way you say it. My father tells me you are from Georgia."

"I am. Sometimes I don't realize how strong my accent still is."

"It is a nice sound. It dances off the tongue, like Spanish."

Savannah refused the fiddle-dee-dee trying to work its way into her head. She walked up the steps, feeling him too close behind her. If she stopped, he would bang into her.

"Bathroom's right there. Sorry, we have to share, but there's a half-bath downstairs next to the kitchen. I'm persnickety about my books, and I'm persnickety about my bathroom. Keep it clean or you can use your father's."

"You will find me a fastidious houseguest."

Of course he was. Savannah couldn't imagine him dirty, or even messy. What the hell was he doing here?

"Your room." She opened the door and stepped aside for him to go in first.

He took in the futon, the mini-fridge, the TV on the dresser and the fan in the window. "Much better than my father's couch. Thank you, Savannah."

"You are very welcome, Adelmo." She paused, a beat too long. Those eyes were just so…so riveting. "I'll leave you to settle in, wander around, do whatever you like. Lunch is at noon, if you want anything. Today is yours. Tomorrow, we work."

"And tonight, we dine."

Savannah pursed her lips. "Yes. I'll go down and make that reservation. How do you feel about Italian?"

"It is the food of the gods." He laughed. "My favorite cuisine."

"Good. Mine too. D'Angelo's it is."

In the kitchen, trying to find the phone number she knew by heart until she picked up the phone to dial it, Savannah heard him moving around upstairs. Her heart pittered. Why was she feeling like a kid on Christmas Eve? A kid who peeked in her parents' closet and already knew she was getting the microscope she asked for? It was the confusion, she decided, that made her say yes to going out with him, even if it was a job interview and not a date. Certainly not a date. She'd not been out with more than a handful of men since Doc. He had been the love of her life, until he became someone she no longer knew. Someone who could hurt her. Someone who could do what he did.

Savannah took a deep breath, and let it go slowly. It always came back to that. To Doc. The girls. She wouldn't wallow. She had sworn she would never, ever wallow. Adelmo being a peculiarly attractive man her own age had thrown her off. That was all.

Putting her sorrow back where it belonged, she opened the junk drawer for the tattered phone book residing there. The drawer jammed. The book ripped even more than it already was. She tugged and tugged, tried prying it loose with a butter knife, but it wouldn't budge. Completely frustrated, she leaned against the counter. Something in her back pocket clicked, hard surface to hard surface. Savannah laughed at herself, softly, so that Adelmo wouldn't hear her, then took the smartphone from her pocket and looked up the number.

* * * *

Ade paced in his room. The floor creaked. He bounced on a board. Grimaced. Flying coach, a farmhouse in the back of beyond, and in of all places, rural Connecticut. But for the semester he guest-lectured at Yale and a long weekend spent in Mystic, he barely knew Connecticut existed. How was it possible? Savannah Callowell was obviously intelligent, articulate, but she hadn't known who he was, or even his proper age. And while he suspected his father had purposely led her to believe his son was fresh out of college, Ade could not fathom a woman of business not taking the time, or making the effort, to research who she had hired. He had certainly researched the lovely Dr. Savannah Callowell.

She was smaller than he'd imagined. Fine-boned and slight-framed. In the pictures he'd found online, she seemed more…substantial. They were old pictures, of course, and she'd been younger. The short, spikey hair of her past had grown into long coils she kept tied back off her round, smooth face. Though slight, she was not all lean lines and hard ridges. Though curvy, she was not soft. And online photos did not do her eyes justice. Deep brown, heavily lashed, and not a stroke of makeup to enhance them.

Adelmo Gallegos knew women, but this one? It was going to take a little more time to unwrap the truth of her.

Sitting on the edge of the futon, he concentrated on breathing until his thoughts stopped tumbling. Maybe she was faking it, waiting for him to expose his past to her. That was far more likely. Well, he wouldn't indulge her.

He tested the mattress. It was a little on the hard side, but quality. The mini-fridge tucked into the corner would hold a six-pack well enough, but a bottle of wine would never fit. The windows were fitted with shades— no curtains—unmistakably mismatched. Water stains marred the second-hand dresser down one side. If she was faking it, she had gone to some expense to be convincing.

Ade took another cleansing breath, let it go slowly. He had left a sixth-floor apartment overlooking the Charles River, in one of the most luxurious buildings Boston had to offer. For this.

No more fine dining in the city he had grown to love. No more evenings discussing agricultural practices and global warming with colleagues he respected even if he didn't like them so much. It was all gone. Every crystal glass. Every cashmere sweater. Even his car, gone. He supposed he was grateful, considering the humiliating circumstances. None of it had been real. None of it had been his. He gave it all back willingly because what he wouldn't hand over was his pride.

He flopped backwards onto the futon, arm covering his eyes, making it instantly night. Conflicted. That was what he was. He was glad to be out of the university, away from the backstabbing and lies, but he missed Boston. He was grateful for the solace of this farm, but it disgraced a career he'd worked ruthlessly to build.

Find who you were, my son. Let go of who you became. His mother's words crept into his head. Despite their combative relationship, he and *la jefa* had always been especially close. She demanded more from him than she did the others, because—once upon a time—all their hopes rested on him. His earnings, his learnings, pushed the family farm out of bankruptcy and into a thriving venture exceeding all expectations, but he had lost much of himself along the way, in little bits and unnoticeable pieces. He had failed his mother. He failed himself. Because he let it all go to his head and became someone he never meant to be. Because of a faithless woman with the power to ruin him, and the will to do exactly that.

* * * *

Mom and Pop wouldn't be happy with me. Then again, they're not around, so I guess it's fine. They moved out of Bitterly after…you know…

and took my little brother with them. I don't blame them. There are times I just want out of this town too. Mom, Pop and me were just starting to talk about college when I got so twisted up in love that wasn't really love at all. Not that I knew it then. They thought I was mooning over that nice boy...what was his name? I think it was Victor. I let them think so, anyway. I was such a dimwit.

I followed her home, the Negro lady. Her name is Savannah. Isn't that pretty? She has one of those Gone-with-the-Wind accents. Golly, I loved that movie. I think I saw it a dozen times. She sounds just like Scarlet O'Hara. She lives on a farm outside of town called Savvy's. Oh, hey! Savvy. Savannah. That's really keen. I like her even more now.

Mom and Pop would scold me for following her. Hadn't I learned my lesson? But what else can happen to me? I ask you. Well, gee, plenty, I guess. But I just couldn't help myself. It feels...good...yes, good to be something other than bored and lonely and scared. And I really want to know what that angry thing always near her is.

Going into people's houses can be tricky. I've seen some get stuck to a house, the way the old lady seems stuck to the cemetery. I am stuck enough to Bitterly, but at least I get around. When I went back to her bedroom, she was asleep at the bottom of her bed. The angry thing was just a black spot in the corner, and the little girls were sitting with her, one at her head and one at her feet, like little guardian angels. Now this new man is here with his Ricky Ricardo accent, and something tells me to stick around a little while longer. But I won't stay long. Honest to Betsy, I won't.

Chapter 5

star-strewn firmament

Edgardo and Raul spent the day out in the fields. Savannah had Adelmo take their lunch to them. She ate her own in her office, alone, caught up on paperwork, recorded sales from the Fourth, and placed an order with Darla and Sandra to restock her shelves with the herbal remedies they were locally famous for. That, in turn, reminded her of her promise to give them her very small but luxurious supply of lambswool left over from last season. They were going to spin a portion of it for her in exchange, and dye it purple so she could finally make a pair of booties for Benny and Dan's baby girl, as she had meant to do before the child was born. Now Irene was eight months old and still, no booties. For the colder months, Savannah told herself. Shucking off the flannel shirt she'd thrown over her tank top, she left the air-cooled office.

As it always happened, the earthy, sweet and comforting aromas stopped her in her tracks the moment she stepped into the drying shed. Herbs hung from the rafters in all states of preservation. Flowers, too. She had bouquets of roses tied up with ribbon, delphinium, hydrangea, and Russian sage. Soon enough, goldenrod and Queen Anne's lace would hang there as well, awaiting the autumn wreaths she and Benny would make. Autumn was Savannah's favorite time of year, and a big reason she stayed in the north when months and months of snow made her long for the sunny south.

The box of lambswool sat on the edge of the loft space, just a little too high for Savannah to reach it. One of the high school students put it up there. A basketball player, if she remembered right. The last thing she wanted to do was go out to the barn, fetch the ladder and maneuver it through the shed, hoping not to break any of her drying plants. But she'd been meaning to get the lambswool to Darla and Sandra for almost a year. Now or never. She went for the ladder.

As she crossed the yard, Edgardo, Raul and Adelmo were coming back from the fields. She waved over her head and continued on.

Adelmo shouted something, waved to his father and uncle, and jogged over to her. "You have a beautiful piece of land," he said, not even slightly out of breath. "Just the right size to supply the area with good, seasonal produce."

"A lot of the farms around here went big," she said, "and ended up going under. That's why I have this farm to begin with. I have more land than I use for growing. I let nature have it back."

"Ah, I did not know."

"Your father and uncle probably don't either. It's not something that ever came up."

"Perhaps you would show it to me. As good as the soil is, there are benefits to rotating sites that soil amendment does not allow for."

"Sure, but just remember—I don't want to go bigger. What I have is plenty."

"Duly noted."

Duly noted? Savannah was close to certain no such phrase existed in Edgardo or Raul's vocabulary, English, Spanish, or the rural tongue they shared. Savannah shrugged it off. She'd known the man a few minutes within scant hours. He had a story. She simply didn't know it yet. "Do you want to go now?"

Adelmo checked his watch. "It is already three o'clock. Is there enough time? You can show me tomorrow, if you wish."

"Are you saying I need four hours to get myself presentable for dinner?" She looked down at her jeans. They were actually quite dirty, even if she'd only been doing paperwork.

"Forgive me, no," he said. "Only that I don't know how extensive your land is, and where it is. In Ecuador, our family farm is dotted all over the mountain. One field is a full hour away from the farmhouse itself."

"I was teasing you," Savannah covered. "Mostly. I can't tomorrow. I volunteer at a childbirth clinic a few towns over on Wednesdays. There is plenty of time left now, if you want. Or we can go on Thursday."

"Let us go now then."

"This way to the coot." She waved him onward. "Oh, damn. I almost forgot. I have to get this box down first before I forget again. You want to give me a hand?"

Adelmo wasn't tall, but he was taller than Savannah. Ditching the ladder idea, she led him back to the drying shed.

He, too, was stopped in his tracks upon entering, his smile one of bewildered joy. "My Lita had a shed like this. She is the one who first taught me herb lore."

"Lita?"

"My grandmother. A gifted herbalist. She has forgotten more than I will ever know about plants and their medicinal uses."

"How much do you know?"

Adelmo blinked, his boyish joy slowly fading into something...else. "You really know nothing of who I am, do you. My father never told you what I have been doing in the United States all these years? You did not Google me?"

"Google you?" Savannah laughed softly. "What kind of person does that? No, he never told me."

"Well, then." Adelmo clapped his hands, rubbing them together. "We have much to discuss at dinner. Let us save it for then, shall we? Where is this box you need?"

He wasn't quite tall enough to reach the box on the loft shelf, but Adelmo easily pulled himself onto the small landing and handed it down to her. Like his father, his spare frame boasted no softness. Savannah took the box and watched his carefully executed swing to the ground more avidly than she'd intended.

After depositing the box in her office and sending an email to Darla that it was waiting there for her, Savannah took Adelmo out on the coot—an ancient, all-terrain vehicle she bought along with the farm. It had been a long time since she surveyed her own holdings. Fields that used to grow corn, corn, and more corn were overgrown with weeds, what appeared to be pumpkin vines, and, of course, corn growing wild. Savannah pointed out landmarks and told Adelmo what stories she knew of the old farming family that had owned the land since Bitterly was first established back in the 1800s.

"Apparently, the Larsons were one of the original families here." She switched off the engine so she no longer had to shout over it. "They, and the Farcuses, the Gardners, the Bossys, and the Wells. I'm told they all moved out here together from some coastal town that doesn't exist anymore, founded Bitterly, then lorded over it right up until I bought this farm from the last of the Larsons."

"Are there none left?"

"Sure, but diluted. And this—" She motioned to the landscape. "—is all that is left of one of the great Bitterly empires."

Adelmo smiled. Bright, July sunlight squinted his eyes. He hopped out of the coot, inspected a pumpkin vine snaking its way out of the bramble.

"This land reminds me of a fairy story Lita used to tell to all the children when we were young. *Jaqayman*, the forgotten garden tended by the little folk. All manner of food grew there, hidden by the bramble humankind wouldn't look beyond. They tended and harvested and helped the animals stay alive all through the winter."

"*Jaqayman*," Savannah repeated. "I like that. And I had no idea there was so much growing here. The animals are welcome to it. I imagine they've come to depend upon it at this point."

"Oh, yes. I am certain they have. And perhaps that is why you never have trouble with them in your working fields."

"I wouldn't say never." Though Savannah couldn't remember the last time more than a stray deer or two caused any damage. She supposed it was the fence—even though it was a flimsy thing, easily jumped. Or maybe it was something Edgardo and Raul did either with scent or noise. Whatever it was, Adelmo's theory was an interesting one.

"Would you mind if I explored up here," he asked. "I will be of more service to you and this farm if I find heirloom varieties of corn, tomatoes, and pumpkins than I can be doing the menial tasks my father wishes me to do."

"Menial?"

Adelmo's brow furrowed. "I chose the wrong word. What I meant was, you really don't need me here while my father and uncle are still running the farm. They will find things for me to do, certainly, but you have an expert in agriculture, most specifically, in such things as heirloom vegetables."

"I do?"

He grinned. "You do. For instance, have you any idea how much of the sub-regional varieties we have lost to the global market? Did you know that there were once as many varieties of peaches as there are counties, just here in Connecticut alone? Each town has its own regional peculiarities, even subzones that account for the differences. But certain peaches yield bigger crops, travel better, ripen after picked. It is a sad, sad thing to lose, especially considering what sells in supermarkets is less nutritious, and tastes like cardboard."

"Well, goodness, sugar, tell me how you really feel."

An eyebrow arched and fell quickly into a broad smile. "I find I am regaining my passion for the subject in a more visceral way, here on your lovely farm."

Visceral? And he misspoke a word like menial?

"What you say," she said, "is one of the main reasons I stay small. I want to grow as close to organic as I can manage, and I do many heirloom varieties."

"I have seen your heirlooms, and I am dubious. Forgive me, Savannah, they are not true heirlooms unless the seed comes from a plant variety grown before 1951. Many varieties now say they are heirloom, but they are not."

"Really? Is that scientific fact or your opinion?"

He shrugged. "A little of both. I am an all or nothing man. If you wish to claim you grow organic, heirloom produce, you must truly be growing organic and—"

"I said mostly organic," Savannah interjected. "There are a few fertilizers and pesticides your father and uncle convinced me I should use. Harmless, but not on the list of certified allowances. I'm small enough to claim it anyway, but I don't."

"As you shouldn't." His brow furrowed. "It is a constant battle with Taytay and Tío—"

"*Taytay* and *Tío*?" She chuckled. "Really?"

Adelmo shrugged and tapped his head. "I forget myself when I get worked up."

"I know that tío means 'uncle,' but I've never heard Taytay before."

"It is…rural, as am I, at heart."

A layer unintentionally revealed? Something skeptical nudged at her, but Savannah stored the detail. "I'm sorry. I rudely interrupted you. You were saying? About organic?"

"Ah, yes. What I was saying was that my father and uncle, and too many others, see cost and ease as an acceptable alternative to doing things right."

"They don't run the farm right?"

Adelmo's nose crinkled. "Let us say, they don't run it entirely as I would."

"And as we say in Georgia, those are fighting words."

"Fighting words that have caused many fights among us." He winked. "It is one reason I am still here in the United States when I was supposed to be educated here, and then return home some twenty-five years ago."

"That's a long time to carry on."

"Long enough for them to get old and have some of the fight go out of them." Adelmo turned a full circle, arms spread. "The natural world is still a mystery to us, but I believe the artificial things we put into our bodies are the cause of many ailments. Advocating a paleo diet is the other extreme. We are no longer cavemen living on raw meat and tubers."

"I take it you are against bio-engineered produce?"

"To an extent, yes. But not completely." Adelmo paused, held her gaze in that discomfiting stare. "And we are getting ahead of ourselves again. We will have nothing left to discuss this evening."

Savannah cocked her head. In the hours they'd been riding in the coot, exploring the fallow fields, the conversation had not faltered. Not once. For Savannah, who lingered more in silence even as a child, that rarely happened. She was used to Benny, who could carry on a conversation all on her own, and the Coco sisters, who competently dominated any gathering they were in. This was alien. It was new. Out in the wild part of her farm, she'd been able to talk unwarily, unafraid of stumbling into a past that would muzzle her. And she found she rather liked it. She glanced skyward.

"It's getting late anyway. We should get back and clean up."

"Will you show me how to drive this vehicle?" he asked as they approached the coot. Savannah turned the ignition, and slid over to the passenger's side.

"See that lever," she pointed. "Slow or fast. That's pretty much it."

* * * *

White jeans, a floral button-down, and the silver, strappy sandals she almost never wore seemed appropriate attire for dinner with a colleague. Savannah felt both professional and pretty without being dressed-up—as if for a date. This was definitely not a date. But she was interested in solving the mystery of this new man in her life. Slipping in a pair of silver hoops as she breezed out of her bedroom, she pretended it was a mindless act done on the fly.

"Ah, you are punctual as well as lovely." Adelmo was just coming out of his bedroom, fastening the bottom buttons of his lavender shirt. Lavender. What man in Bitterly would wear lavender? What man in Bitterly would wear anything more colorful than plaid? Between his shirt and the clogs on his feet, his otherness stood out. He wore it well.

"Thank you. You clean up pretty nicely too."

"I try. Are you ready to go?"

"Ready. And hungry. We'll take my car."

"As I have no vehicle of my own, that would be a good idea."

His smooth, musical voice held no sarcasm. His smile was not a sneer. Savannah let her raised hackles ease. It had been a long, long time since

Doc's always-veiled insults chipped away at her self-esteem. Savannah thought she'd gotten over it.

"After you." He gestured to the stairs and Savannah realized she'd been staring.

Instead of trying to explain, she murmured a thanks, sailed down the steps through the kitchen, and grabbed her keys from the rack on the way out the door. In the fresh air, the relative cool snapped her out of whatever sudden panic had her in its grip. She took deep breaths.

What the hell is wrong with you, sugarbeet? She heard her Auntie Bea's voice as clearly as if she were standing beside her. Savannah had no answer. Maybe later when she couldn't sleep for the pounding in her head. She got into the car as Adelmo, seemingly unaware of the mad dash she imagined she'd just taken, did the same.

"Seatbelt," she said.

"Always. I have an American driver's license, if you'd prefer I drive."

"That's okay. I got it."

Chivalry was not necessarily chauvinism, she reminded herself. He was just being a gentleman. That firmly in mind, she clicked on the lights and headed down the driveway.

They chatted casually the short distance to town. Adelmo was polite and good at making small talk seem less trite. The afternoon in the coot made falling back into that unwariness easy. He asked about the gazebo on the green, and the disparity of the army tank always covered in little children climbing.

"It is strange, isn't it?" Savannah answered. "I have no idea why they'd put a World War I tank on the Green. Benny, one of my full-timers, was born and raised here. She and her husband live in the old town center. Actually, Dan grew up here too. They'll tell you just about anything you want to know. I'm sure you'll meet them soon."

"They are friends of yours?"

"They are. Good friends."

"I would like to meet them. I would like to meet as many people as I can. It will help me to acclimate to this town. It is far different from any I have lived in before."

"What kinds of places have you lived in?"

"Cities, mostly, except when I go home."

"To Ecuador?"

He nodded.

"Do you get there much?" she asked.

"I make sure to spend four months a year back home. For various reasons."

Savannah pulled into a spot near D'Angelo's. His reasons were his own. His to offer, not hers to ask. The alluring scent of garlic already pulled at her. Inhaling deeply, she conjured the plate of linguine and clam sauce she would order. It wasn't always on the menu, but the chef never objected to the request.

"A lovely little trattoria," Adelmo said, coming around to her side of the car. "Smells delicious."

"It used to be a family pizza joint." Savannah got out of the car and closed the door before he could do it for her. "A few years ago, the original family sold the place, and it got a makeover. The pizza is still amazing, though."

"I am a pizza connoisseur. Perhaps I should try it."

"You won't be disappointed. But I have to be honest, I only get it as take-out. The dine-in menu is just too good to pass up."

Adelmo got to the door first and held it open for her, pulled out her chair and waited for her to sit down. The swell of pleasure battled the need to do it all for herself. Savannah was conscious of people looking their way. Several waved. Talk would be all over town before morning. Placing her napkin on her lap, she let it go.

Vehemently.

* * * *

"Wine?" Ade plucked the wine list from the table. The labels were surprisingly respectable. In his pocket, his cell phone vibrated.

"I have to admit, my palate is that of a five-year-old," Savannah was saying. "If it tastes like juice, it works for me."

He looked at her over the top of the wine menu. Ingenuous. That was the word milling about in his head since riding in the coot. Outside of childhood, such people didn't exist. Not in his world. When he had spotted her in the hall, the coils of her hair still glistening from her shower, the word hit him again. How could her innocence be real after she had suffered so much?

"Would you allow me to choose a bottle?" he asked.

"Just be prepared for me not to like it."

Ade signaled to the waiter, and ordered a Malbec he discovered in Napa several summers ago. Scanning the menu while they waited for the wine, he chanced glances Savannah's way. She smiled without seeming to realize she was doing so. He noticed that about her earlier. Even now, as she looked over a menu she probably knew by heart, her lips curled gently, deepening the dimples of her smooth cheeks. Yet the tension in her body evidenced itself around her eyes.

She set her menu onto the table, leaned over it. The view of her substantial cleavage snagged his attention. A mystery of spiced-rum skin. He could almost taste honey, almond, cinnamon, bourbon. His groin twitched. No shifting of shoulders, no quirk to her smile still soft and unaware. No seduction. No pretense. Just a lovely women who had no idea how desirable she was. Ade looked quickly away as the waiter returned to show him the bottle, uncork it, and pour a splash for him to taste. The wine washed away the phantom rum lingering on his tongue, distracted his baser instincts. Scrumptious as Savannah was, he'd made a promise to Taytay—and had no intention of breaking it.

"Excellent. Thank you."

The waiter poured, smiling at Savannah as he filled her glass. "Hey, Savvy. How's things?"

"Crazy, as always, Brian. We miss you at the farm."

"No offense, but I make a lot more here and still have time to bike."

"How's the cycling going this summer?"

"Not bad. Giving up weekends here at the restaurant has put a dent in my bank account, but if I place in the big one in October, it'll be worth it."

Cycling? A bittersweet subject. Another passion lost to his career, another possession lost alongside his ego. Boston's winding streets and a bicycle that cost more than most cars had kept Ade in good shape, and soothed the frustration always too close to the surface. He asked the waiter, "How is your time?"

Brian wiped the mouth of the bottle. "Good enough to qualify, not enough to win. Yet. You race?"

"I used to, many years ago. I had aspirations, but alas, it was not in my stars."

"Injury?"

"Age, choices that had to be made, but I do enjoy it still in a non-competitive capacity."

"We have some good trails around here. Nice smooth ones for sightseers—and then the kind I like." Brian mimed steering a bike, bouncing like his head would shake off. Ade laughed.

Savannah joined in. "Remember when you thought it was a good idea to transport seedlings using the back-up trail, on your bike?"

"Poor little seedlings. At least they weren't the chicks."

"They would've been had I sent you out to deliver those first."

Ade sat back in his chair, listening to them go back and forth, unhappy with himself, with his lusty conjuring. It happened unintentionally. Even as a boy, his libido had been…healthy. He had no compelling reason to deny it. Despite his Catholic upbringing, he wasn't a true believer, or even a marginal one. No threat of eternal damnation quelled the insatiability of a boy's libido—or a man's. Those who thought otherwise were fools. In his youth, he feared no unwanted children to trap him in an honorable marriage. As he became a man, that lack of fear took on a bitter taste, even if it served him well. Until Boston. Until Anita.

His cell vibrated again. Did she even know when he thought her name? Cursed woman. He had half a mind to throw his phone into the nearest body of water. Run it over with a car. Somehow dispose of it. But he couldn't. Not yet.

"I no longer have a bicycle." His response to the waiter's suggestion they ride together came automatically. Another skill that had served him well—listening even while his mind was elsewhere.

"I might be able to hook you up with a good deal," Brian said. "A friend of mine doesn't ride anymore. He's a scuba guy down in Florida. His bike sits in his dad's garage. I can ask him if he's interested in selling it."

A bicycle. Yes. Better than a used car. More affordable. Now. "Thank you. I would appreciate that."

The cell phone in his pocket vibrated once again. As Brian read them the specials, Ade reached into his pocket and switched it off. He had work to do. He'd deal with Anita later.

Maybe.

Chapter 6

down the night

Savannah ordered *linguine con vongole*, red and spicy. Her mouth watered in anticipation of the tang and the spice and the tender clams Tony, chef and proprietor, always cooked perfectly. Adelmo opted for *pollo quarto formaggio.*

"And, to start," he said, "may we please have the pear and candied walnut salad. Arugula instead of romaine, if that is possible."

"No problem." Brian tapped it into the handheld order ticket. "Anything else?"

"The *baratta*," Adelmo answered. "And the wild mushrooms with avocado. And fried calamari."

"You got it."

Savannah leaned back in her chair, eyeing him up and down. "Where are you going to put all that?"

"You will help me, no? Was it wrong to presume we would share the first course?"

"It's a bit...intimate, isn't it?"

"Food is meant to be shared," he said. "Among family, friends, lovers, even strangers. No?"

Smooth. Was he flirting with her? Had he stressed the word *lovers*? Or did her imagination make it seem so? It'd been a long time since anyone flirted with her. At least, a long time since she noticed. "Well, I might be persuaded to have a bite or two. But that's a lot of food."

"You have never seen me eat." Adelmo raised his wine glass, twirled it gently. "To new endeavors."

"To new endeavors."

Their glasses clinked. Savannah brought the wine to her lips and sipped. Fruity, yet not sugary, spicy without being heavy, the wine coated her tongue with little bursts of flavor she couldn't track, but culminated in a surprised, "This is wonderful."

"I hoped you would enjoy it. It is a perfect summer wine. Say what you will of European vintages, California produces some of the best in the world."

"I wouldn't know about that, but I do know I like this."

Brian brought their salad and set it onto the table between them. Though he gestured for her to eat first, Adelmo dug in with gusto while she nibbled politely through the salad, then the appetizers. It was usually all she could do to eat a full meal at D'Angelo's, where the portions were hearty. If she wanted to save room for dessert, she had to go slow. CC's provided all the baked desserts, and there was no way she was going home without a slice of Johanna's cake.

She moved food around the plate while Adelmo plowed ahead. Who was this man who knew how to choose a wine, and yet who ate with the abandon of a ranch hand after a cattle drive? Charming and stylish, dressed in lavender and clogs, yet able to swing from a rafter into a loft space to fetch her a box.

"What is it?" Adelmo's fork paused halfway to his mouth.

He caught you, sugarbeet. Savannah sat straighter. "I didn't mean to be so obvious."

"We are here to come to know one another." He set his fork down. "And this is my official interview. Ask whatever questions you like."

"I was just wondering"—*why a man as obviously cultured and accomplished as you are has agreed to be foreman on my little hick-town farm*—"why you came to America to study."

Adelmo dipped a calamari ring over and over. Popping it into his mouth, he leaned slightly forward. "My family sent me to study here in the United States. I have many siblings and cousins, but there were only funds for one of us. I was the brightest, the most ambitious. I would learn all there was to offer and bring my knowledge home to the family farm. At first, I did. Then I learned more. I learned things about farming practices and how they impact the world at large. I am an environmentalist, first and foremost. My father and uncles were not pleased after I changed my major, but I have sent a good portion of my earnings from teaching and lecturing back home to the family."

"Like they do."

"Exactly."

Savannah laughed. "Well, not exactly. I've never been able to pay them what they're worth."

"A little goes a long way where we're from," Adelmo said. "But I was able to send home substantially more. Ease my conscience, so to speak, for staying in the States. Because of this, our farm has grown from an obscure rural operation to a well-respected organic farm. I am passionate about the farm-to-table movement, and I believe in staying local. Part of the reason much of the produce found in supermarkets has no flavor is that it is picked before ripening so it can be sent around the world. The process, the varieties, the chemicals needed to feed a global environment not only creates flavorless food, but cripples small farms like yours. Makes them unsustainable."

"I do well enough."

"Because your locals can largely afford to pay a bit more for quality. An ancient way of life has become a boutique industry."

"You said something about it being an ongoing issue with your dad and uncle."

"Older minds." Adelmo waved a hand over his head. "They open reluctantly. Doing things the right way is not always the most profitable way. Neither is it necessarily the most expedient. In the end, the process is worth the extra time and expense. They agree when it pleases them to agree, and fight with me when it does not. This is why I spend four months home every year. To make sure they are complying with agreements made."

Adelmo pulled the *baratta* closer, cutting the stacked cheese, orange slice and basil into deliberate quarters. He ate a piece, chewed slowly, and then had another before spearing a third mini-stack to hold out to her. "Try this. It is extraordinary."

Savannah hesitated, but she ate it off his fork. "Oh, wow. That's something."

"Finish it. And taste the mushrooms."

"I'm good. Our dinners should be coming out soon." She sipped her wine, gathering her own composure. His passion for the subject, eating off his fork, just sharing a meal and conversation with this man made her feel both comfortable and wary—as if she were just waking up from a prolonged slumber. *Sleeping Beauty had a farm, e-i-e-i-o!*

"Your farm offers a chance for me to practice what I preach," he said. "I have been in academia far too long."

"Then why not just go home to your family farm?"

"Ah, the family farm." He chuckled softly. "The family farm comes with *la jefa*, my mother. I love her dearly, but, as my father learned, she is loveable in doses. Small ones."

"And yet Edgardo is going home to her."

"He and Tío are getting too old for heavy farm work. My siblings and cousins have been running our farm successfully for many years. It is time for the older men to enjoy the prosperous life they have made."

"I have to admit, I didn't suspect either of them old enough to have a son your age. Is it rude of me to ask how old they are?"

Adelmo bit into a piece of buttered bread. "Seventy-five." He grinned. "As of June."

"Both of them?"

"They are twins. Did you not know?"

"I had no idea." Savannah flopped back in her chair. "Edgardo led me to believe he's the older brother."

"He is. By about ten minutes."

"Seventy-five." She blew out a deep breath. "Until you showed up, I'd have said they were in their fifties."

"That would be some feat, given my own descent into decrepitude, even for rural Ecuador."

"Wow. I'm going to have to get my head wrapped around this." She nibbled at a mushroom. Charming. Intelligent. Attractive. Elusive. Or had he not just deftly maneuvered away from her clumsy lead into why he'd consent to work her farm? Curiosity burned. Questions brought questions. Pasts brought forth pasts. The need to know warred with the need to hide. Curiosity won. "You are not a farmhand, Adelmo," she blurted. "Why have you agreed to be one?"

He took a long, slow breath, went into himself. Savannah knew how that felt. Sort through what you can say and what you can't. Give enough without giving too much.

"I assumed my father and uncle told you about me." He met her eyes squarely. "It would have spared me having to do so. But you have a right to know who you have hired, and why I sought work on your farm. Perhaps sought is not quite the right word. It was my father's idea, one that appealed to me." He shifted in his seat but held her gaze. "I am hiding, Savannah. After a hard-won career in academia, I got involved with the wrong woman and paid the price. I've lost everything. My position, my credibility, the lifestyle I'd grown accustomed to in a city I loved. As you can understand, it is a sore subject, and one too personal to share in full with someone gracious enough to provide me, essentially a stranger, with the solace of anonymity."

Savannah grasped his hand across the table. "Please, I'm sorry, Adelmo. You don't have to say any more. I had no idea."

Adelmo stared at their hands on the table, his expression flat. Unreadable. Then he blinked, curled his fingers through hers, squeezed and let go. "Please, no apologies," he said. "Humiliating and painful as the circumstances are, it is good there is honesty between us. No secrets to get in the way of a friendship, eh?"

Her gaze fell. Secrets were all she had. They existed in a black hole of time she shared with no one. She left Georgia so she would never have to. And now Adelmo bared his soul, making her silence seem forced. Unfair. Cowardly. Yet silent she would remain. After so many years, if the words necessary to tell her tale did exist, Savannah didn't know where to find them. "I'm glad to offer you a place to hide out for a while," she said instead. "This has all been a bit…overwhelming, hasn't it?"

"How do you mean?"

"You, being, well…you, and not who I expected. I have to be honest, Adelmo, I would never have hired you had I known. Wait a sec." She put up an equivocating finger. "What I mean is, I never could have afforded you, what you're worth."

"I will do what is necessary, whatever you need to run your farm."

"I have no doubt about that. None whatsoever. If you are still willing to stay now that you've seen just how small Savvy's is, I am grateful for your expertise. But I'm thinking you were right about the menial tasks your father and uncle have you doing."

"Forgive me. It was a poor word choice."

She waved him away. "Don't apologize. In light of all you just told me, it was the exact right word, if a bit pretentious."

"You wound me, Ms. Callowell." Ade covered his heart with both hands, let them slide away. "But you are correct. I am pretentious. It happens when one starts out a crusader and ends up a scholar too full of his own greatness he can no longer see his world clearly. I am an expert on matters of sustainable cultivation processes when I rarely get my hands dirty. The change in my circumstances happened against my will, but, perhaps, in the nick of time."

"How so?"

Adelmo tugged at his lower lip, gaze on the tablecloth. "I think," he said, looking up, "I have been on the wrong path, Savannah. It is something that has been trying to free itself from my mind for a long time.

Today, walking the fields with Taytay and Tío, riding in the coot with you, it all just…clicked."

Savannah blushed. She dabbed nonexistent wine from her lips. "I imagine your life has been…urbane."

"It has. And I assure you, I am ready for a change."

"I understand that all too well, sugar," she murmured.

"There it is again," he burst, banishing the solemnity. "*Sugar.* I knew that's what you were saying. You've called me that several times today."

Covering her face with her napkin, she laughed into it. "It's a habit. I call everyone sugar."

"I like it." He winked. "It tells me much about you."

"It does?"

"First, it tells me you are from the south—"

"My accent does a good job of that."

"Ah, you've caught me. I know nothing of dialects and colloquialisms. I was trying to impress you."

"As if being an expert in sustainable cultivation processes wasn't enough."

"I write, too."

"You do? Anything I can read?"

"I am about to disappoint you again. I've not finished my masterpiece, though I have spent at least a decade researching it. It is my hope to work on it this winter, and the main reason I plan to stay here in Bitterly instead of going home with Taytay and Tío…"

Savannah wasn't fooled. The conversation shifted too quickly, his manner too purposefully, and she let it. He'd been honest with her, and she had no right to pry. It felt good to go back to casual. Flirty. Amusing. Safe.

The front door opened, letting in warm, summer air. Savannah turned to it, and her heart thumped into her stomach. In came the family McCallan. Some of them, at any rate. While Charlie and the twins took boxes straight into the kitchen, Johanna made a beeline for their table. An infant on her hip, a toddler by the hand, she sidled up to them, her sly grin perched, as ever, on her lips. She kissed Savannah's cheek as Adelmo rose to his feet.

"Sit, sit." Johanna waved him back down, and said to her little one, "No, Valentine, not you. Savvy and this nice man are having dinner." Then to Adelmo, "You must be Edgardo's son."

"Adelmo, yes."

"I'm Johanna. I own CC's, the bakery here in town. My husband and I just stopped in to deliver a few cakes. I'm glad I tagged along. It's so nice to meet you."

"The pleasure is mine."

Her gaze shifted to Savannah. She waggled her eyebrows. "Benny was right. Handsome. And a sexy accent to boot."

Savannah quelled the groan. The things Johanna said without even blinking. "How would Benny know anything about anyone? She's up in Maine, camping,"

"She was," Johanna said. "The flies were too much for her."

"Benny and her flies." Savannah shook her head. How had Benny even met this man? The answer was, she hadn't. Word got around fast in Bitterly. "Anyhow, I suppose I don't have to tell you that Adelmo is my foreman."

"I know who he is." Johanna turned to Adelmo. "You look nothing like your dad."

"I look like my mother."

"She must be beautiful."

Savannah didn't manage to quell the groan this time. "Johanna, please."

She only laughed, startling the baby in his sling. "Don't mind me," she told Adelmo. "It's summer. I'm a little nutty in the summer."

"You're a little nutty all the time, Jo."

"True enough, I suppose. So did Charlotte tell you about the barbeque?"

"She did. She asked me to bring watermelon and tomato salad."

"She did what?"

"I offered," Savannah amended. "It's so good to see her."

"It always is," Johanna sighed. "She makes me miss Cape May."

"Lovely little town," Adelmo interjected. "Winter and summer."

"It is. I used to have a bakery there. Well, I still do, but Charlie's daughter runs it these days."

"Is it also called CC's?"

"It is. You've been there?"

"Just once." Adelmo smiled that expensive smile. "But it was memorable. There was a cookie, a chocolate one—"

"Chocolate mud cookies."

"Yes, that's exactly the one. Extraordinary."

"Well, I bake them here too. If I had any left, I'd go get one for you. No matter how many I make, they sell out daily. But I just brought Almond Joyful cake. Save room for dessert. You'll love it."

"Almond Joyful?" Adelmo asked.

"Almond cake, chocolate frosting and coconut flakes."

"Oh, I see, Almond Joy—"

"—ful. Copyright infringement and all." She turned to Savannah. "Your favorite, isn't it, Savvy?"

"I might have to hate you, Jo."

"I can't help it I work my art in delicious calories."

Charlie came through the swinging kitchen door with his kids. Johanna waved him over.

"Hey, Savvy."

"Hey, Charlie. This is Adelmo, Edgardo's son and my new foreman come next spring. He's here learning the lay of things this season."

Adelmo rose, shook Charlie's hand.

"Charlie McCallan. Welcome to Bitterly."

"Adelmo Gallegos. Thank you."

"You've just been welcomed by the mayor himself," Johanna told him. "New in town and already moving in the highest circles."

"I'm not mayor," Charlie said. "Not yet, anyway. The election isn't until November."

"Hot food, coming through." Brian arrived with two plates of steaming, aromatic food. Charlie and Johanna stepped back to let him through, making apologies for disturbing their dinner.

"I'll see you on Friday at six o'clock," Johanna called as she and her family headed for the door. "And, Adelmo, you come too."

After Brian left them with their food, Ade leaned in, spoke softly. "That was…something."

"To say the least. That's Johanna for you. Never a dull moment."

Savannah struggled to find the right words. Dinner with a colleague was one thing. A barbeque at the McCallan's smacked of a date. Not even a day since his arrival, and already Bitterly was talking.

"I'm sorry Johanna put you on the spot like that," she said at last. "You don't have to come to the barbeque. I'll make excuses for you."

"Would you rather I not come?"

Savannah's gaze moved from his eyes, to his lips, to his eyes again. Was he amused? Flustered? Peeved? For her life, she couldn't say. "Do you…want to?"

"I would. Unless that makes you uncomfortable."

"No, no. Don't be silly." *Oh, yes. Yes it does, but, fiddle-dee-dee, such lovely discomfort.* "It'll give you the opportunity to meet Benny and Dan."

"Benny, your full-timer who said I am handsome and sexy, yes?"

Savannah blushed. "She said your accent is sexy, but yes, that would be her."

"I look forward to it."

"You'll like her. You'll like all of them. You won't be able to help yourself."

"I'm certain I will."

"I'm blabbering." Savannah pressed her palms to her cheeks. "Sorry."

Adelmo laughed softly. He pointed to her plate of food. "That looks delicious."

Savannah let her hands fall. "So does yours. I don't think I've ever ordered that, myself."

"Shall we share?" Eyebrow quirked, grin working its magic, Adelmo waited.

Savannah gave up trying to subdue the warm sensation pooling in her middle. Attempting to tame the idiotic smile trembling her lips, she twirled the linguine, speared a tender clam from its shell and held it out to Adelmo. "Food is meant to be shared. Sugar."

* * * *

Ade finished everything on his plate and a whole slice of Johanna's Almond Joyful cake, minus the bite Savannah managed to eat after finishing her own meal. He insisted she take a piece home. "For a midnight snack," he said, and though she demurred, she thanked him instead of insisting otherwise.

The drive home was quiet, but companionably so. Ade rested his head against the headrest, closing his eyes to the cool air coming in through the window. Boston had never been so quiet, its air never so fresh. The earthy scent reminded him of Ecuador in a way other rural environments never had. A trick of the mind, perhaps. He had not lived with his father and uncle outside of visits to the family farm in decades. That surely had to account for the comforting sensations of home.

Savannah pulled her car around to the back of her house and switched off the engine. Ade pulled himself out of the doze he had succumbed to. He sat straighter, tried to pretend he had not been dozing. He glanced at the dash just as the clock blinked out.

Ten after ten?

Ade shifted in his seat. Three hours had gone swiftly. Easily. Pleasantly. In Boston, time speeding along came with an adrenaline rush, barely contained fervor and polite aggression. Not so in Bitterly. Not so with Savannah. "I am surprised by your little town," he said. "That was an extraordinary meal."

She chuckled softly. "We country bumpkins like to eat too."

"Bumpkin," he repeated. "I am not sure I know this word."

"Local yokel?"

"That one, I have heard."

"Well, then." Savannah tapped the wheel. "Much as I hate for the evening to end, I have to be up early tomorrow."

The absolute dark of a country night of no moon made watching her easy. No calculating purr accompanied the glance through her lashes. No seduction masked in innocence. A woman like her, one without a cunning pore on her delicious skin, was easy to manipulate. And yet Ade could find no reason to, no desire to. Perhaps that was the reason his carefully rehearsed honesty had become spontaneous garble about being on the wrong path. It had startled him, speaking the words he recognized as the embarrassing truth the moment he said them. But he was back on his game now. Mostly.

"I, too, must be up with the sun. My boss is a cruel taskmistress."

"You should report her." A smile came and went just as quickly. Instead of getting out of the car, she picked at the stitching of her steering wheel. "If I get to the clinic an hour early, I can go over the charts before patients start arriving."

"Then by all means, you should get some sleep." Ade got out of the car, grabbed her slice of cake from the back seat, and went to her side. He opened her door, offered his hand to Savannah.

She hesitated, but she took it. "Aren't you going to ask what I do there?"

Heat rushed to his cheeks. She was a doctor. An OB/GYN. His Internet search had given him that detail, along with the rest. "I did not feel it was my place to pry," he covered. "You are my cruel taskmistress, after all."

Savannah shoved him playfully. "I'm a doctor. Obstetrics and gynecology."

"Ah, so I am not the only doctor posing as a farmhand."

"I suppose not." She averted her gaze. "I don't really broadcast it, but it's not a secret or anything. I just thought I owed you the truth, seeing as how you…well, we seem to have a lot in common."

Much, and nothing at all. Ade offered his arm, like the gentleman he promised Taytay he would be. Savannah took it.

"Does it surprise you?" she asked. "That I'm a doctor?"

"Why should it?"

"I was surprised to find out you're not only a grown man, but a highly educated professional. Aren't you wondering what an OB/GYN is doing on a farm in Bitterly?"

"I didn't know," he lied, "until a moment ago."

Something bad happened in Georgia, Taytay had said. *Very bad. Savvy's heart is old. Very old and fragile.*

Ade had been too wrapped up in his own drama to pay close attention to the promise his father demanded. Only once he decided to discover all there was to know about his soon-to-be employer had he remembered his father's words, and understood the promise he extracted. And only now that she was no longer an abstract means to an end did Ade regret prying into the horror of her life.

He motioned her to precede him up the steps. Savannah went inside and flipped on the lights that flickered, went out, and flickered back on again. She grimaced up at the fixture.

"Bet that bulb is loose again. You'd think I had elephants tromping around, loosening all the bulbs and sockets in this house."

"I can look at that if you'd like."

"Are you an electrician too?"

"Hardly, but I did grow up on a farm that ran mostly on generators and outdoor plumbing. Allow me to take a look."

"Well, all right. Thank you."

Savannah took the boxed cake from him and set it into the refrigerator, leaned protectively against the door. "Don't you go snitching my cake."

"I can't make any promises."

She wagged a finger at him, but laughed softly. "This was a really nice evening. Thanks."

"Then I am hired?"

Her smile faltered, but didn't fail. "Ah, I forgot. This was an interview." She pushed off the door. "I'm getting the bargain of a lifetime, Adelmo. If you still want to be here, I want you."

The grin happened before he could squelch it.

"Here," she amended quickly. "I want you here. On the farm. That came out—I didn't mean—Oh, forget it. I'll just say good-night before I start blabbering again."

"Good-night, Savannah," he said more softly than he should have, than he meant to. "I look forward to working with you."

"Me too."

"Sleep well."

"I'll do my darndest to." Savannah stopped in her tracks, tilted her head from side to side.

"Is something wrong?"

"Wrong? No. It's just that…my headache's gone."

"I was not aware you were feeling ill. You should have said something. We could have waited—"

"If we waited until my headache went away, it might have been months."

"Months?"

"Unfortunately."

"That doesn't sound good."

"It's not, but I've been getting them for a long time. I'm used to it. Something about tonight made this one go away, though. I wish I knew what it was."

"It must have been the cake," he said. "Johanna's Almond Joyful cake can cure all the world's ills, I am certain of it."

"I did have the one bite." Her dimples deepened.

His heart stitched. Ade pretended to have an itch. "I think it was two bites."

"That must be it, then." Walking past him, she wagged her finger again. "Stay away from my cake now, you hear?"

"Yes, cruel taskmistress," Ade called after her that one beat beyond the tease he imagined, and fumbled into schoolboy flirtation. Hallway shadows swallowed her bit by bit, until she was a hint of light cloth vanishing around the stair rail. Her tread shuffled up the steps. Water in the bathroom. Creaks across the floorboards above. Only after her door clicked closed and all sound ceased did Ade realize he still stood rooted to the spot where she had left him.

He half-heartedly contemplated snitching a piece of her cake, just to make her laugh when she saw it. Instead, he took out the pitcher of sweet tea and poured himself a glass.

Savannah was a woman. He was an expert in that field. What was it about her that brought forth honesty he didn't know he possessed anymore? Why did he fumble like a schoolboy because of a dimple?

Because he was tired. Defeated. Just back from too much time home with *la jefa*. Savannah was a woman, an attractive, intelligent woman. Despite his body's pulls and jolts responding to her as such, he had promised Taytay he would be in all ways a gentleman. His time on this farm was to heal him, provide solace after so hard a fall from grace.

Inhaling deeply, exhaling long, Ade leaned against the counter in Savannah's kitchen. He reached a hand into his pocket. His fingers slicked along the phone's smooth, glassy face. Cold. Comforting. He pulled it out. He switched it on. It vibrated, lighting up with texts:

> *Call me.*
> *Call me.*
> *Where are you?*
> *You can't hide anywhere I can't find you.*

Make this easier on both of us. Call me.
Call me!
I'll find you, you bastard. Don't think I won't.

The voicemails waiting for him would say the same. Ade had no intention of listening to them, or calling her back. She wasn't even getting a text. The woman was a viper and a liar. An adulteress. Even that, he might have forgiven to preserve his position, status, wealth. He'd forgiven worse for less. Adelmo Gallegos was not beyond deceiving a colleague without qualm, or a woman without guilt. They were players, just like he was, in a game necessitating such things. But there were some things he would not do, and deceiving an innocent child was at the top of that list.

* * * *

I couldn't help it. I couldn't. He's just so foreign and dreamy. I was hoping to see them kiss, otherwise I would've stayed outside this time and never seen what I did. Oh, I wish I hadn't. Good golly, I wish I hadn't. That thing squished into an angry ball wanted at Savannah so bad, but it stayed back, getting madder by the minute.

What is that thing? Like some kind of monster under the bed waiting for a stray hand or foot to show over the side? I get all jittery, but I'm just so curious. What is it? Why does it hate Savvy so much? Those little girls know, I betcha. I can try asking them, but they never say anything. They just stand guard, always ready and waiting.

Chapter 7

every look love gave us

Ever since Benny happened into the childbirth clinic in East Perry, Savannah had been less secretive about being a doctor. It didn't take long for word to spread around Bitterly. Though it seemed to be common knowledge she volunteered over in East Perry, no one asked why she no longer practiced medicine outside of her Wednesdays in the clinic. No one speculated. No one whispered behind their hands when she appeared. It was a matter of fact that no one but she bothered about, so Savannah stopped.

Upon arriving home Wednesday, as always, far later than she hoped, Savannah had found a dishtowel-covered bowl on the table, a note on top:

> *This is my own version of locro, a traditional Ecuadorian potato and cheese soup. Taytay and Tío challenged me, and I was goaded into stealing potatoes from your pantry and cheese from the storefront. Considering I used your food, I made enough for you as well. I hope you do not mind.*

Savannah had lifted the dishtowel, the aroma of cheese and spices filling her up and making her mouth water. The bowl was still warm. She grabbed a spoon from the ever-full dish rack, and ate standing at the sink. Intoxicating was the only word she could come up with to describe the soup. She left him a note in return:

I have to hate Johanna for her cake, and you for this soup.
Insanely delicious. Thank you.

And that was all she saw of him until Friday afternoon when he came in from the fields covered in burrs, clumps of dried mud, bramble, and sweat. Savannah turned from washing the dishes she left in the sink after breakfast, dripping hands on hips.

"You're like a little boy up in that field."

"I forgot how enjoyable it is to get dirty." Adelmo untied the laces of his work boots and kicked them off. "I will sweep this up, I promise. If you would be so kind as to turn your back, I'll leave my jeans here as well instead of leaving a trail through your house."

"Oh." Savannah's cheeks burned instantly. "S-sure."

She turned back to the dishes, washing again the things she'd already scrubbed clean. In her periphery, Adelmo stripped out of his jeans. His belt hitting the floor was a muffled clunk that echoed in Savannah's rapidly beating heart.

How silly. She was a doctor. And he slept across the hall from her, lived in her house, bathed in her bathroom. *Get over it, sugarbeet.*

Her own voice in her head became her aunt's, became a chuckle echoing out of the past but somehow, in the present. She missed Auntie Bea at that moment, more than she had in all the years since leaving Georgia behind.

A bump upstairs lifted her head, opened eyes she hadn't realized were closed. The shower turned on, making the old pipes of her house groan cranky protests more endearing than anything else. Savannah rinsed the twice-washed dishes and set them into the rack to dry. Adelmo was upstairs in her shower, where she would be soon after scrubbing off the day's work. She tried not to imagine anything lusty, and failed. Miserably.

"Watermelon and tomato salad," she reminded herself. "Make the watermelon and tomato salad."

She sliced the watermelon, heirloom tomatoes—true ones, she checked—and red onion, tossed them in olive oil, salt and a squeeze of lemon before drizzling in the red-wine vinegar. It needed to marinate just long enough to meld the flavors without breaking down the fruits and making them mushy. On top she sprinkled the sweet pea sprouts she preferred to the mint in the original recipe. The earthy taste complemented rather than competed with the other flavors, in her opinion. Just before leaving, she'd sprinkle the crumbled farm cheese on top.

The water went off upstairs. Savannah covered the salad and left it on the counter, waited to hear the footsteps across the hall and the door to Adelmo's room close before she went up herself.

"You finished in the bathroom?" she called from outside his room. He opened the door, wrapped only in a towel. Savannah stumbled back. Adelmo didn't seem to notice.

"One moment."

He hurried to the bathroom, his back still wet and the muscle that allowed him to swing himself into the loft deliciously evident. Savannah curbed that line of thought only to get snagged on his chest hair being the sort of just-enough she appreciated on a man.

"I will be ready to go when you are." He came back with a toiletry bag. "Is it silly of me to be excited about this gathering?"

"Silly? No. But...why? It's just a barbeque."

"Guest lecturing from college to college does not give one time to make many friends. I will be here in Bitterly at least a full year. I am...hopeful."

And his expression was hopeful. Hopeful and happy. He seemed more relaxed since their dinner together. Less guarded. That was a feeling she knew as well. Bitterly had a way of soothing even the most troubled spirit. Savannah returned his smile that became almost shy. Endearing and sexy at the same time. And he was still only wrapped in a towel. Savannah lowered her gaze and took a step away, then another.

"We'll head out about a quarter to six. It doesn't take long to get across town."

In her own room, Savannah leaned against her door. Eleven years. Eleven years, and in all that time, the occasional date to satisfy Margit or Auntie Bea was the closest she had gotten to being interested in a man. And now, within days of meeting him, she couldn't curb the naughty thoughts her Auntie Bea would howl over.

She exhaled deeply. It was the intimate proximity, his accent, loneliness finally catching up with her that she wouldn't have noticed if he weren't living in her house. Maybe it was the just-enough chest hair, or the potato and cheese soup he made. Whatever it was, Savannah didn't simply lust after Adelmo, she liked him. She liked knowing he was near, and not in the same way she did his father and uncle—men she loved. There had been others, in Georgia and in Bitterly, who tried to attract her attention. She'd even toyed with the notion of a colleague at the clinic, but it never went further. Why Adelmo? Why now?

Maybe you simply like him in that special way, sugarbeet.

She showered, dressed and managed to snap out of it enough not to startle when Adelmo came out to the car dressed in cargo shorts, a polo, and those clogs. His highlighter-yellow shirt worked to ease the inner frenzy building up inside her. Savannah could smile genuinely as he climbed into the passenger seat. "You sure like bright colors."

Adelmo plucked at his shirt. "Is it inappropriate?"

"Not at all. Down south, men dress much more colorfully than these Yankees do. It's refreshing."

"Is refreshing a nice way of saying silly?"

"Are you fishing for compliments or truly concerned about the color of your shirt?"

Adelmo flashed that smile. "Both."

"Well, your shirt looks great and so do you. That should cover it. Now hold on to the bowl of salad so it doesn't tip on the way."

"What is this?" he asked, lifting the cover.

"Watermelon and tomato salad. Don't you go sticking your fingers in there."

"They are clean." Adelmo plucked a chunk of watermelon from the bowl. Chewed. His eyes rolled and his shoulders slumped. "That is outstanding. What would make you think to combine these things?"

"I didn't," she confessed. "It was a recipe left on my website-slash-blog thing back when Benny first created it for me."

Savannah spoke of the site Benny created, and how the blog had become a place where growers, consumers, cooks, and casual visitors shared information, stories, and recipes. She caught him snitching more bits and pieces from the bowl, and though she chastised him every time, she'd catch him doing it again.

"Give that here." She said when they got to the house on County Line Road. Lifting the lid, she saw the sprinkling of cheese still sitting pretty on top. "At least you were polite enough to snitch from the edges."

"I couldn't help myself. This is my new favorite thing to eat. Even more than Johanna's Almond Joyful cake."

"Just see to it everyone else gets some." She laughed. "And don't think I didn't notice the snitch you took from my cake while I was at the clinic on Wednesday."

"Me? I would never do such a thing."

"Liar. You can't fool me. I measured precisely, and there was a good quarter inch missing. Admit it."

He placed a dramatically stricken hand over his heart. "But I made you soup."

"And that's why I forgave you."

"All right." Adelmo hung his head. "I admit it. Now may I have one more snitch before we go around back?"

And this is why I like you. She snapped the lid closed. "Let's not get carried away, sugar. It's easy enough to make. Most of the ingredients are right in the garden or at the farmstand. All but the watermelon. I've never had much success with them."

He nodded. "Yes, growing them can be tricky here in the northeast. The cool nights lower the soil temperature more than melons like."

"I tried plastic to up the temperature a bit, but the weeds were out of control."

"Ah, you used clear."

"To let in sunlight."

"Yes, yes, but the clear plastic acts as a greenhouse to weed seeds too. Black plastic keeps the soil even warmer, and it doesn't allow the weeds to grow. You must water very carefully though when using plastic. Watermelons need a lot of water."

"Interesting," Savvy said. "Too bad it's so late in the season."

"We can try it next year."

Savannah met his gaze, tried to figure out if the sudden dip in his tone was real or imagined. He was out of the car before she could decide, coming round to her side and opening the door.

"Thank you," she said.

"May I take that for you?" he asked. "I promise not to sneak any more."

"I don't trust you for a moment." But she handed it to him all the same. Adelmo closed the door behind her, his arm encircling her. Briefly. He smelled like pine and spice and fresh air.

"You look lovely this evening," he said. "As always."

Savannah lifted a Birkenstock-sandaled foot. Cut-offs, tank top and Birkies. Her casual outfit of choice from the first scent of the earth warming to the first bite of autumn. "Well, thanks, but I have to say, your standards might be a bit low."

"I assure you, they are not."

No question this time. His voice dipped lower. His eyes narrowed slightly, and his smile sent a shiver across Savannah's shoulder blades. She murmured sounds she wasn't quite sure qualified as actual words and preceded him around to the back of the house where the family McCallan was already gathered, along with two of Johanna's three sisters, Benny and Dan, and Benny's younger brother, Peter Grady.

"Are we late?" Savannah asked after the greetings were made.

"Nope," Johanna took the bowl from her hands. "We're still waiting on Nina and Gunner. Why don't you go introduce Adelmo around while Charlie and I get the food out. The kids are starving, as always."

Savannah introduced Adelmo to Johanna's sisters, Emmaline and Julietta, and their husbands, Mike and Efan. She didn't bother with the little ones racing about, whose names she rarely kept straight anyway, but included eighteen-year-old Caleb and, of course, Charlotte in the introductions.

"Nina and Gunner are always late," Charlotte pulled Savannah in to whisper, which in this young woman's world was nothing of the kind. "They always breeze in with some wild story about being abducted by Somali pirates or something. Half the time it's true." Charlotte caught Adelmo's hand. "Adelmo, is it? What a great name. Come and meet Benny. She's been dying to see you in the flesh after Johanna's description."

Dragging him over to meet Benny, as well as Dan and Peter, Charlotte left Savannah staring after her. Caleb was shaking his head, chuckling softly.

"She seems a lot more..." Savannah sought the right word.

"...manic?" Caleb suggested. "Yeah, she is. It's getting worse. Will says it's because she's super-unhappy but won't admit it. That's how our mom got just before she left Dad."

"Where is Will these days?" Savannah asked. "Is he doing a summer semester?"

"Internship. He's staying in Florida with Mom for now."

"No bakery for him, huh?"

"Nah. He wants to be a professional scuba diver or something."

"Caleb," Charlotte laughed, dragging Adelmo back to Savannah. "Marine biology, Savvy. Don't listen to my little brother."

Caleb rolled his eyes.

"You're starting at the Culinary Institute soon, aren't you?" Savannah asked him.

He beamed. "Associates in Baking and Pastry Arts. Dad wants me to do a Bachelors program, but I don't see the point."

"Education is never wasted," Savannah insisted.

"But time is. I've got plans."

"You do?"

Caleb grinned. "Big plans not just for myself. For CC's."

"Plans he won't share." Charlotte feigned a pout. "Not even with me."

"So you can steal them? No way. The world will have to await my genius."

Brother and sister teased and argued. Children played. Adults talked and laughed. Johanna and Charlie called the older kids in to help carry things out. Julietta and Efan started a rousing game of duck-duck-goose with the little ones. Before food came out of the kitchen, Nina and Gunner arrived, a sullen teenaged girl in tow. Dark hair and eyes, her skin like sunshine on burnished wood, she was even more exotic in Bitterly than Savannah herself. She stuck close to Nina, smiling only cautiously as introductions were made.

"Savvy, this is Tabitha. Tabs, this is Savannah Callowell."

Tabitha's jaw worked, but she didn't say whatever words made her scowl.

"I'm pleased to meet you, Tabitha." Savannah stood aside to pull Adelmo forward. "Ladies, Gunner, this is Adelmo Gallegos, the new foreman on my farm."

"I am pleased to meet you. Tabitha." Adelmo extended a hand, kissed it gallantly when she gave it. The teenager's wide eyes darted from his face to Savannah's and back again. "I am pleased as well."

Her accent was somewhat Greek, somewhat Russian. Savannah couldn't quite place it. "Welcome to Bitterly," she said, and was rewarded by something that might have been a real smile. "How long will you be in town?"

Tabitha's lips pressed into a pouty line.

"Only through the weekend," Nina said. "Gunner and I have to be back in New York Monday morning."

"Charlotte told me you have a curiosities shop in the city," Adelmo said. "That seems a unique line of work."

"It is and it isn't." Gunner laughed. "I've come to know there are a whole lot of oddies out in the world to cater to."

Charlie and Johanna, followed by a line of children, came out the back door carrying platters and bowls, and baskets of bread, utensils and paper plates. Nina hurried off to help, Tabitha on her heels.

"And welcome to you, too," Gunner called to Adelmo as he joined his wife and Tabitha. "I apologize in advance for the headache you'll go home with. My wife and her sisters are a bit...overwhelming. Add Benny to the mix and it's completely nuts."

Adelmo's eyes moved from face to laughing face. Savannah tried to read his expression. Amused? Or...she shook it off. That flickered calculation was her own experiences insinuating themselves. His smile was nothing but kind. Curious, but kind.

"Overwhelming to say the least, huh?" she asked him. "Aren't they?"

"A bit, yes. But nice."

"I know a lot of people in Bitterly, but these? They're my only real friends."

"Why is that?"

Savannah shrugged. "I guess I'm particular about who I let into my life."

"I will keep that in mind." He held her gaze.

Savannah warmed from head to toe, but she didn't look away.

"Come and get it," Charlie called, waving them in. "Hurry, before the kids devour it all."

Adelmo gestured her to lead the way. Despite Charlie's warning, the children didn't break their game to rush the food table. Gathered there with the other adults, Savannah took paper dishes from the pile and handed one to Adelmo.

He leaned over her shoulder. "I thought this was a barbeque," he whispered far too close to her ear. "I have had pasta salad at a barbeque, but never anything like this."

"I should have warned you," she said. "This is an Italian barbeque. That means macaroni and meatballs, not grilled stuff. I'm sure Emma made the meatballs and tomato sauce. No one can beat Johanna's skill with sweets, but Emma's the cook in the Coco family. You're in for a treat."

They ate. And they ate. Having been a guest to such a gathering before, Savannah knew to pace herself. Johanna would have something completely irresistible for dessert. The bottomless stomach Adelmo exhibited at D'Angelo's was again in evidence. When Johanna's strawberry shortcake appeared, he ate a generous slice. Slowly. Savoring every mouthful as if it were the last thing he would ever eat.

"That beats me." Dan Greene patted his stomach, setting his fork down with half a slice left. "I can't do it."

"Allow me to help you." Adelmo snatched Dan's plate and finished what was left on it. He licked the fork clean. "That, ladies, was the most delicious meal I have ever had the pleasure of eating. And I have eaten in some of the best restaurants in the world. Genius, from first bite to last."

"That might be laying it on a little thick." Mike, Emma's husband, pulled his wife closer. "But not by much. The older I get, the more Emma's cooking shows up in my jeans size."

"Tell me about it," Charlie chimed in. "Try being married to the cake queen."

"Adelmo's a good cook too," Savannah blurted, and immediately regretted it. Her face burned. "I mean, he made *locro*, this potato and cheese soup, the other night for his dad and uncle and was good enough to leave a bowl of it for me."

After the momentary but undeniable silence rife with glances passing from Savannah to her new foreman, the party descended upon Adelmo with questions about Ecuador, his work, and the *locro* Savannah mentioned. She took the opportunity as it came, to gather dishes and her composure. Loading up an empty bread basket with things to bring back inside, she pretended she didn't notice Benny trying to get her attention.

In the empty kitchen, Savannah set down the basket and leaned against the counter. She breathed in. And out. Deeply. Trying and failing to tell herself she was being silly, that her reactions were only creating more misunderstanding of the situation she currently found herself in. These sisters, Benny and Dan, were the stuff happily-ever-after was made of, one and all. Naturally, they were looking for it. Everywhere. They loved her, and she loved them. But they had no idea she already had her happily-ever-after, and that it became the stuff of nightmares in the end.

"Another headache?"

Benny came through the door, pushing the screen open with her foot and carrying a platter of dirty utensils. Savannah hurried to hold the door for her.

"Strangely enough, no," she answered. "I haven't had a headache in a few days."

"That is strange. They're usually really bad in the summer. Probably the heat."

"In Bitterly?" Savannah laughed. "Sugar, you never felt heat until you've spent a summer in Georgia."

"Allergies?"

"Checked and checked again. Just the headache. But it's not plaguing me now so let's not jinx it."

Benny put the platter and utensils into the sink and ran the water until it was hot. "I'm just going to wash these."

"I'll dry." Savannah grabbed a dishtowel. The two women stood at the sink in companionable silence. Savannah caught Benny peeking at her twice before she took the last utensil from her soapy fingers.

"He's just my new foreman," she said through an expelled breath. "He didn't turn out to be the college kid I thought he was, but that changes nothing. Johanna invited him tonight, not me."

"But you did have dinner with him on Tuesday."

Savannah rolled her eyes. "I knew the whole town would be talking about that."

"Not the whole town." Benny crinkled her nose. "At first anyway. Johanna called me from her cell on the way home that night. I did hear about it at the coffeehouse though."

"Bitterly is way too small-town sometimes."

"Come on, Savvy. It's cute. You have to admit it's like something out of a romance novel."

"If there was any romance, maybe. But there isn't. Overqualified as he is, Adelmo's my foreman for the next year on the farm. End of story."

"Whatever you say, boss."

Savannah knew better than to believe that was the end of it, but, hanging the dishtowel over the oven handle, she pretended for the moment that it was.

"So how was your abbreviated camping trip with the little princess in tow?" she asked. "I hear the flies were too much for you."

Benny wrinkled her nose again. "July is black-fly season. I didn't know. And camping with a baby is a lot less fun than it sounds. I think we'll do a hotel next time, save the camping until she's four or five."

"Where to next?"

"New Brunswick and Prince Edward Island. We met a couple up in Bar Harbor who were just coming back from there. The pictures." Benny clutched her heart. "To die for, Savvy. You've never seen anything so beautiful."

"Isn't it cold up there?"

"Gloriously. You know me. I'm a polar bear at heart."

"And I'm a tropical bird."

"In Bitterly, Connecticut. You poor dear."

And the subject of Adelmo thankfully and truly dropped. Savannah followed Benny outside where dusk settled and fireflies rose up into it. Julietta and Efan, as always, led the children off like a pair of benevolent Pied Pipers. The jars Savannah noticed lining the porch rail were handed out, holes were punched into the lids, and off they all went to catch little glowing bugs in makeshift lanterns.

Still gathered at the picnic tables, the adults chatted less animatedly than before. Dan's arm rested across the back of Benny's chair. Baby Irene slept on her mother's chest. Emma and Mike sat likewise tucked, Julietta's infant son snuggled into the crook of his aunt's arm, while Nina and Gunner pointed out the ways constellations were different all over the world. Charlie and Johanna, heads together, whispered and laughed softly over jokes no one else heard. Charlotte and Peter, Tabitha and Caleb leaned in, no longer children yet not yet full-fledged adults. And Adelmo sat amidst them all, one leg slung over the other. Casual and relaxed. He already fit in more naturally than she did, even after all her years among these wild sisters and their extended others.

Children squealed, turning her attention to the clutch gathered around Efan, who was holding up something small and wriggling. A mouse. A bat. Something he should not be touching, Savannah was certain. There were so many children from toddlers to adolescents. Happy. Carefree. Alive.

The thought struck with the terrible force it sometimes could when she was least expecting it. Savannah turned away, her eyes filling and tears falling. She clenched her teeth, forced the tears back. Conjuring her twin daughters as they had been, smiling and sweet and just as happy as the kids still squealing over whatever Efan had in his hands, she breathed deeply until the sting of tears abated. A warm and soothing sensation began in her middle and spread. Savannah almost felt them there at her hips, little arms encircling her. In her mind's eye, she placed one hand on Sally's dense curls, one on Ginger's silky locks, stroking their heads as she used to. *You are always in my heart, my sugarbeets.*

The warm sensation reached her cheeks. Savannah didn't care if she looked foolish, standing so still among the children's chaos. She would have happily stayed just as she was, absorbing whatever of her girls was left in the world, if only out of her own mind. But the sensation ebbed and, like arms falling away, was gone. Savannah's eyes opened, followed the sound of children racing about the yard. Ginger and Sally would be closer to Caleb's age, or Tabitha's. But for one, split moment, they were racing about with all the little ones. Their shadows, if not their selves.

She spotted Charlotte just as Charlotte spotted her and waved her nearer. Savannah let go of her little ghosts and made her way to sit beside the young woman who always made her glad. "When you going back to Cape May?"

"Tomorrow, unfortunately."

"I was hoping you'd changed your mind."

"I always change my mind once I'm here." She laughed. "But Cape May calls. Matt's been slammed. I had to beg Caleb to come back with me and help out a few weeks."

"You had to beg an eighteen-year-old guy to spend the summer at the beach?" Savannah pursed her lips. "Must be tetched, as my auntie says."

"Caleb is that." Charlotte shrugged. "He doesn't like Matt. He tries to push Peter on me every time I come home."

Savannah glanced at Peter Grady. Every young woman—and some of the older ones—found his bright blue eyes and dark hair as irresistible as the cleft in his clean-shaven chin.

"I can think of worse things than having Peter Grady pushed on me, sugar."

"Savvy." Charlotte lowered her voice. "We've been friends since childhood. I swore off hometown boys when I was in middle school. Katie and I have a pact. Local boys overly attached to Bitterly lead to never stepping a foot outside this town. No, thank you."

"When's the last time you spoke to Katie?"

Charlotte gripped her arm. "Don't even say it…Who?"

"Grayson—"

"McKenna? No way." Pulling the cell phone from her pocket, Charlotte rushed Peter. "Why didn't you tell me about Katie and Grayson?"

And like that she was gone, shrieking laughter into her phone. Savannah was suddenly exhausted, yet she didn't have the heart to pull Adelmo away when he was so obviously having a good time. Instead of joining the adults, she found an Adirondack chair, leaned into the curve of it, and closed her eyes.

* * * *

"Savannah?"

Her brow furrowed. Her lips moved with words she didn't speak, then frowned. Ade waited while Savannah blinked all the way back from adorable slumber.

"Was I snoring?" She shouldered higher in her chair.

Ade chuckled softly. "No, you were not snoring."

"I was dreaming. I think it was a bad dream."

"I'm glad I woke you, then. You are tired. We should go."

"It was all the food." She groaned. "It made me sleepy. I'm okay now. We don't have to leave."

"It seems the others are starting to go, anyway." Ade gestured over his shoulder. "Dan and Benny want to get the baby home."

Savannah took his offered hands and let him haul her to her feet. She swayed just a little, and he held on to her until she steadied. Though he wasn't tall, he was still taller than she. For one, split moment, he imagined her head coming to rest against his shoulder, the perfect fit they would make, and dismissed it as quickly. He was not a man of soft feelings and heart patterings. Normally. But he was anything but normal these days.

"Are you all right?" he asked.

"Fine, but—" Savannah fished the car keys out of her pocket and held them out to him. "You mind driving home?"

"Not at all."

Ade took the keys. He held his hand lightly on the small of her back as they joined the others in saying good-night, kept it there as they walked to the car, telling himself it was to make certain she didn't fall, and not because he wanted an excuse to touch her. The battle with his self-control was, he felt, the stuff of legends, and it had only been a few days. He'd met, bedded and forgotten women in less time. He told himself it was his promise to Taytay, the fact that Savannah was his boss. That's why he stayed away when he wanted to be near, why he made her *locro* when what he wanted to make was love. It had nothing to do with resisting this forbidden thing, or that doing so made him happier than he had been in many years.

"You will have to remind me of the directions," Ade said as he got into the car and turned over the engine. "I was not paying attention, and now it is dark."

"Sure thing," Savannah said. "Take a left at the end of the driveway."

They chatted as he drove, about Charlie's mayoral campaign and Dan's landscaping escapades, Johanna's baking skills, Emma's meatballs, the literary banter between Julietta and Efan that he couldn't follow but appreciated all the same. Simple, wonderful topics with simply wonderful people he didn't have to guard against, or outwit. He'd discovered that within moments of walking into the yard. There were no nuanced phrases that meant nothing. As refreshing as he found Savannah, Ade also found her friends. In fact, Bitterly seemed full of such people, just like Taytay assured him it was. He liked these people truly, and that was another something that had not happened in too many years.

He pulled up the driveway. The night was young, and he wasn't tired. Savannah, however, seemed drowsy. Content, but drowsy. Ade parked, and hurried to her side of the car. She took the hand he offered, and allowed him to keep it as they ambled to the porch steps. Whether he was slowing her pace or she was slowing his, neither of them were in any hurry. Ade opened the screen door, gesturing her ahead of him.

"Oh, you have the…" Savannah spun to him, into him "…keys."

She was so close. All he had to do was tip her face and their lips would meet without any effort at all. Ade's heart hammered. His lip beaded sweat. He was a boy again, or the man before women became an obstacle to overcome. A way to a means. Savannah was neither. She was a woman with a sorrowful past, opening up to him as his conscience said she shouldn't.

Her face tilted. She searched his eyes, found his mouth and Ade gave into his hammering heart. She tasted like summer. She smelled like a breeze coming down off the mountains. In his arms, she was the perfect balance of softness and sinew. Savannah's arms wound about his neck. His wrapped tighter about her waist, hands wandering to her lower back and no further. This kiss was enough. And it broke no promises made by a more jaded man. A man who didn't think it possible to feel anything more than calculated desire.

Savannah pulled gently away. "I'm sorry," she said. "I didn't mean to…"

"I did."

That dimple deepened. His gut lurched.

"I've been alone a very long time, Adelmo—"

"Ade." He caressed her lips with his thumb. "Now, you must call me Ade."

"Ade," she said, and the power of that music dwarfed all other words she spoke. Savannah's lips trembled. "I've been alone because that's how I wanted it, because something terrible happened in Georgia, many years ago. Now I am kissing you, a man I've known only a few days, not to mention an employee, and I'm scared. I don't want to be, but I am."

Ade stroked her cheek with the backs of his fingers. *Something terrible happened in Georgia.* The horror, read indifferently weeks ago, hit him full in the face. Confessing what he knew wasn't an option. Not after that kiss. Not after her trembling words. Ade leaned in, kissed the corners of her eyes, and stepped back. "It is a kiss in the moonlight after a wonderful night spent with friends," he said. "Nothing to fear, Savannah. I am nothing to fear. I promise you that."

"Nothing to fear," she whispered back, as if his promise made it so.

He dropped the keys into her hand.

Savannah opened the door. "Whoa!"

She slammed backwards into him, arms flung wide and feet flying. Ade caught her before she crumbled. Eyes fluttering, lips working, Savannah slipped out of consciousness before he lowered her to the ground.

"Savannah? Can you hear me?" He patted her cheek, looked beyond her into the dark kitchen. No sign of an intruder, no sound to indicate an escape in progress. Lifting her into his arms, he held her close. He whispered,"*Ojalá que esté bien,*" over and over, as he carried her into the parlor, placed her tenderly onto the sofa, and called 911.

* * * *

Oh my gosh! Oh, no! It just…I've never…those brave little girls. And me, so scared I couldn't move to help them. It—he. I know that dark ball of anger is a he now. I saw him clear as those little girls trying so hard to keep him off. They didn't stand a chance. Not against him. Ricky Ricardo kissed Savvy, and the ball of simmering anger boiled over. I felt it like an electric shock, same as when my brother told me to stick a hairpin into a light socket. Same as I felt that day, just before the hammer came down on my head. Evil has a feel to it, I guess.

He came at Savvy and the little girls got poofed away. He slammed into her so hard. So hard. And I didn't do anything to stop him. Again. All this time dead, and I haven't learned a gosh-darn thing.

Chapter 8

making music for my heart

"You should have told me they were getting this bad."

After a night in the hospital and days being doted over by three Ecuadorian men, Savannah now had to patiently endure Margit's agitated pacing in the parlor.

"It never hit me like that before." Savannah sat on the couch, covered by a thin blanket despite the warm day, knitting with the fine, lavender lambswool Darla and Sandra had spun. "Not ever. In fact, the headache I had when I called you last week went away and stayed away for a couple of days. Then all of a sudden—slam!"

"Did you eat anything out of the ordinary? Drink? Can you think of anything that might have brought it on?"

Not a thing, sugar. Unless you mean kissing my new foreman under a starlit sky. "I did overeat at the McCallan's. But I've certainly done that before. And I wasn't drinking anything stronger than lemonade."

"You're sure it wasn't spiked?"

"Unless Johanna is now feeding her kids alcohol, yes, I'm sure."

"Savvy, don't joke." Margit sat on the edge of the couch. She pulled the mass of dark, curly hair off her neck, leaned into the breeze from the table fan. "You really should get air conditioning in here."

"We don't usually need it but for a week or two every summer."

Margit's blue eyes twinkled. "Of course the week I come to visit. Is this your way of discouraging me from ever coming back?"

Savannah set her knitting down and reached for her friend's hand. Until seeing her again, she hadn't missed Margit. Now, sitting together in her parlor, she missed her so much. "I would love if you came back in the autumn. Or during the holidays. It's really lovely up north then."

"I've consorted with Yankees before, sugar-pie." Margit winked. "Remember Logan Rabbinol?"

"Oh, wow. Yes, I do. I thought I was going to finally be your maid of honor."

"Yeah, well, two weeks playing house in Providence was enough for me." Margit rubbed at her throat, her eyes slightly dreamy. "Maybe I could use another two after we see him."

"See him?"

"In New Haven. I made you an appointment."

"Yale?"

"Yes, Yale."

"With Logan."

"He is the best. It was good of him to squeeze you in. He's usually booked months out. Good thing he still has the hots for me."

"Every man you leave in your wake has the hots for you, Margit." Savannah groaned. "I'm fine. Really."

"Not cutting it this time, missy. We're going. I'll drive."

"I've driven with your before, sugar. I'll drive. When?"

"Wednesday morning."

"Good thing I already have someone covering my shift at the clinic." Savannah conceded defeat. "I'll call Benny to mind the store for me."

"I hid your cell in the towel drawer in the kitchen. I'll go get it."

"I really do feel better now," Savannah called after her. "Barely any headache at all."

The dull throbbing was so common, she hardly noticed it anymore. As a doctor, she knew that wasn't good, and, as a doctor, she also understood if these headaches hadn't killed her after all those years, they were not likely to. At least, after tests that would reveal nothing, she and Margit would have a nice day together, maybe go to the beach. And Pepe's famous pizza on Wooster Street was an absolute must. Maybe she'd bring a pie back for Edgardo, Raul, and Ade.

She couldn't even think *Adelmo* anymore. Along with the abbreviated name came a warm and sexy tingling Savannah had no desire to quell. He had been so gentle with her, so kind. Edgardo and Raul deferred to him like careful schoolboys, ready to fetch and carry but not make any move unless directed by the younger man. Savannah found this curious, but not enough to bother about. It simply felt good being taken care of.

"Were you able to get my prescription made?" she asked Margit after she returned with her phone.

"The hospital docs were good enough to take my recommendation and prescribe it for you." She pulled an amber vial from her pocket, shaking the contents. "This is better. Faster. Under your tongue, missy."

Savannah tilted her head up and did as she was asked. The bitter taste made her grimace.

Margit capped the bottle and handed it to her. "You need a physician up here to prescribe it for you. You let it go too far and it went out of control. You're a doctor, Savannah—"

"Oh, now it's Savannah, is it?"

Margit ignored her. "You know it's better to keep the pain under control than it is to try getting it under control."

"I told you. It went away."

"Sure it did."

"I'm not lying, Margit."

Shoulders slumped, her friend let out a long breath. "I love you, Savvy. You're my oldest friend. I say this with all that love—I don't believe you."

"Fine, don't." She lied to Margit enough in the past. She didn't take offense now that she wasn't. There was some sort of karma at work. She was fine with that too. Ade's attentions, Margit's visit, and the dull ache in her head already subsiding, Savannah tossed the blanket aside. "I'm tired of resting."

"Savannah Callowell, you get back onto that couch."

"Come on, Margit." She danced out of the room, teasing her friend after her. "Let's go up to the fallow field and see what treasures Ade has found."

* * * *

The rash in the crooks of his elbows itched. A thorn embedded itself so deep into his palm that it was going to take more effort than prodding to get out. He also made an enthusiastic dive into a patch of what he thought might be some nearly-extinct variety of squash, and brushed against a patch of nettles. The sting still burned, hours later while he played cards with Tío and Taytay. And yet Ade would happily bump, bruise, and skewer himself in the wild bramble of Savannah's upper field day after gratifying day without qualm.

Late each afternoon, he returned to the creaky little house and his juvenile room to clean up. He, Taytay, and Tío made certain Savannah took her medication, ate, slept, and always had the TV remote and a book nearby. She seemed happy to see him, reluctant to see him go, but go he did. The anticipation of her smile when he walked in was worth more than anything else he could imagine.

Once Margit arrived, he backed off caretaking. She was a doctor, Savannah's doctor. And though they'd both protested, he gave up his room to her. He would sleep on the couch in the doublewide until Margit went home.

"You're just afraid we'll keep you up all night, guffawing like a couple of college girls," Margit had teased. "As if you actually need beauty sleep."

Ade pretended not to hear her.

In another time, another place, he would have flirted back, ended up in her bed. His bed. They were kindred of a kind, he and this curvy, pixie of a doctor from Savannah's past. People who knew how to play the game and enjoy it. Sex for a purpose, or done and forgotten before the week was out. This wasn't another time, another place. It was a farm in Bitterly, Connecticut, and he was a new man.

Wary as he had always been about feeling anything, let alone feeling so much so soon, Ade's whole body thrummed with the excitement of this new sensation, this hope for love. The instant gratification of a one-night-fling couldn't compare to the exquisite thrill of anticipation. Seduction had become a sacrilege he would not commit. He had only to glance at the countless and continuous texts on his phone to remind him of where the calculated wariness had gotten him.

"Who is she?" Taytay demanded in the rural language they spoke at home, after yet another text interrupted their nightly game of *cuarenta.* "Tell her to go away."

"I've tried, Taytay." Ade snapped his cards onto the table. "*Limpia.*"

Edgardo scowled at the empty playing field. "You cheated."

"I did not. You're not paying attention."

"It is difficult with your phone lighting up every five minutes. Turn it off."

"Savannah might need—"

"Savvy has her doctor friend. Give it here."

Blowing a breath through his lips, Ade switched off his phone. He ignored the threats and exclamation points on the texts still glowing on his screen, and slid it into his shirt pocket. "Play with Tío," he said. "I'm going to see about getting this thorn out of my hand. It's starting to throb."

His father's best treatment for any wound entailed washing it, bandaging it, and leaving the rest to his body to decide. There would be nothing helpful in his medicine cabinet. Ade crossed the dusk-lit field and went to Savvy's for the calendula and comfrey salve he'd seen on the shelf there. The salve would help, though he wished for the *sangre de drago* Lita would have smeared on his wounds and rashes.

Rummaging around the shelves, he found the right jar without switching on the lights. He left a note in the cash box, and went into the windowless bathroom in Savannah's office. The overhead light—a bare bulb on a wire—gave off harsh but substantial light. In a well-stocked first-aid kit tucked under the sink, he found the tweezers necessary for extracting the thorn.

Red. Angry-looking. He'd let it stay in too long. Digging at it now, he gasped and groaned. Sweat beaded his forehead, his upper lip. Ade gritted his teeth and dug deep. Pus oozed out, and with it, the thorn, instant relief, and a long exhale. He washed his hands.

So small a thing, this alien invader, to cause such pain. He read the ingredients on the jar of salve—safflower oil, essential oils of calendula and comfrey, beeswax, and vitamin E. Simple. Effective. Expensive. Consumers bought a tube of antibiotic ointment for under a dollar. Few would consider paying seven bucks for the jar in his hand. They didn't think about the petroleum jelly in the tube as a bi-product of the oil industry, its impact on the environment, or that the widespread use of antibiotics was creating stronger and stronger bacteria. Like it did for his father and uncle, expedience and cost outweighed the greater good. The science behind the thorn, the pus, the salve intrigued him no less now than it did when he was a child learning at his grandmother's side. The thirst to know more drove him.

And drove him.

Right out of the life he had aspired to.

Pocketing the jar of salve, Ade leaned against the sink. He pulled out his phone. Switched it back on. All the texts were largely the same. He deleted them. He found two that were not from the viper—one from his cell-phone provider about his data usage, and one from the wine-of-the-month club he belonged to, saying his subscription was about to expire. Ade deleted them too.

The voicemail icon showed six messages waiting. Inhaling deeply, he touched the screen, and listened.

"You think you can just leave me, but you can't. You think you can hide, but you can't do that either. Not forever. Make it easier on yourself and call me. We can work this out. If you don't piss me off any more than you already have."

Delete.

All but one of the messages were much the same. That one set his heart racing, and not in the good way he'd been experiencing since arriving in Bitterly. He listened to it again.

"Hey, Ade. It's me. Carl. I don't know where you're at, and that's probably a good thing. My job's been threatened about a thousand times because Anita thinks you told me. All I said was I figured you'd gone home to Ecuador. If that's where you are, stay put. I just thought you'd want to know—"

Ade checked the display. The call hadn't dropped. Carl's voice came back, softer.

"Sorry. Someone came in. I just want you to know that she's making it look like you quit of your own free will. We both know no one's buying it, but that's how it works around here. A Durst says it's so, it is. I wish I could say I got your back, buddy, but I need this job. I'm too old to find another position. Call me if you need to, but only if you need to. The less I know, the better."

Tempted as he was to return the call, Ade deleted the message. Carl didn't need the drama. They'd only been friends in the broadest terms. Colleagues slightly friendlier than most. The kind that would warn him away from the Durst family, give him a heads up as to the goings on, but not stick his neck out any further. Ade harbored no ill will. He hadn't earned the man's loyalty. Carl was a history professor, not young, not old, no one of importance or influence. Ashamed as he was now to admit it, even within the silence of his own mind, garnering friendship for friendship's sake had not been important enough to warrant the effort.

He powered off the device, watched the screen blink out. Anita had bought it for him. She paid for his plan. Knowing she couldn't suspend service without losing all contact with him completely gave Ade the foolhardy courage to keep using it. Contacts. Old messages. Pics and passwords and links stored within. His last and only link to Boston, to the life and people there.

Cool air puffed at his neck. Ade turned to the door still mostly closed. No air-conditioning drone, only crickets see-see-sawing at the night. He slipped the phone into his pocket, put the first aid kit away. The cool air on his neck slithered down his arms, raised goosebumps on his skin. He stood silent, stood still. Waiting.

Cricketsong hushed, leaving a lone insect chirping. The chirping elongated, became constant. A buzz, like a fly circling his head. Ade swiped at it, ducked, and the buzzing ceased. In his periphery, something in the mirror moved.

Cold sweat beaded his skin. He moved first his eyes. Was it…could it be? A face beside his own. A girl's face. He turned his head to look straight on, gasped, jumped back. And Ade laughed at himself, the sound banishing the goosebumps and chill. The face in the mirror was his own. The girl's face was only a towel hanging on the hook behind him.

"I need a good night's sleep," he told the mirror. Once he brought Savannah the flowers he'd picked for her that afternoon, her smile would send him into less troubled slumber. Long days, too many thoughts, his heart in constant turmoil, it was no wonder he was seeing things.

* * * *

That didn't go very well. I guess I got a little carried away. Ricky Ricardo almost saw me. I really didn't mean to scare him. Honest to Betsy. Even if it was sort of fun while it lasted. I was just trying to get his attention, to see if he was one of those people who could actually see me. If no one can see or hear the dead, why are there so many ghost stories, huh? But then I went and got sloppy and I don't know if he actually saw me or just felt something creepy. Gosh. I've been at this haunting thing a while. You'd think I'd be better at it by now.

But, oo-la-la! Ricky Ricardo is even dreamier up close. I thought his eyes were brown but they're green, like a Christmas tree. I might be a little on the hook. For all the good that would do me, huh?

Sometimes, I crack myself to bits.

Chapter 9

roses, red and amorous

Savannah loved the hour between dusk and dark, when sunshine faded and cooled into evening. Not even July's mosquitoes could keep her indoors. Armed with repellant, a citronella candle and a glass of sweet tea, she sat out on her front porch with Margit. Talking. Laughing. Even remembering the better times in Georgia, when they were young women in high school, college, med-school. The lingering headache infiltrated, but didn't obliterate the happiness, the hope. Neither did it keep her heart from fluttering or her lips from smiling when she spotted Ade coming up the path carrying a bunch of wildflowers.

"How is our patient, doctor?" he asked Margit.

"She says she's fine, but I don't believe her."

"Dull ache," Savannah confessed. "Nothing I'm not used to."

Ade handed her the flowers. Wild daisies and phlox, Queen Anne's lace and clover. Perfectly simple, homespun and lovely.

"Thank you, Ade."

"You thank a thief," he said. "I robbed your field to get them."

"I told you, you're welcome to whatever's up there. I'm only sorry you haven't found any of the heirloom varieties you were hoping for."

"I did spot another pumpkin patch. There is hope yet."

Margit took the flowers from Savannah. "Maybe the Great Pumpkin will choose it as the most sincere," she said, winking over the top of the bouquet. "I'll put these in water."

"Thank you."

Margit's glance flicked from one of them to the other, eyebrow quirked.

Repressing the urge to roll her eyes and groan behind her friend's back, Savannah patted the spot beside her. "Sit, Ade. You must be tired. You've been keeping late hours up in the field."

"But Margit will be—"

"She's not coming back." Savannah laughed softly. "Subtle and Margit are mutually exclusive terms."

Ade sat beside her, but on the edge of the couch. "I will not pretend the opportunity for a moment alone is not attractive." He averted his gaze. "I've been very worried about you, Savannah."

"I've been getting these headaches for—"

"That makes it even more worrisome." He shook his head. "I was glad to hear you did not refuse the trip to Yale."

"They're not going to find anything. It's just to satisfy Margit."

Ade fidgeted, didn't quite look her in the eye. "I do not mean to pry," he said, "but the other night you mentioned something very bad happened to you, many years ago."

"I don't talk about that."

Silence lingered a moment too long. "I would never ask you to. But you know you can, if ever you wish. Yes?"

Savannah could almost bear the telling now, almost wanted share this secret she shared with no one. Because when she opened her eyes in the hospital, Ade's had been the first face to materialize out of the blur. "Thank you, Ade. I'll keep that in mind."

He blew out a long breath, brought her fingers to his lips, lingered there. Footfalls on gravel turned his head. He dropped her hand still tingling.

Benny waved, shifted the baby slung on her chest, and came up the front steps. "Hey, Savvy. Sorry I couldn't get here earlier. Irene refused to take her afternoon nap today and she still shows no signs of going to sleep. I hoped taking her out in the car would do the trick, but as you can see—" She showed them a wide-awake baby girl. "No dice."

"Maybe on the way home."

Benny crossed her fingers, gritting her teeth dramatically. Ade offered his pinky to the baby. Irene took it, looking as quizzically as only an infant could. She leaned toward him.

"I don't have much experience with babies," he said, "but may I?"

"Be my guest." Benny untied the wrap. Irene went to Ade without so much as a glance her mother's way. "That's really strange. She never wants to go to anyone. Sometimes I even have a hard time getting her to go to Dan."

"I'll leave you ladies to talk." Ade bounced the baby. He walked slightly down the path, stopping at a flowering bush. "These are hydrangea, little one. They are pink because Savannah likes pink, and because the soil is more alkaline. We could turn them blue, just like your eyes, if we raised the acidity level…"

"Well, fiddle-dee-dee," Benny teased the moment he was out of earshot. Savannah rolled her eyes. "You make a terrible Scarlet O'Hara."

"I was going for Savannah Callowell." Benny shooed a bug, ducking a little. "You say that all the time."

"I do?"

"Yes, you do. And I won't even torture you about Ade or how cozy you two looked on the couch when I got here."

Savannah shook her head but the denial didn't make it past her lips.

Benny swatted again. "What's with the flies? I thought they left us alone after the mosquitoes came out."

"I don't see any flies."

"So annoying. Can we go inside? I'm like a ripe peach out here."

"Sure." Savannah glanced Ade's way as she uncurled herself from her chair. Irene's downy head rested against his chest. He crooned and swayed. Savannah sighed, and held the door open for Benny. "After you."

"Don't let them in."

"Who? Oh, the flies. I still don't see any."

"Well, I hear them. Scoot! Scoot!"

Upstairs, Margit sang "Hopelessly Devoted to You" in the shower. Savannah led Benny to the kitchen where the list of instructions, earlier written, awaited. She handed Benny the notebook. "Thanks for doing this. You're the only one I trust to run the store unsupervised."

Benny scanned the list of dos and don'ts. She turned the pages. "I can't believe you're still going into the clinic this week. You should call out."

"It was hard enough switching my day," Savannah said. "If I don't show up, all those women don't get seen."

"Barbaric."

"Tell me about it, sugar."

"You know," Benny turned another page, "if I had any idea you were going to leave me a whole book of instructions, I'd have come yesterday."

"They're just-in-case things." Savannah laughed. "And it's easier for you to mark sales in the notebook than keying them into the computer. I'll do that after I get home."

"You're such a control freak."

"I don't deny it."

"You need an accountant."

"I can't afford one."

Benny ducked suddenly, dodging a fly Savannah couldn't see for the life of her.

"You let it in."

"I don't see anything."

"Get the swatter."

"I don't have one. Benny, there's nothing there."

"There is! There is!" Benny squealed, racing about the kitchen as if chased by a tiny, zapping demon. She blew out the back door and down the steps, stopping near the parked cars.

"What's up with you, sugar?" Savannah came more slowly down the steps. No flies, not even a cloud of gnats in sight. Benny stared beyond her, at the screen door slapping, eyes wide and jaw slack and her face pale as the moonlight blooming. Savannah hurried down the steps to grasp her elbows. "What is it? Benny, what's wrong?"

"There's something in your house," she whispered. "There's something…"

Benny shuddered, broke away from Savannah's grasp and ran to the front of the house where Ade was still swaying, crooning. Softly. He put a finger to his lips. Benny's shoulders slumped.

Savannah turned her around. "What happened? What do you mean there's something in my house?"

"Don't think I'm strange."

"Too late."

"I'm serious, Savvy."

"So I am. What happened?"

Benny bit her lip. "I saw something."

"What did you see?"

"I'm not sure, but…" Benny pulled Savannah in closer. "Listen, I know this is going to sound nuts-o, but I have a little experience with otherworldly things. I'm sensitive to them."

"And you saw something otherworldly?"

"The buzzing, Savvy." Benny shushed herself. "You said it yourself. There was nothing there. But there was. I swear it. I'm not kidding."

"I don't believe in spooks, Ben."

"That doesn't mean a thing to them. I'm telling you, there's something… someone there. And that someone is bad. Really bad. Murderously bad."

A shiver sliced through Savannah, clean as a newly sharpened knife. She clenched her jaw, refused to react further, refused to even think the thoughts trying now to scream to life.

"I know this woman," Benny was saying. "She lives in Brooklyn but she had family here in Bitterly once. Her grandfather was married to a Weller girl. He built the house I live in. She's better at this sort of thing than I am. Will you let me bring her here?"

"For what purpose?"

"To show me up for the nut I am. Come on, Savvy. Please? You've got nothing to lose."

Only my mind, sugar. "I don't see the point."

"The point is, what if this…bad energy is what's causing your headaches?"

Savannah groaned. "Come on, Benny. You can't be serious."

"I'm dead serious. And I didn't mean the pun until I said it. Pretty good, huh?"

"Brilliant." Savannah took her friend's hands. "You know I love you, Benny, and I mean no disrespect to your system of beliefs, but there is no spook causing my headaches."

"I know what I saw, Savvy. I know what I felt. And you said yourself that these headaches started once you moved here to Bitterly. What if something was already living in your house? What if something bad happened there and needs to be…oh."

"Oh?"

Benny squeezed her hands a little too tightly. "The drowned girl. What was her name? Augie told me…Tilly. Tilly Tully. I wonder if this is where she lived. Or if this is where she was murdered."

"Mur—?" Savannah choked on the word. "In Bitterly?"

"I was surprised to find out too. But yes. There was a murder in Bitterly back in the 1950s. Come on, Savvy. Let me call my friend. She's old and she probably won't leave Brooklyn but let me try. Okay?"

The rock and the hard place Savannah was standing between closed in on her. Benny made no secret about her belief in those otherworldly things Savannah had no patience for. Neither did she want a strange woman coming to her home, telling her there was some kind of evil energy drifting about that was causing her headaches. It didn't make sense anyway. The headaches followed her from the house, to work, to town. Everywhere. And she'd lied. To everyone. The headaches didn't start in Bitterly. They started after she sold the house she lived in with Doc and the girls. No one knew that. Not even Margit.

"Please?" Benny said. "Appease your crazy friend?"

"You're not crazy." Savannah let go of Benny's hands and rubbed at her temples as the throbbing suddenly became intense. "All right, fine. If it makes you feel better, call her."

"You all right?"

"Tired. I need to take a pill and go to bed."

"I didn't mean to upset you."

"You absolutely did not upset me, sugar." Savannah kissed her cheek. "And thanks for minding the store."

They went quietly to Ade still swaying a sleeping Irene but no longer crooning. He carried her to Benny's car, strapped her expertly into her car seat and closed the door quietly.

"I'm going to call you at four in the morning when she decides it's playtime." Benny crossed her arms. "What did you do?"

"I sang to her," he said. "An old Spanish lullaby. *La jefa* swears by it."

"*La jefa?*"

Ade grinned. "It means the boss. That's what the family calls my mother. Affectionately, of course."

"To her face?"

"If we are feeling brave."

They all laughed softly, careful not to wake the baby. Benny kissed Savannah's cheek, hugged Ade and got into her car. "I'll take care of everything here while you're in New Haven. Just don't worry. And I'll let you know about my friend as soon as I hear."

"I know you will, I won't, and okay," Savannah whispered back. She and Ade waved as Benny pulled away. She was sweet and slightly nutty, but she meant well. If the woman from Brooklyn came out to the house, she could work whatever spook-banishing ritual she wished. It would make Benny happy, if nothing else.

"Irene certainly took to you," Savannah said as she and Ade walked back to the porch. "You have no idea how unusual that is."

"As unusual as it is for any child to like me. They tend not to."

"Really? Why?"

"I've just never been…good with them." He looked away. "That is a small lie. I've never had an interest in them. Children are sensitive to such things."

"That's true. Well," Savannah sighed, "things change."

"People change," Ade added. "Things change with them."

"Deep."

Ade looked away.

"Hey." She touched his arm. "I was just teasing."

"I know." He looked up, sorrow in his eyes. "My couch awaits. Good-night, Savannah."

She loved how he said Sah-vah-nah, not Sa-*van*-na, like everyone else pronounced it. No accented syllable, just a name rolling like a chant off his tongue. She almost called him back. "Good night, Ade," she whispered, but he didn't seem to hear.

* * * *

Well, isn't this a revolting turn of events. They think I'm the one giving Savvy headaches? That I was the one who chased them through the house? I wasn't even in there. I was listening to Ricky Ricardo sing to the baby. Of all the nerve. It would serve them right if I just left them alone with their ghoul. I should go back to haunting stupid teenagers and fiddling with the traffic lights.

Dang it. Who am I kidding? I can't leave Savvy just when everything's getting juicy. But nobody better accuse me again. I like scaring people but I'm nothing like that thing. I'm smarter too. I accidently almost let Ricky Ricardo see me in the stupid mirror, but Savvy's ghoul did it on purpose. And not just a fleeting glimpse either. He wanted that other woman to see him. It felt like a challenge. Maybe he doesn't know he's not allowed to do that. Maybe he just doesn't care.

* * * *

It was no use. Ade's eyes wouldn't stay closed. At three o'clock, he got up, shuffled into the kitchen, and opened the refrigerator door. The thing was packed full of prepared food his mother and aunt would never believe their husbands consumed when not in their care. Fishing a beer out from behind a take-out container of Chinese food, he cracked the cap and took a deep gulp.

"Revolting," he murmured, but he took the bottle out to the tiny landing that served as a porch for the double-wide and sat on the top step. Sipping the beer, listening to night sounds, Ade attempted to ease his mind. More than Anita's ongoing harassment, more, even, than Savannah's headaches was the deepening sense of betrayal burrowing into his gut.

Ade tossed back the rest of his beer. Hindsight was ever cruel. Caution had kept him quiet about Savannah's past. The lesser, meaner Adelmo Gallegos had tempered that caution with cunning. One never knew what information was going to come in handy. By the time he realized his mistake, it was too late, and it got worse with each day, with each glance, and every smile.

A light went on across the yard in Savannah's kitchen. She passed from window to window. What was she doing up at such an hour? Same as he, more than likely. Ade set the bottle down, rose to his feet. Whether it was sleeplessness or courage, he started through the yard. "*Más vale tarde que nunca*," he muttered. Maybe, just maybe, she would be as weary as he and the ungodly hour would work in his favor after he confessed his sins.

He moved quietly up the stairs, peeked in the window. Savannah stood at the stove, stirring something in a small pan. Though the door was closed, the kitchen windows were open. Her soft humming joined the cricketsong serenading the night. Ade tapped softly on the edge of the screen door. Savannah jumped, dropped the spoon, and spun about, hand to heart.

"What are you doing up at this hour?" she asked as she let him in.

"I came to ask you the same question."

"I suppose neither of us can sleep." She gestured to the pot on the stove. "You want some warm milk and honey?"

Ade moved to the stove, sniffed the steam coming out of the pot. "This reminds me of Lita."

"Everything here seems to remind you of her."

His heart stitched. "She used to make it for us before bed. I'd love some."

Savannah turned off the burner, poured milk into mugs and handed one to Ade. She gestured him to the parlor couch. Only the light coming from the kitchen illuminated the room full of shadows and moonlight. Ade waited for Savannah to sit before doing so himself. The confession he came to make suddenly did not seem like a good idea. Maybe he didn't have to. Maybe there was another way.

"Who used to make you warm milk and honey?" he asked. "Parent? Grandparent?"

"My Auntie Bea," Savannah answered. "She's actually my great-great-aunt on my father's side. Or something."

"She must be quite old."

"Very." Savannah sipped. "She'll be one-hundred-five next May."

"That is old. Lita is not quite there yet."

"Is she your father's mother? Or your mother's?"

"My father's," Ade answered. "We have almost no contact with my mother's family."

"Oh, that's a shame."

"It is." Ade sipped, licked away his milk-mustache. "I met my maternal grandmother once when I was thirteen, at my older sister's *quinceañera*. We are Ecuadorian on my father's side, mountain people for as far back as anyone can recall, but my mother's people are Spanish aristocrats so bent on maintaining the purity of their line that when my mother married my father, she was disowned completely. A *quinceañera*, however, is a very big event in our culture. Abuela insisted upon not only attending for this granddaughter she never met, but paid for an elaborate celebration the community still speaks of."

"And that was the only time any of you met her?"

"Constantina, my sister, visited her several times after that. Through her, I came to understand that despite the fact that we lived in the twentieth century, it was quite brave for Abuela to disobey her husband. Doing what she did for my sister was an act of rebellion. I admire her for that, and I honor her even if her rebellion never extended to me."

"I imagine your mother was well on her way to being disowned when she married your dad. She must be strong-willed to have earned her nickname."

Ade laughed into his cup. "That is putting it mildly."

"I think I would like your mother."

"I know she would like you," Ade said. "My father and uncle have been talking about you for years. Everyone knows you by now."

"Well fiddle-dee-dee." Savannah fluttered her eyelashes. "How many fans do I have?"

"Too many to count. I honestly don't even know how many cousins there are at this point."

"What was it like," she asked, "growing up in such a large family?"

"Chaotic. But happy. Taytay and Tio started splitting their time between the United States and Ecuador when I was twelve or so. I missed them terribly, but there were other uncles, aunts, cousins, siblings. And always a lot of work to do. Between the farm and school, I was never bored."

"And you were a good student?"

"I was. Very good. You must have been as well, no?"

Savannah nodded, eyes downcast. "I was, thanks to Auntie Bea."

"How so?"

"My parents died when I was a baby," she said, her eyes still on her cup of milk instead of him. "I barely remember them. I think I only do because of pictures. My father's cousin took me in, raised me with her own kids, but I was always aware that I was only a favor to a poor, dead cousin. I didn't get to play sports or take dance lessons. Any money there was for that kind of thing went to my cousins.

"Auntie Bea took me to the library once a week. She was kind of a stray too. I'm not even sure whose aunt she actually was, just that she was old for as long as I can remember and lived in the sunporch-turned-bedroom of my aunt's house." Savannah looked up, smiling and wiping a tear from her cheek. "I don't mean to sound ungrateful. I'm not. At all. It was good of my aunt to take in the strays no one else wanted, especially considering money was so tight."

Ade's jaw clenched. Strays? He sipped at the warm, sweet milk. "Did you get along with your cousins?"

"Well enough." She shrugged. "We didn't fight or anything. I was a lot younger, and they pretty much ignored me. If it weren't for Auntie Bea, I'd have been a very lonely child. I miss her something fierce."

"When did you last see her?" he asked, though he could guess. Even Taytay and Tío, who claimed to know little of what happened in Georgia, knew she had not been back in all the years she lived in Bitterly.

"Too long." Savannah's eyes met his. She bit her lip. "I should probably go see her. Is that what you're thinking?"

Ade reached for her hand. How easy it had been to call up the skills he'd renounced. Another few moments and she would tell him all those terrible things he already knew. She never had to know he'd snooped into her past before they ever met. He'd be free of one burden, only to shoulder another. In another life, with other women, the trade-off would have been acceptable. With Savannah, it was not.

"I'm thinking"—he brought her fingers to his lips—"that you are very beautiful."

Savannah looked away, but let him keep her hand. "Thank you?"

"Is that a question?"

"No?"

"That sounds like another one."

Savannah snatched her hand away. She gathered their empty cups, dropped one that bounced on the carpet but didn't break. Ade suppressed the urge to pull her into his lap and kiss her fluster calm.

"Allow me." He took the cups into the kitchen and rinsed them clean instead. Secrets and more secrets. Which was more painful? Keeping them, or telling them? Until he figured it out, he would let them stand. His. Hers. There would be time, the right time. He simply had to be patient.

Ade turned off the water, dried his hands. Sleep still eluded him. Tomorrow was going to be a long and exhausting day. For him, and for Savannah too.

"I suppose I should…" He stopped in his tracks. Savannah sat on the edge of the couch, head in hands. Ade went to her. "Savannah, what is it?"

"Nothing." Her voice trembled. "I'm just so tired, Ade."

"Then you must sleep. I will help you." He grabbed a blanket from basket beside the couch. Shouldering himself more comfortably into the cushions, he gestured her into the crook of his arm.

"Ade, I can't."

"Of course you can. Come. If I can get Irene to sleep, I can do the same for you. It won't hurt to try, right?"

He held out his hand.

"Oh, all right."

Savannah curled into the crook of his shoulder, her head resting upon his shoulder. Ade covered them both with the blanket. She fit so perfectly into his side. The feel of her, the scent of her should have undone all resolve to chivalry, but the need to protect and comfort held strong against his body's response. Gathering her close, Ade sang:

> *"Cierras ya tus ojitos.*
> *Duermete sin temor.*
> *Sueña con angelitos*
> *Parecidos a ti.*
> *Y te agarrare tu mano.*
> *Duermete sin temor.*
> *Cuando tu despiertes,*
> *Yo estare aqui."*

Savannah relaxed into his side. Her arm slipped across his waist. Ade's heart filled to capacity, quite possibly for the first time.

> *"Close your eyes little one,*
> *Sleep without fear,*
> *And dream while the angels*
> *Watch over you.*
> *I will hold your hand.*
> *So sleep without fear.*
> *And when you wake with the morning,*
> *I'll still be here."*

Spanish, then English. English, then Spanish. Ade sang. Softly. Words became whispers. Whispers became sleep. Sleep became dreams of who he was, who he had been, who he wanted to be.

Chapter 10

out of recollected places

The visit with Yale doctors proved, for Savannah at least, fruitless. Dr. Rabbinol—Logan—ran all the tests that had been run before, and then some, the results of which he wouldn't have back for weeks. Those results would tell her nothing new. She was perfectly healthy. Her brain was fine. Blood pressure and glucose levels, blood cell counts and hair strand tests and any other possible poke or prod they could perpetuate on her person would come back fine, fine and more fine. For Margit, however, things turned out better.

"You sure you don't mind if I cut out on you early?" she asked as they waited for their pizza. "I probably should have asked before I said yes to him."

"Don't be silly, sugar. Of course I don't mind. I think you and Logan make a—"

"Don't even." Margit clamped hands over her ears. "He's amazing in bed, his house is on the beach, and he cooks like a pro. Sex. The Beach. Food. In that order. That's all there is to it. Besides, after what I found on the couch, I'm pretty sure I'm expendable back at your place."

"Let it go now, will you?" Savannah rolled the icy-cold soda glass along her cheeks warmed as much by Margit's insinuation as the hot summer sun. "We fell asleep talking."

"Whatever you say. Sugar."

From Pepe's Pizza on Wooster Street, they went to Hammonasset where they whiled away the afternoon on the beach. Fried clams, scallops and oysters fresh out of the ocean, washed down by a pitcher of beer ended a day otherwise well spent. Except for the bruise in the crook of her elbow from the IV, Savannah had no regrets.

"You should have just stayed," she said as she drove them home in the fading light. "It's silly for you to make the long trip back to the farm only to come all the way up here again in a few days."

"I want to see the clinic. And besides"—Margit pinched her side—"all my things are at your place."

"You're terrible," Savannah teased. "I'm going to miss you."

"Me too. But life goes on, right? And Ade will be happy to have his bed back."

"Futon," Savannah corrected.

"A comfortable futon. Where'd you get it?"

"Thrift store. There are some very wealthy New Yorkers who buy the best and then sell it rather than store it for the winter. What?"

"You bought Ade a bed from a thrift store?"

"I thought I was furnishing a room for a college kid."

"So would you have bought him a proper bed if you'd known he was…bed-able?"

"Good Lord, sugar, you led me right into that one."

"One of my many talents. Come on. Tell me you don't want to."

"I'm not even dignifying that with a response."

"That, missy, is all the response necessary."

"You're terrible."

"You said that already. And you're smitten. Admit it. To me, at least."

Savannah concentrated harder on the road. The harder she concentrated, the more aware she was of Margit's stare.

"Yes, all right. I'm smitten."

"So is he. You know that, right?"

"This is all very juvenile, don't you think?"

"Oh, stop." Margit slapped her shoulder. "It's been too long, Savvy. It's time you had a man in your life again. And in your bed. Good Lord, woman. How do you stand it?"

Savannah took a deep breath. And another. "What if I don't want one?"

Margit's hand came to rest tenderly on her shoulder now, a soothing gesture that worked. "You didn't. For a long time. But now you do, and it's okay."

"Is it? I'm not sure about that."

"I am. Look, I know you think you put it all behind you but—"

"But I haven't." Savannah gripped the wheel harder. "I don't think it's possible."

"You've done your girls proud," Margit said. "You've never wallowed. Not for a single moment. I agreed with your decision to move out of Georgia, but you pretend it never happened. None of these Yankee friends of yours know it did. Isn't that kind of…reverse wallowing?"

"I'm not sure that makes sense."

"It probably doesn't, but you know exactly what I mean. Can you even say it out loud? To me?"

The words skewered her, pins into a pin cushion. Sharp. Stinging.

"Say it, Savannah. Doc killed your girls and nearly did you in too. Come on."

Eyes on the road, body maneuvering the car along the dark twists and turns, Savannah's mind curved through her past. Not this. Not now. Not ever. Could she? "They died," she said, her voice steady, "and I lived. I couldn't save them."

"Close enough." Margit's soft, surgeon's hand moved up and down her arm. "No one could have saved them. Doc knew what he was doing."

Please. Stop. Savannah gritted her teeth.

"I knew him, too, remember?" Margit continued. "I loved him. The man who went to the desert died there, Savvy. The one who came home…"

"Was a monster," Savannah whispered. "I should have taken them away then. I should have known what was coming."

"You could never have predicted it. Ever. After the first time he put you in the hospital, you did take them away. He found you."

The road blurred, just for a second. Because she didn't hide well enough, kept her job and her family ties, her girls were dead. Eleven years dead. Her leg. Her ribs. Ached. Savannah gripped the steering wheel harder. She forced herself to breathe without gasping. "I know what he did, Margit. Everything he did. Everything he was, then wasn't."

Margit slumped back against the seat. "I'm sorry, Savvy. We were talking about Ade. How did we get here?"

Savannah relaxed her grip. She sighed. "You're just being a friend who wants to see me happy."

"Does Ade make you happy?"

"He does," Savannah admitted. Her fingers on the wheel ached. She loosened her grip, tried to unknot her shoulders. "I barely know him. He arrived on the farm and I got slammed in the gut. I don't get it, Margit. Why him? How is it happening so fast after all these years?"

"A question for the ages. So does this mean you're not going to push him away?"

"I've hired him through next year's growing season, contract and all."

"That's not what I meant and you know it."

"Let's leave it there anyway, okay?"

Margit cracked the window. Cool air blew in, rattled the soda cans in their cup holders. "It's so nice outside. Turn off the air conditioning, Savvy, will you?"

Subject closed. Savannah gratefully opened all the windows. Margit switched the radio on. The raw and gravely sounds of nineties grunge blared to life.

"Number One Crush," Margit squealed like a teenager, and growled the angst-riddled, love-saturated lyrics Savannah still knew by heart. Before the song ended, she, too, was belting out lyrics she hadn't heard in years. Smashing Pumpkins, Presidents of the United States, The Refreshments. Song after song. Memory after memory. This time, good ones, when she was young and working hard toward a goal, like her kind and wonderful husband stationed overseas. He was there doing his part, putting men and women back together again. She was stateside, tending those left behind. A baby born. A soldier mended. They were going to change the world, one patient at a time.

What I've seen...I can't unsee it, Savvy. I can't unlive it.

She cut off his voice, that bloody memory trying to worm its way out of her mind. Cut it clean just as she took stance, and fired. She sang louder. Harder.

Savannah left her demon in the dust, somewhere on the roadside in rural Connecticut. It would find her again. It would always find her. For the first time since that horrific night in Georgia, the thought wasn't fear, but a dare.

* * * *

Ade's hands trembled. It just never ended. Of course it didn't. He'd been a fool to even pretend Anita would just go away and leave him be. He wanted to chuck the cell phone in his hand, but he hit play and listened to Carl's message again.

"I swore I wouldn't do this, but...she's behind it, Ade. You have to know she's behind it, even though the board is saying it's been in the works for over a year. She made sure I knew because she knows I'll tell you. Probably thinks I'm just some addled old prof. Maybe I am. But it's a shot, understand?

"Your name is on the roster for the fall semester. Full professorship. Ecological Studies and...there's a lab. I don't remember. I've heard rumors of tenure too. And a sizeable grant for that field study you've been petitioning for. We both know the Dursts can pull the right strings to make it all happen. It's what you've worked for, Ade. It can be yours, if you're willing to pay the price. Think on it."

He tucked his phone back into the breast pocket of his work shirt. Light dappled through the trees, leaving patches of sunshine like stepping-stones along the path ahead. Behind him, the upper field he'd poured his passion into since arriving in Bitterly. No heirloom varieties yet, but a testament to nature and her ability to renew, to survive, to thrive.

What had Anita promised Carl to deliver the message?

Ade was a man changing, but he hadn't changed all the way yet, and the old Ade knew a set up when he saw it. Carl's message went against everything he knew about the man, and was in keeping with everything he knew about Anita. It had nevertheless gotten the job done.

Closing his eyes, Ade inhaled deeply. Wildflowers and dirt and trees and heat, and the ever-present odor of gasoline from the coot idling where he'd stopped it. These were the scents of long-ago summers, when he was a boy in Ecuador. The chaos and always-exhaustion of those days had been the best of his life. Until now. A year ago, he would have laughed had someone even suggested such a thing. A year ago, he was a famed lecturer, scientist, enviromentalist, sought after for knowledge gleaned over decades of hard work, cunning, and compromise.

He shifted into gear. The engine kicked in and the coot rolled on. Adelmo Gallegos, compromise? He prided himself on being uncompromising in his views on nature, ecology, conservation. Endorse an effective but toxic pesticide because of a donation to the university? No way in hell. Seduce the lobbyist to get the donation anyway? All the time. Had he considered it compromise, then? A means to an end? A necessary evil? In the end, a better result for the common good.

Compromise. Yes. He had. He'd compromised himself, if not his views. Integrity came in all colors, all scents and sounds and deeds done in the pursuit of achievement. He'd drawn his line and over again, always moving it slightly further along the path that led him to his ultimate goal— lecturing in the most prestigious establishment of higher learning, attached to the most influential family in the city, a family capable of buying and selling most others in the United States. He had it all, and let it go.

But he could have it back again, and then some.

Ade pulled the coot into the tractor barn and switched it off. Birds still sang. Tractors rumbled. Sprinklers *schk-k-ked* among the rows. Students weeding and debugging as per his instructions sang slave songs they learned in their high school chorus. Did they even consider the irony?

Would it occur to them not to sing those songs when Savannah was home? But she wasn't home. She was in New Haven with Margit.

Heading into the house to use the shower there, Ade unbuttoned his shirt. He shucked it off in the kitchen along with his boots and pants and crusty socks. Alone but for the flies he let in, he dropped his briefs as well, retrieving his cell phone and his wallet from the dirty pile.

They weighed almost the same. Slim as was the phone, so was his wallet. Anita had taken everything from him, even what was left of his own savings after sending money home to Ecuador. A single call from a Durst was enough to freeze his account. All he'd been able to retrieve was the one ATM withdrawal. Five hundred dollars, and that was nearly gone.

Ade clicked the cell phone display on. Carl's voicemail illuminated.

What he worked for.

All he wanted.

If he was willing to pay the price.

Standing naked in Savannah's kitchen, Ade swiped out of the voicemail screen, to the text screen. No new texts, though he already knew that. She was waiting for him to get Carl's message. To make a decision. For all the things there were to despise about her, Ade could not help admiring her strategy. Tell him lies. Cut him off. Harass him. Let him feel the pain of poverty and the loss of respect. Dangle a carrot that was more like a winning lottery ticket. A million dollar lottery ticket. A billion. And all he had to do was accept her lie, pretend the child she carried was his, and go back to living the life he'd worked so hard to make.

The antique mantel clock in Savannah's parlor chimed five. The field kids would start heading home. Taytay and Tío were probably already in the doublewide calling out for dinner. More Chinese food, and not from the upscale restaurant on the Green, but the hole-in-the-wall place that used way too much MSG. And Ade still stood naked in Savannah's kitchen, cell phone in one hand, wallet in the other.

He placed them both onto the counter, took a glass from the cupboard, and got himself water from the tap. Cold. Mineral. Restoring. In Boston, the water tasted like a swimming pool. He and Anita had used a delivery service, one of the many luxuries he never thought twice about.

Chugging the water, savoring the cool of it sliding down his throat, Ade closed his eyes. Back and back he tipped his head. Water sloshed down the sides of his face, rolled down his neck, along his torso. He drained the glass and stood panting, staring at the empty vessel.

Ade set the glass into the sink. He turned the faucet on. Watched it fill. Turned it off again. He took the battery out of his cell phone, and dropped the pieces into the water glass.

The old phone he'd come across in the drawer in his father's kitchen would suffice. If he hurried, he could shower and still get to town before the cell carrier closed. Maybe he'd go to D'Angelo's. Maybe he'd drive out to County Line Road and see what Charlie and Johanna were doing that evening. Or maybe he'd just make himself something and wait for Savannah to come home.

* * * *

Oh, swoon. Oh swoonery-swoon-swoon! Am I wicked? Scratch that. Of course I am. That's what got me into trouble in the first place. But, Honest to Betsy, Ricky Ricardo is the dreamboat of dreamboats. Even the old lady in the cemetery would swoon over him if she saw all those muscles, all that skin. I don't know that I've ever actually seen a man's butt before. Maybe I have, but, golly, not like his.

I didn't come in here looking for an eyeful, though thank you very much for that. I figured, since Savvy's not around, it would be a good time to see if that ghoul exists here in the house, or only where she is.

After all this time dead, I'm finally learning a few things about my kind. He's not here, the little girls aren't either. But they are. Like shadows. No, not shadows. They're like…like…what's it called when you look at something a long time, then close your eyes and it's still there but like a negative for a photo? After-image? Maybe I made that up. Or I learned it in science class. Anyway, that's what they're like. They're still here, but they're with her too. I bet they're in a lot of places, like wherever it was they came from, with other family members who miss them. Or fear them.

Am I, too?

Golly, that's some thought, huh? I'm here, but am I down at my rock? Am I scaring kids there even when I'm not around to enjoy it? Am I stuck to the shack where he killed me? I haven't gone anywhere near the place. I don't even remember where it is. But it makes me wonder if I left a piece of myself there, like the ghoul and the girls are here. And if that's true, are any of us ever really gone, gone?

Chapter 11

remembered forms and faces

She was longer at the clinic than most days. Margit shadowed her, lent a hand here and there, but the law prohibited her from actually doing more than assist. Officially. She left for Providence by mid-afternoon. Savannah cringed a little when her dearest friend climbed into the sweet little convertible, albeit rented, in front of a clinic full of women who mostly couldn't even afford a second-hand car.

July was proving to be a fertile month in her part of Connecticut. Seven women had come into the clinic with an inkling, and left as ascertained mothers-to-be. And that was just the new patients. The list was longer than there were hours of operation, more so than most days. By the time Savannah got home, she was almost too exhausted to take pleasure in the sound of Ade moving about upstairs.

She picked up the notebook of instructions and sales Benny had left on the kitchen table. Fair enough sales for the end of July. It wouldn't take long to key them into the computer. Paging through the notes, she found one from Benny:

> *Savvy,*
> *My friend from Brooklyn will be in Bitterly on Friday, and will stay the weekend. She wants to see the house her grandfather built. She is also very curious about what I saw. I hope you're up for this. I'll bring her by about three o'clock on Saturday. Is that enough warning?*
> *Love, Benny*

Savannah closed the notebook, cursing softly under her breath. Snap decisions, especially those made under duress, were rarely sound ones. Now the woman was already in Bitterly and Savannah had no way out of it without insulting the poor old thing. Thank goodness Margit was already gone. If she knew, or worse, were around for whatever it was Benny and her friend had in mind, her next Margit-arranged doctor visit would be to a psych ward. And Ade. Savannah groaned. She'd find some way to get him away from the house. At the moment, she was just too fried to even think about it.

Savannah grabbed leftovers from the fridge, shoveled a few bites of cold spaghetti into her mouth, and swallowed it down with a glass of cold milk. Bed awaited. Cool sheets. Soft pillow. The ceiling fan whirring a breeze. Savannah almost felt herself drifting off as she trudged up the stairs.

"You're home."

Ade's voice startles her eyes open all the way.

"I am." She chuckles, halting on the top step. "How was your day?"

"Uneventful. And yours?"

"Exhausting. And no, I haven't gotten any test results back. I promised to tell you when I do."

"I know. I'm sorry."

"Don't apologize for caring. Seriously, Ade."

His gaze falls, but not before Savannah sees his smile.

"What?"

"Ade," he says. "I like the way you say it."

"How do I say it?"

He laughs softly. "Not the way my mother does. I don't know if I can say it the way you do."

"Try."

"Edday."

"I do not."

"I told you I could not say it as you do."

"Well, how do you say it then?"

"Ah-day."

"That's how I say it."

"No, it's not. But I like your way. It is uniquely you."

"Not if we were down south."

"But we are not in the south. We are here. And here, you are the only one who says my name the way you do. That is poetic in its way, don't you think?"

Savannah tilts her head. "How so?"

His smile softens. Ade moves closer. He traces her jaw, the slope of her nose. Savannah breathes in and out, in and out, trying to do so normally. When his fingers caress her chin, she gasps.

"You are the only one who says my name as you do," he says, "and the only one who makes me feel like this."

Without pausing for a breath, Ade kisses her tenderly, and so quickly she doesn't have time to respond before he steps back.

"Sleep sweet, Savannah."

"Don't go," she blurts. Her cheeks burn, but she does not pretend she hasn't said it. She does not take it back. Savannah holds out her hand for his. He takes it and she draws him to her, into a kiss that does not remain stationary at the top of the stairs, but moves down the hall, to her bedroom, to her bed. Sheets are thrust aside. Clothes are shed. Kisses and caresses are given and taken and given back again. Savannah has never been more aware of her own body, every sweat-slicked inch of it. And his—oh, his—comes alive under her small, work-worn fingers. Ade moves in her, she in him, a synchronicity of parts and pleasures buried so far back in her past they are brand new again.

Straddling his hips, moving as he moves, as his hands travel from her hips to the curve of her waist to her breasts, Savannah's insides alight, blazing orgasmically outward like sunshine rays, like starlight. Beneath her, Ade's eyes are open. Watching her. Waiting for her light to dim before letting his own burst. And then they are in one another's arms, out of breath and laughing softly. Speaking words of love, of the future, and Savannah understands in that last, cold-water moment before...

She gasped awake. Alone in her bed still rumpled with strenuous dreaming. She half-remembered listening for him at the top of the steps, brushing her teeth, getting into bed. Only half. Sinking back into the pillows, she held tight to the dream, and wept because it was already fading.

* * * *

Carmen Iapalluccio, Benny's friend from Brooklyn, was nothing like what Savannah expected. She was quite a bit older. She wasn't a long-skirt-wearing, bead-clicking, crystal-carrying mystic either. Tiny and slight, she sported a helmet of dyed-black hair, sensible shoes, orthopedic stockings and a black, polyester dress straight out of the 1970s. Carmen was every sweet, little-old-lady Savannah had ever watched on sitcom reruns. She carried no crystals but, rather, a white marble bowl in one hand, and what appeared to be olive oil stored in an airline-sized whiskey bottle in the other.

"Welcome." Savannah tried her hardest to smile sincerely as she came down the back porch stairs. Benny held the old woman's arm, though she stood straight and steady on her own.

"Thank you. What a lovely place." Carmen's voice matched her appearance, high-pitched and birdy. "I love this town. Benny has been so good to show me around. Not like Brooklyn at all. Quaint, like a Norman Rockwell painting."

"The Rockwell Museum isn't far from here," Savannah said. "You should get Benny to take you while you're here."

"Oh, do you think we could, Benedetta?"

"Sure, Carmen. I'd be happy to."

"What a treat this has all been."

"Would you like a tour of the farm?" Savannah offered. "It's not much, but…"

"It's lovely dear." Carmen handed Savannah the bowl and bottle. "But you are not happy about the reason for my visit, so why don't we get it over with, all right?"

"I'm not—"

"—a believer in such things." Carmen and Benny exchanged a glance. "It's all right, dear. I don't require that anyone believe anything that makes them uncomfortable. If you'd rather I leave, I will take no offense. Benedetta did say you were reluctant."

"No, of course I don't want you to leave." Savannah reached for Benny. "Why don't you take Carmen inside. I was just going to the store to get some of the mint and chamomile tea we mixed last week."

"Would it be all right if Benedetta showed me around a little?" Carmen asked. "I don't want to wander through your house without permission, and it's better if I get a feel for things."

"Not at all."

But of course, Savannah minded. She crossed the yard and slammed into the store, startling the young ladies who worked for her into motion. She gestured them to resume chatting, grabbed a box of the tea and started back to the house.

Why was she so angry?

Savannah halted in her tracks, fingers pressed to temple and taking deep breaths. The ache pounded a moment then eased back to dullness. Carmen seemed sweet, sincere and spiritual. Letting her do her thing harmed no one, and maybe…

No, there was no maybe. Savannah took one last deep breath. The tractor rumbling and clicking in the distance was a huge relief, at least. Edgardo and Raul were showing Ade how to work around all the little idiosyncrasies of her second-hand equipment. Having him witness to this whole…exorcist thing was at least one embarrassment she didn't have to face. It was bad enough, looking him in the eye after that dream.

Up the steps, into the kitchen where Benny and Carmen already sat at the table, Savannah barely got to the sink to put the kettle on before Carmen said, "I sense something here. It got stronger when you came in, Savannah. But there is something else. A curious something, and not what I'm here to see to. Now, if you wouldn't mind, dear, may I use your powder room before we start?"

"Carmen," Benny clucked. "You should have said something sooner."

"I didn't want to be rude, dear."

"It's this way." Savannah showed the elderly woman to the bathroom and went back to Benny.

"Are you sure you're okay with this, Savvy?" Benny asked. "I wouldn't have brought her if you told me you changed your mind."

"It's fine." She grimaced. "I don't believe in any of this. I'm doing it for your peace of mind."

"Well, thanks for that." Benny put her hands on her hips, arching backward and groaning. "Even when I'm not carrying her around, I feel Irene in the small of my back. I hope she learns to walk soon."

"Then you have a whole new set of problems." Savannah turned her friend around, kneaded the muscles along Benny's lower back. "Does this help?"

"Mmm…yes."

"Get a tennis ball and have Dan roll it along your back at night, like when you were pregnant. Keep it with you and you can do it yourself against a wall."

"Can't I just come to see you?"

"No, you can't." Savannah stopped kneading. "My hand is already tired. Baby-wearing might be a thing, sugar, but there's an alternate meaning to those words."

Benny blinked. She snort-chuckled. "I never thought of it that way. But you're right. It's totally wearing on me. But she's not happy otherwise."

"I'm not sure how I feel about it. If you look at most other cultures in the world, it's a natural thing to do. We Americans are so set on independence, we force it on our kids too young. Baby-wearing wasn't a thing when my girls were infants, but I…"

"Girls?" Benny gripped her arms. "As in children?"

Savannah's stomach lurched.

"Savvy?"

She couldn't speak. It was Margit's visit. Talking about her twins. About Doc and what he'd done. What he became in a far-off place. Because of horrors he could not unsee. Careless, careless. And already the pity in Benny's eyes was too much to bear. How quickly would that pity turn to horror if she knew what Savannah had done?

Her friend's voice was a buzzing somewhere in the distance. Carmen flittered into the room, her words like chirping. Savannah kept her eyes on the old woman, on her sensible shoes and black dress, and the smile that became concern the nearer she came. Her lips moved. Benny's buzzing ceased. Frail and birdy hands came up, came to rest upon Savannah's shoulders. Old and glistening eyes looked from one side, to the other.

"I won't ask for your secrets." Carmen's voice snapped sound back into being. "I will only tell you what I see. Wings. One is like a shadow. One is like a cloud. Here." She spread her fingers from Savannah's shoulders. "And here."

How to breathe? How to breathe? Savannah couldn't remember how.

"I don't know if they are there to lift you up, or if you are grounding them? I think you must decide." Carmen's gaze went beyond Savannah, and to the screen door. She smiled. "She won't come in, but she's watching."

"Who?" Benny asked. "Who's watching?"

"Savannah's guardian."

"If that…that thing is Savvy's guardian then it's a rabid Doberman."

"So young," Carmen continued without comment. "She doesn't want me to know she's here. She makes me feel a heaviness in my chest, like I can't breathe…"

"Are you all right?" Savannah fell automatically into doctor mode. "Take a deep breath."

"I can breathe just fine. It is she who can't…couldn't." Carmen's hand moved to her head. She winced. "Oh, goodness. Goodness."

"What is it?" Benny asked. "Carmen, talk to me."

"Pain and fear. Blood, water and…the moon. So cold. I don't…I can't. Not this. Forgive me, but I can't do both."

"Can't what?"

"I have to let it go."

Carmen closed her eyes tight. Her thin, pastel-pink lips squinched up into her wrinkled face. And then she relaxed with a breath exhaled.

"No matter what the poets say," she told them, "death is never beautiful."

The old woman looked at the screen door, gave a little shudder but squared her shoulders like a fighter in the ring. She held out her hand for the bowl and oil. Savannah gave it back to her.

"Come, ladies," she said. "Let us begin."

* * * *

I didn't tell that old bat anything. She guessed. She read about me or something. What did she have to go and tell Savvy about me for, anyway? How'd she know I was even there? I didn't let her see me. I didn't. Why me and not that thing making Savvy's life miserable, huh? He's right there. I don't get it. I didn't get life. I don't get death. I don't know how any of this works and I'm damned tired of it.

Now I said a cuss word. Mom and Pop would wash my mouth out. It'll probably keep me out of heaven or something. Stupid, stupid old lady. I have to get out of here for a while. I'm too wrapped up in all this. Maybe I'll go spook some kids. No. Too humdrum. The traffic lights have been working way too well lately. It's time for something delinquently swell. That'll make me feel better.

Guardian, schmardian. I'll show her who's watching over who.

* * * *

Savannah had turned off the ceiling fans, as requested. Already, she was sweating, but the old woman seemed perfectly cool. Carmen filled the marble bowl halfway with cool water. Her whispered Hail Marys, three of them, were the only sound except for far-off farm noises and cicadas heralding the heat. Her rheumy gaze moved from face to face, window to window, taking in the surroundings.

"Anger," Carmen whispered. "So much anger. And sorrow."

"Me, or…?"

"Savvy, shh," Benny warned.

Carmen uncapped the little bottle, and let three drops fall onto the surface of still water. She stirred with one fingertip and sat back. The oil swirled, spread, and reformed. Smaller and smaller drops surrounded one slightly larger one.

"So broken," Carmen said. "Shattered. Oh. Oh, oh." Fingers kneaded wrinkled cheeks.

Savannah wanted to grab her hands, make her eyes focus, make her explain. She curled her hands into fists and jammed them into her pockets instead.

Carmen's fingers moved up to the corners of her eyes, to her temples. "Pain. Here." She gasped. "No mercy. No pity. Stop it. Please. Stop."

The overhead fan moved, slowly at first, and then picked up speed. There were no lights on, but daylight itself seemed to dim, chill. The hair on the back of Savannah's neck stood on end. She broke out in a cold sweat.

"What's happening?"

Benny pulled her closer.

"Nothing good."

Carmen whispered words Savannah couldn't make out. The bowl on the table rocked. Like the fans, slowly at first. Water and oil spilled over the sides. Carmen's lips moved soundlessly now. Her face pinched. The rocking intensified, dumped the contents that pooled on the table, dripped onto the floor. The old woman trembled, desperate eyes flicking from Benny to Savannah and back again. She reached for Benny.

"Out!" Benny shoved Savannah toward the door, grabbed Carmen's hand and yanked her nearly off her feet. "Out, now!"

Savannah held open the screen door. She stumbled through after her friend and the old woman. She barely kept herself from toppling down the stairs from the force of the heavy door slamming closed behind her. The screen door flapped, flapped, and was still.

"What the fuck was that?" Benny growled. "Sorry, Carmen."

"Cursing has its purpose." Her voice shook. She sought Savannah's hand, gripped it tightly when she found it. "That thing means you harm."

"What thing? What is it?" *You know what it is. You know who.* "What the hell just happened?"

"I wish I knew." Carmen's trembling hands moved up her cheeks. "Sometimes they speak to me. Sometimes I get images from what is left of them. I'd have never tried to contact it if I'd known." She shuddered from head to toe, shook it off. "I can usually protect myself from such malevolent energy, but I have never encountered anything like this before. It is hatred. It is sorrow. And it means you harm, Savannah."

Real fear. Pure concern. The woman wasn't faking it. Savannah couldn't explain what happened inside her house, but neither could Carmen. Why, then, was she so chilled, gooseflesh and all?

"Is it part of the house?" Benny asked. "Is it the drowned girl I told you about?"

"Oh, my, no. I don't believe so." Carmen fanned herself. "Whatever that malevolence was, it is attached to Savannah, not the house."

Savannah sank to the bottom step. She put her head in her hands. None of this was possible. What had she been thinking, letting Benny bring this sweet but delusional old woman to her home? The two of them put things in her head that didn't belong there. She wasn't Benny, prone to the whimsical. She was a doctor. A scientist. A woman who left the home she knew and loved to strike out into the unknown. Such a woman didn't believe her dead husband was a furious ball of energy slamming doors and causing her head to ache. She didn't believe Sally and Ginger were her wings. Whatever happened in her kitchen had a scientific explanation. A meteorological one. Over the mountain, storm clouds thickened. Electrical summer storms wrought all kinds of crazy havoc in the Berkshires.

The sound of the tractor's rumbling lifted her head. Ade waved from the seat of the ancient tractor he'd mastered. Savannah got to her feet, brushed herself off. Ade. The tractor. The farm. Solid things. Real things, no matter how badly she wanted to believe her girls were truly still with her, and not just memories in a box.

"She is a fine old work horse," Ade called over the roar, and cut the engine. He climbed down from the high seat. Benny and Carmen stood beside her in a clutch. Savannah focused on Ade, on the way his calf muscles bunched. His brow furrowing as he came closer. Even called up the dream that was no more real than...

"Something wrong?"

"Not a thing," Savannah said quickly. "Ade, this is Carmen Iapalluccio, a friend of Benny's visiting from Brooklyn. Carmen, Adelmo Gallegos."

"Brooklyn, New York?"

"Is there any other?" She laughed, small and shaky, her gaze flicking to the house and back. "Pleased to meet you."

"The pleasure is mine," he said. "I did not mean to interrupt. I'll..."

"The ladies were just getting ready to leave." Savannah's cheeks burned, but being rude was better than having them stay. "I was just going inside to get some things Carmen left in the kitchen."

Trotting up the steps, she cut off any protest, real or imagined, that might follow her. Savannah yanked open the screen and pushed open the door with more force than necessary. All was quiet within. Brilliant daylight. Just her house, her lovely little house, getting stuffy because she'd turned off all the ceiling fans.

She flicked on the one in the kitchen, cleaned up the spilled water, and grabbed the bottle of oil and the marble bowl. Savannah brought them out to Carmen chatting amiably with Ade, as if nothing at all had just happened.

"Savvy never lets me drive the tractor," Benny burst as if they had been talking of it all along. "Just because I didn't really drive much until recently doesn't mean I can't handle a tractor, right?"

"It is a bit temperamental," Ade warned.

"Psh." Benny grabbed his hand. "I can do it. Show me. I'll be right back, Carmen."

And off she hauled him without even a glance over her shoulder. Benny's talent for subtlety was even more lacking than Margit's. Savannah couldn't help smiling, or being embarrassed. She handed Carmen her things.

"I'm sorry for being so rude. I don't want Ad…my workers knowing about any of this. It'll freak them out. Please, stay and have tea."

"I would rather not, dear." Carmen patted her arm. "Not because I am offended. You aren't the first to react this way. I'm a little shaken, is all, and think I need to lie down."

"I'm so sorry, Carmen."

The old woman shrugged thin shoulders. "It's happened before. The spirit world does drain, and I'm old. And because I am old, I will ask your indulgence, even though you don't want to know."

Savannah quelled the sigh, the shuddering. "All right."

Carmen leaned in closer. "Your malevolent spirit is not happy about your houseguest, but he is wary of him too. Maybe even a little afraid. Take notice, do your headaches ease when Mr. Gallegos is around?"

All the hair on Savannah's arms stood on end. The pounding ache earlier squinting her eyes was gone. Not even the dull ache remained.

Carmen grinned. "I had a hunch. The air around you changed when he arrived."

Ade started up the tractor again. Benny rode on the running board, jumped off as he drove past. He waved and continued on to the garage where Raul and Edgardo stood waiting.

"We good?" Benny asked, her gaze darting from young woman to old.

"We're good," Savannah answered.

Together, they assisted the old woman, less sturdy than she had been earlier, to the car. Savannah settled her into the front seat. The walk had pinked Carmen's cheeks, but her smile was wan. She reached for Savannah's hand through the lowered window.

"Sometimes a soul is broken beyond fixing." Carmen said. "It's a sad and terrible thing when anger is all that remains. It doesn't allow healing, Savannah dear, no matter how we might wish otherwise. Whatever you believe happened or didn't happen, remember that."

"I will."

Carmen squeezed her hand once, and let it go. Leaning back into the car seat, she closed her eyes. Savannah bent low to wave Benny goodbye. Her friend only nodded, a grim expression her only other response.

* * * *

The old bat has a point. Anger just makes everything worse. Maybe that's why I'm still here. Maybe I'm still too angry about what happened. About being stupid enough to believe his lies. Yeah, I'm scared of that monster, but why would he be anywhere I get to go? I was a good kid. Stupid, maybe, but I was good. Unless throwing rocks at barking dogs or ditching drips before the flutterbums catch you talking to them is bad. I guess it is a little, like scaring kids and messing with the traffic lights is a little bad. Whooee! It's going to be a while before they fix what I did this time. And it didn't even make me feel better. But then I heard them, the little girls. I didn't even know they noticed me, but they called somehow, and I heard. It took all three of us to slam that ghoul inside the house, but we did it. That made me feel better. It made me feel really good, in fact. Less alone and…and powerful, I guess. Like I could actually do something other than what I've been doing. So I guess I'll stick around a little longer. Besides, there's always the chance of seeing Ricky Ricardo naked again.

Chapter 12

love's ardent hands

Another day in the upper field. Another failed yet satisfying attempt to find agricultural treasure. With this, patience, diligence, and care were key. He had absorbed that alongside everything else he had learned, twisted it to his needs, his ambitions. In Bitterly, he was untwisting those lessons and relearning them all over again. *La jefa* would be proud. And Lita, who the old woman visiting from Brooklyn reminded him of. They looked nothing alike. It was something else. Something not quite definable. Benny had the same quality Ade neither understood nor dismissed.

"So how do you feel about spirits and shit?" Benny's question had taken Ade aback, as had the obvious but effective effort to separate him from Savannah and the elderly woman the Saturday prior. Whatever Savannah assured him, something was most definitely wrong. Ade had answered, "I am an optimistic skeptic. Why?"

"What does that mean?"

"It means that I need more proof than faith, but I never say never. Again, why?"

Benny had pursed her lips then, pretending interest in the workings of the tractor she'd hauled him off to show her.

"There is an otherworld all around us," she said. "I've enough proof to satisfy even you, but I understand it's a personal thing. You can't take my experience at my word. You'd have to have your own."

Benny had quickly told him about the old woman, the bowl and the oil, and the strange and terrible happenings in the kitchen. Ade could easily have explained the science of the static sensation and spinning fans with the electrical storm brewing and earth tremors too faint for active bodies to feel. But he kept those thoughts to himself. Hadn't he felt the eerie and definite sensation of being watched the night he stood naked in Savannah's kitchen? So much so that he dressed before cleaning up the mess he'd made in the entry. Despite his years in America, he was raised in a culture that venerated the dead, believed they watched over loved ones for all eternity.

"I'm just making you aware," Benny finished. "You do with it what you will."

Ade had kept his skeptical mind open all week. Whether alone in his room or playing a board game with Savannah, he watched, listened, felt. Nothing. The only goosebumps he got were Savannah-related. Whatever Benny thought she saw made no second appearance. Of the experience, Savannah said nothing at all.

Ade turned off the shower and pulled his towel from the rack. Savannah's voice came muffled but audible through the floorboards of the creaky old house. His heart swelled, stuttered, soothed. The weeks he'd been in Bitterly seemed like years. Good years. Boston was a distant and blurry past, even if he'd only cut ties with his life there little more than a week ago. Pleasantly restorative as were evenings spent playing games or watching television or simply talking, it was too much like comfort. Comfort quickly became friendship, and Ade—impossibly, strangely, wonderfully—wanted more. After drying, dressing quickly, he headed downstairs.

But he halted when he neared the kitchen. Savannah was on the phone, her back to him. She had the old, corded phone balanced on her shoulder, away from her ear. He could hear the muffled, heavily accented voice on the other end.

"Well, my goodness, sugarbeet, it was good talking to you."

"I've been remiss way too long, Auntie Bea." Savannah's voice was clear. "I'm sorry for that. No excuses, just sorry."

"Sorry enough to come visit?"

"It's hard to even think about it."

"Sure it is, sugarbeet, but hard never stopped you. Never once, even when you were a little girl. Maybe if you bring that handsome Spaniard with you, it'll be easier."

Ade bit down on his lip to keep from laughing. So she was talking about him. Excellent.

"Auntie Bea." Savannah laughed. "I never said he was handsome."

"Isn't he?"

"Well, yes he is. But I'm not sure Spaniard is politically correct these days."

"Just think about it, all right? I'm not getting any younger, you know."

"Ah, the infamous Bea guilt."

Ade leaned on the doorjamb, wanting to hear more.

"It's a fact, young lady. I'll be one-O-five this May. How much older can I get?"

"You'll live forever," Savannah said softly. "I'll think about it. And I'll call you next week." She hung up the phone. Moving to the counter, she let go a sigh.

Sorrowful? Relieved? Ade could not be certain. He cleared his throat.

"Oh." She grimaced. "How much of that did you hear?"

He pushed off the doorjamb. "Spaniard is not offensive, but inaccurate. I am Ecuadorian."

"That much, huh?" Savannah laughed. "Auntie Bea's voice certainly carries."

"I thought you had her on speaker until I saw the phone you were using."

"She doesn't hear well, so she shouts. Can't keep the phone to your ear when talking to her, that's for sure." Savannah glanced at the ancient phone on the wall of her kitchen. The cord, stretched out and tangled, hung nearly to the floor. "I never use the landline," she said. "I only keep it for Auntie Bea. Same number the Larsons' used to have. I've given her my cell number a hundred times." She spread her fingers. "She only remembers this one, and she won't answer a call if she doesn't recognize the number on caller ID."

"Then you called her?"

"I don't do it nearly enough."

Ade ruffled his wet hair. "Will you go?"

Savannah shrugged. "I haven't been back in a very long time. But I know if I don't, I'll never see Auntie Bea again. She's too old and frail to make the trip north."

Ade went to her, took her hands in his. He kissed one, then the other. "I would go with you, if you asked."

Savannah averted her gaze. "I won't ask."

"Why?" But he knew. He searched her silence for some sign that now was the moment to confess. Any sign at all.

"If I go, it'll be alone. It has to be. But thank you, Ade."

Sign enough to hold his tongue. "The offer stands, all right?"

She nodded.

"Excellent, then let us change the subject to how very handsome you think I am."

Savannah looked up at him through her lashes, coy and cautious. Ade had not well and truly kissed her since her blackout. The urge to do so now overwhelmed him, which made it imperative he did not. Instead, he tugged her gently toward the door.

"Let us go out tonight," he said. "A real date. No pretending it is just business."

No more coy and cautious, Savannah met his gaze dead on. She didn't speak, only stared. Her hands in his twitched but didn't let go. "I'd love to, Ade. Very much."

"Where would you like to go?"

"D'Angelo's again?" she said. "It really is the best in town."

"D'Angelo's it is. Do we need a reservation?"

"Probably not, but why don't you call while I freshen up a bit."

"Seven o'clock?"

"Seven o'clock."

Ade let her hands go. He pulled his new-but-ancient cell phone from his pocket. "Ah, no Internet capabilities on this thing. Can I use your cell?"

Savannah handed it over. "I'll be ready by a quarter of."

She had to know what he'd done to his smartphone. He'd found it on the counter the following day. And the glass he'd dunked it into was dry on the rack. But she hadn't said a word about it. Ade was no fool. Questions begat questions Savannah didn't wish to answer. They both hid painful pieces of their pasts. The difference was, he'd been curious and cautious and the Internet supplied an outlet for both. Even if she looked, Savannah's online search would find nothing about his troubles. Anita had made certain of that, and it would remain so until she either got what she wanted or knew without question she would not. The Durst power reached that far.

The shower went on upstairs. Ade found D'Angelo's in her recent calls and made the reservation. Sitting in the parlor, waiting for this woman who had come to mean so much to him, he made a decision. He wouldn't give Anita the chance to ruin him for a second time. Savannah had the right to know what she was getting into. Who he was and all he had done. If he had any chance of a future with her, in Bitterly, he had to come clean. Tonight.

* * * *

Cool water countered August's heat on her skin, but not the heat inside. Savannah's fingers still tingled. Her body ached. He had kissed her hands, asked for a date, and the conversation with Auntie Bea popped like a soap bubble. In the moments following, the years of her lonely vigil swept through her mind and out again. They lived together, enjoyed one another's company. Safely. Ade's simple request pulled away that safety, leaving Savannah to freefall into, *I'd love to.*

Evenings spent domestically contented gave fodder to her lusty dreaming, had long since tumbled into daydreams. The evening ahead allowed Savannah to luxuriate in the conjuring. In her mind's eye, Ade parted the shower curtain. He stepped into the tub behind her, nuzzled the nape of her neck. His hands moved up and down the curve of her waist. Slowly. So sensually. To her breasts…

Soon enough, Savannah. She smiled, and then she laughed. Softly, lest he hear. He wanted her, and she was ready. Savannah had no doubt. Maybe tonight would turn dreams into reality, or maybe she would hold on to the excruciatingly gorgeous anticipation of it all. Now, next week, next month, it didn't matter. They had two whole seasons with nothing more to do than decide how to spend them.

Back in her room, she dressed quickly. A dress this time. Full and flowing. And no Birkenstocks. Savannah didn't pretend to slip earrings on, but chose the turquoise dangles so blue against the dark of her skin that Auntie Bea had sent for her fortieth birthday. Twirling her hair into careful coils she pinned up and off her neck, she spotted her laptop in the mirror, still open to the page that had prompted her to call her aunt in the first place.

She smoothed a little moisturizer into summer-burned cheeks, her eyes drawn again to the computer screen. *Spirit Reckonings.* She had first seen the page as a suggested interest at the bottom of *Savvy Gardening*, the blog site Benny had created for her. Clicking through it, she discovered Spirit Reckoning, a regular commenter. Savannah had clicked on the suggestion, telling herself adamantly, out of common courtesy. It was good manners to show like interest.

The posts and following discussions mostly dealt with the way a human mind worked through grief, responded to cues, and came up with acceptable answers for those inclined to believe. No pointers on how to spot ghosts, quell hauntings, or which crystals to use to conjure otherworldly phenomenon. Thought led to thought, and Savannah's had traveled to Auntie Bea, who couldn't possibly live forever despite her efforts.

She turned away from the mirror, sat on the edge of her bed and put the computer on her lap. Swiping her finger across the screen, she accidentally moved it to the next page instead of closing out.

*The human mind is an awesome thing, capable of creating
worlds both physical, and mental. There is usually a scientific explanation for everything, but sometimes we simply have to accept
that there are things that can't be explained by what we, as hu-
mans, know now. Keep an open mind to the non-sensible. Peace.*
    *"Round about what is, lies a whole mysterious world of what
might be." ~Henry Wadsworth Longfellow*

A smile worked at Savannah's lips. She saved the page in her favorites
and closed the laptop, ran her hand across the cover. Electronic warmth
tingled through her palm, up her arm, to her shoulders where, Carmen
said, she had wings. One like a shadow. One like a cloud.

Savannah closed her eyes. A deep inhale. A long exhale. She carried
the memory of her daughters in her heart. Would it be so terrible, so
tremendous a leap, to believe they were still with her in spirit? Was it
wrong for a mother to want such a thing?

No longer her laptop, but the Box rested on her lap, and Savannah had
no recollection of moving. The scent of the cedar trunk, open beneath her
windows, soothed and filled Savannah's head, left no room for the ache
trying hard to bloom.

She opened the Box. Serenity twirled about inside her like a tiny
whirlwind. Tears welled. Savannah didn't wipe them away or quell them.
She took the booties out, kissed them one at a time and set them aside.
Drawings. The princess valentines the girls gave out in kindergarten,
one made out to her and one to Doc while he was still overseas. Tiny,
articulated dolls they got with their kids' meals at Christmastime, their
favorite things in the world.

They'd both gotten the white doll and Sally cried. It wasn't fair that
five of the six collectables were white. Ginger traded with one of her
preschool friends who got the black one and didn't want it, but when she
presented it to her sister in trade, Sally refused.

"You keep that one. I'll keep mine. Okay?"

Tiny as were the toys, the twins never lost them. The hair was always
tangled and the faces mostly rubbed off. Ginger and Sally never went
anywhere without them, just like they never went anywhere without one
another. Savannah remembered searching the house for those dolls, once
she'd been released from the hospital, after the funeral and burial. She
found them where she should have looked in the first place, under their
pillows, in beds still and forever unmade because that was where she

found them. Unresponsive. Already gone. Her consolation being that they hadn't suffered, only fallen asleep to never wake again. Doc, in his twisted way, loved them. He loved them so much he couldn't let them live in a world as evil as the one he knew existed.

Sometimes, life breaks a soul beyond fixing.

Savannah could no longer see for the tears. Wiping them away, she placed the dolls aside with the booties and the valentines. She pulled out the clipping. The only one she kept. Because it had come closest to the truth during that time of speculation and exaggeration:

WAR VET AND TWIN DAUGHTERS DEAD IN APPAR-ENT MURDER/SUICIDE

An unexpected shift at the hospital had saved Savannah's life. It made Doc impatient. Changed his plan. Getting home to find the babysitter asleep on the couch had surprised Savannah, tipped her off. It had only been just after ten.

Finding the girls, dialing 911, fighting off Doc who'd been hiding in the closet full of their daughters' shoes and clothes. His anxiety rising. Flashbacks pelting. His reason obliterated. Already wrecked on the opiates he'd injected that no longer worked to silence his demons. It was all a blur that ended with her fighting for her life and Doc dead from a gunshot wound deemed a suicide because of the note he left behind. The note Savannah didn't see until after all was said and done, and then never again. It was a lie. Her lie. Because Doc hadn't killed himself.

The babysitter recovered from the high dose of benzos Doc had hidden in the smoothie he'd brought for her. She didn't remember anything, but the guilt followed her to a mental break a year later. That was when Savannah left Georgia. There would be no peace for her there where memories lived in every nook and cranny. No peace. No escape. The pity in every eye, and the knowing she had deceived them all.

A soft rap at the door, accompanied by Ade's voice asking if she was asleep, banished terrible images. Savannah lifted a hand to wipe away tears, only to find there were none. "No. I'll be ready in a minute."

"Take your time. I will call D'Angelo's and move our reservation to 7:30."

The clock at her bedside showed 6:57. Savannah stood up, the clipping in her hand. She read the headline once, twice. MURDER/SUICIDE became TRIPLE MURDER. The headache always behind her eyes pulsed. She saw Doc in her mind's eye, his hands raised, hers trembling.

She felt the trigger, a phantom bit of slippery metal. If she tried hard enough, she could smell the metallic scents of blood and steel.

Her head pounded. Savannah took long, slow breaths. Tucking the clipping back into the Box, Savannah pushed Georgia, the girls, and Doc away. Tonight was about having a real date, about creating a better future, not reliving the tortured past.

The headache eased back to a dull throb. Dabbing on a little lipstick, she held one hand still with the other. A swoop of mascara on lashes that had never needed it. War paint. Or simply ritual to calm that part of her never at ease. The woman in the mirror studied her as she was studied. Her eyes were as fierce as Savannah suddenly felt. She dared the mirror-woman to look away first, dared her to even try ruining dinner with Ade.

"I didn't think so," she said, and headed downstairs.

* * * *

Ade opened the door of D'Angelo's, stood aside to let Savannah enter first. She didn't glance nervously around the restaurant like she had the last time. A good sign. Tonight, she affectionately greeted those she knew, introduced him without hedging, and didn't draw her hand back when he took it in his.

How life could change in so short a time.

After ordering, she asked about the upper field and the progress he was making there. Appetizers brought a discussion concerning the academic tome he would spend the winter writing, and of his father and uncle and their soon-to-be-permanent reunion with home. By the time their dinners came, they were on to Halloween and the pumpkin contest during Harvest Fair Days, and how blissfully quiet it would be on the farm once the season was over. Each new topic excited and contented Ade, as well as distanced him further from his purpose. It was too easy to forget unpleasantness when he was with Savannah.

Instead of making his confessions, Ade regaled her with the deeds and misdeeds of his youth in Ecuador. His struggles through American academia came close to giving him an in, but Savannah always managed to steer the topic elsewhere. Not that he was trying overly hard to guide it back.

She told him about the clinic and the poor but tight community of women pulling together to raise their children. Some showed up pregnant in her office almost yearly despite the various forms of birth control she made available to them. For some, it was a choice. For others, it wasn't.

"There was one woman, I'll never forget, whose husband used a box cutter to remove the implant I put in after she gave birth to their sixth child. She was forty-two at the time. He demanded to see where he signed a consent form. I couldn't get him to understand that she didn't need his permission."

"*Qué chingados*," Ade muttered. "How does one person do such a thing to another? To someone he supposedly loves?"

"You'd be surprised to know the things I've seen." Savannah dabbed her lips, averted her eyes. "Not just here, but in…in Georgia."

Heat slithered up Ade's back. He hadn't thought. He didn't mean to. He'd drawn confession to the table, but Savannah's, not his. That pinched look when a headache was coming squinted her eyes. Ade did not have to be particularly astute to know what tumbled through her head. He could let her speak and she would never know he'd dissected her secrets long ago. That was what the old Ade would have done, but he was no longer such a man.

He reached across the table for her hand. "I have a confession to make."

"You do?"

"I have an ulterior motive for this dinner."

Eyes widened. Lips parted. "You're leaving Bitterly."

"What? No, of course not. Although"—he grimaced—"you might want me to, after I tell you what I must."

Savannah laughed softly, a little tremulously. "There is nothing you can say that will make me want you to go away."

"Even if you discover I am not the man you think I am? Even if you learn I have been a cold, manipulative, glory-seeking scoundrel who has used people, mostly women, including you, to get what I want?"

Savannah sat straighter. "That isn't the Ade I know."

"It is the man I was until I got played by a woman way out of my league and ran home to *la jefa* like an angry child. When I came to Bitterly, I was still that man, prepared and planning to use your farm and you to work my way back to the top."

"But…you've always been so…so…"

"Charming?" He shook his head. "It's what I do, Savannah. It is who I wanted you to see, but not who I actually was."

"Then this has all been"—she closed her eyes, took a breath—"an act?"

Truth balled in his throat. He brought her fingers to his lips, lingered there when she didn't pull away. "At first? Yes. It was an act. I tried to keep it up. I tried to convince myself that you already knew all about me and my past, and that you were biding your time, waiting to use my troubles to your advantage."

"Why would you think such a thing?"

"Because that's what I would have done." *What I did*. The confession stuck in his throat. *Primero lo primero.* "But you defeated me without even trying, without me even realizing, when we first sat in this restaurant sharing a meal. Your farm gave me back my passion for my work, but you? You gave me back the heart I didn't think I had any use for. All within days of my arrival."

Savannah looked away, but she didn't pull her hand from his. "I thought it was just me."

"It was not." He tugged at her hand until she looked up. "A year ago... *qué carajo*. A month ago, had anyone said I would be here, with you, confessing the sins of a changed man, I'd have laughed. Maniacally. But it's true, Savannah. I have changed here in Bitterly, because of this town and its people. Mostly because of you. And that is why I must tell you about Boston, and how I ended up here in the first place."

"You don't have to."

"I do, Savannah. Please. Will you listen?"

She nodded.

In his head, Ade gulped for air. Self-preservation battled in all its past and present aspects. This was it. Either the Ade he'd become in Bitterly would triumph, or he'd crash and burn. He tapped into the poise that allowed him to speak before thousands without breaking a sweat. That Ade still had his uses.

"I have always been ambitious. It is no accident I am the one who was schooled in the United States. My passion for my chosen field was never in question. Not by me or my family. I was going to change the world, Savannah. But somewhere along the way, it stopped being about the environment and became about me. My glory. I have been ruthless. Heartless. I never harmed anyone physically, but there are worse ways to leave one's mark. I didn't care. I used people, got what I wanted, and did not look back. Boston was supposed to be just another conquest, another step to my higher goals. I targeted a woman, Anita Durst, for—"

"Wait a second." Savannah gripped his hand harder. "You mean *the* Dursts? The America's Royal Family Dursts with all those Governors and Senators?"

"Yes, those Dursts." He grimaced. "I aimed high, Savannah. And I struck my mark. I needed research grants, and positions out of my reach. Anita was my means to an end."

"But you rose in your field by your own merits," Savannah said. "You couldn't have otherwise."

Ade's heart twinged. Was she trying to assuage him? Or herself? And then it twinged again for thinking she'd be anything but selfless, even for a moment. "That is true. I have many accomplishments to my name, and I am proud of them. But I got what I deserved in Boston. I can say that to you now and be embarrassed that it is true. Boston was supposed to be just another conquest. I was not counting on Anita having an agenda of her own."

"And that was?"

"She wanted to be married to a scientist she could groom for nothing short of the Nobel Peace Prize."

Savannah's eyebrows lifted. "Well, fiddle-dee-dee, if that isn't a lofty goal. Would she have succeeded?"

"Given time, I have no doubt. Perhaps it is immodest of me, but I've never had room in my life for modesty. I had the ambition, intelligence and skill. She had the power and influence to get me there."

"You're starting to scare me a little, Ade." Her laughter trembled. "Just what happened in Boston that you'd give up all that?"

The busgirl cleared away their dishes and the empty bottle of wine, refilled their water glasses. Savannah leaned back so the girl could work. Her hand slipped from his. The smile on her lips but not in her eyes was as strained as her laughter. Still, she thanked the young lady by name.

Gathering his flagging courage, Ade launched right back in the moment the table was cleared. "I did nothing that could get me arrested. I only played the part of a man head-over-heels in love with the perfect woman. We were first on every society list. I was happy, I thought. No, not happy. I was getting what I wanted, accomplishing a goal."

"Then you didn't love her? Even a little?"

"There was passion and ambition but not love. Not on either of our parts, as it turns out." He took a deep, deep breath. "She became pregnant by another man. She had lovers stashed all over the area. At first, she tried to make me believe the child was mine. She demanded I claim it as my own or she would ruin me. I refused to lie to an innocent child to further my career. To prove she could do it, Anita didn't just strip me of my whole life in Boston, she erased me from it."

Savannah silently contemplated the tablecloth for a moment, and then she took both his hands in hers, squeezed them gently. "I get why it was so hard for you to tell me about the sort of man you've been," she said, "but refusing to lie to an innocent child only proves that the man I know, the man sitting with me right now, was there all along, waiting for that crossroads to present itself."

Ade's scalp prickled. "I...I don't understand."

"Ade." She kissed his fingers. "You could have pretended the baby was yours and continued with your life. That was your line, and you didn't cross it. Don't you see? Bitterly didn't change you. It simply brought you back to who you truly are."

The prickling in his scalp coursed through his entire body. Could it be so simple? No. Adelmo Gallegos had fallen too far from the Ade who left for university. And yet, did he not feel like that boy again? Suddenly, and with a clarity beyond his ken, he did see. The sensation was unsettling, and liberating.

Savannah let go of his hands. "So why not take a paternity test? She can't claim the child is yours if science proves it otherwise."

"That isn't her point. She wants me, and if she doesn't get me, I remain as good as erased from every achievement I've made through my years in Boston."

"That can't be right."

"It's not, but I no longer care."

"Of course you do," Savannah said. "And the fact is, birth control is not infallible. As an OB/GYN, I can tell you with absolute certainty that nothing short of abstinence is one hundred percent."

But there was another absolute. One no one talked about, especially him. Something old and vicious was reaching into his chest, trying to pull his heart out through bone and muscle and skin. This wound he didn't know had festered until Anita made her claim, opened up. The fact. The one, undeniable fact no one knew but him. Until this moment of confession. "I had the mumps when I was seventeen," he said. "It is rare that complete infertility results, but I seem to be that rare case. I'm sterile."

"Oh."

His face burned. His stomach flipped. "Oh?"

"I'm not sure what else to say. This is a painful subject for you, I imagine."

"It is," he admitted. "Being unable to father a child made certain things I have done easier. I had no one looking to me as an example of what it is to be a good and noble man. It allowed me to be more ruthless. Until Anita claimed I was what I could never be, I didn't know the extent of my feelings on the matter. I am a man who cannot be a father. That is... emasculating. And heartbreaking, as it turns out."

"Being unable to father a child doesn't make you any less of a man. Children do not make us men and women, only fathers and mothers."

"Yet in a family of dozens of siblings, cousins, nieces and nephews," he said, "being unable to contribute is unimaginable, especially for my mother. She is ever asking for grandchildren I cannot give her."

"Hmmm." Savannah scrunched up her nose. "Interesting."

"What is?" He tried to smile. "Why are you grinning?"

She traced a nonexistent pattern in the tablecloth. "Did you ever think," she asked, "that maybe the path you chose might be overcompensating for this perceived inadequacy?"

"Pardon?"

Her tracing fingers curled into her palm. She laughed softly. "For an intelligent man, you sure are thick in the head. Think, Ade."

He'd been ruthless. Unbending. Ambitious. He aspired to every kind of success to make up for being unable to father a child? The epiphanical prickling dizzied him. New eyes saw what old, closed eyes never could. Savannah gave him more thoughts he'd never conjured, more hope he didn't deserve. "After all I have told you," he said, "why do you find the best in me and make it true? Make me hope it is?"

"Because finding the best in people is what I do, sugar." A tear rolled down her cheek. She wiped it quickly away and smiled all the broader. "It's what helps to keep me sane."

"Are we ready for dessert?" Brian appeared beside their table, hands on aproned hips and oblivious. "We have Johanna's Vanalmond Decadence this evening. I had a piece earlier and have been dreaming about another one ever since."

Savannah held his gaze a moment longer, and let it go. "We'll have two," she said. "And two cappuccinos. Make mine decaf."

* * * *

"I think we've overstayed our welcome." Savannah gestured to Brian leaning on the bar, chatting with Chef Tony, and the bartender. Ade blinked out of his own thoughts, thoughts she didn't have to guess at to know, and smiled.

He washed down the enormous wad of sugar and flour in his mouth with steaming cappuccino. "I'll leave him a big tip."

Savannah ate the last bite of her cake. She savored it, eyes closed, entirely content. He paid the check and they left D'Angelo's for the summer night, the Green, and music outside.

"Oh, it's Thursday." She skipped ahead, hauling him along. "Live music in the gazebo. Let's go down and listen for a while, shall we?"

They strolled to the gazebo hand-in-hand. Ade pointed out Charlie and Johanna surrounded, as always, by children. He waved. Charlie motioned them over, rising from their blanket spread out on the grass.

"Just the man I've been waiting to talk to. I think my tomatoes have some kind of disease." Charlie drew Ade aside, leaving his place on the blanket beside Johanna open. Ade looked over his shoulder, winked, and turned his attention back to Charlie and his blighted tomatoes.

"Fancy meeting you here." Savannah dropped into Charlie's spot.

"You and Ade are looking cozy," Johanna whispered. "I heartily approve."

"Well, sugar, as long as I have your blessing." Savannah shouldered her playfully. "We just had dinner at D'Angelo's."

"Sounds serious."

"I'm not sure what it is yet, but it certainly isn't casual anymore."

"That's pretty wonder—Millie! Millie, don't feed your sister grass. Dammit, excuse me a sec, Savvy."

Johanna grabbed her toddler and was sidetracked by one of the other mothers wrestling with her children. Savannah couldn't imagine trying to get kids to sit on or near a blanket when there were so many other kids around, when the night was warm and fireflies blinked a carpet of stars. When music played and everyone listened even if they chatted and laughed at the same time. She imagined, just for a moment, Ginger and Sally running around, cardigans flapping behind them like tiny wings, and let it go. She was too happy to bring sorrow to the fore. As much as it hurt, she tucked them gently away.

"Looks like it's safe to steal Johanna's blanket." Ade dropped down behind Savannah, a leg on either side of her, and drew her back to his chest. His arms draped around her shoulders, he sang along with the band, softly into her ear, "...found out a long time ago, what a woman can do to your soul..." He kissed her ear.

Savannah leaned into him, kissed one of those draping arms. "I like when you sing," she said, and the Spanish lullaby whispered through her thoughts. "It makes me feel wrapped up in cotton and tucked in a box, as Auntie Bea used to say."

"Now that is a visual."

"She was a premie back when there was nothing to do but let them die," Savannah told him. "The story goes that the midwife tucked her into a shoebox stuffed with cotton and put her on an open oven door. Early incubator."

"That is astounding."

"So is Auntie Bea. I—" She held her breath. "I think I'm going to go see her. And I want you to come with me."

His arms tightened around her. "It would be my honor."

"I think I can do it, go back to Georgia. With you."

He rested his cheek to hers. Savannah closed her eyes and savored the scent of him, the scratch of his cheek, the heat of his body. Ade confessed his past and was cleansed. More than anything, she wanted the same.

Tears stung. She did not let them fall. This was his absolution, not hers, even if the opportunity had presented itself like a gift. She'd let it slide. For him. And was content to carry her own burden a little while longer. Until Georgia, where it all happened. They'd both had enough truth for one night anyway.

Chapter 13

my life's dark tapestry

"You sure you don't want to come over and play some games?" Johanna shifted her sleeping son on her shoulder. "It's only ten."

"We're farmers, Jo," Savannah answered. "We're up before dawn."

"I'm a mother and a baker. So am I."

Savannah laughed with her. "I suppose so. Can we get a rain check?"

"How about Saturday night?"

"Ade?" she asked. "You up for a stimulating evening of board games over at the McCallan's on Saturday night?"

"Sure. Sounds like fun. Just be aware, I'm ruthlessly competitive."

"We'll be there."

They all said their good-nights. Savannah kept hold of Ade's hand. She felt bad about refusing Johanna's invitation, but playing board games didn't seem the right fit to end their evening. Her head pulsed once, twice. She pressed fingers to her temple, closed her eyes. Behind her lids, a gun. Hands up. Fingers trembling. *Bang.* She shook it off. Not now. Not tonight. She handed the keys to Ade. "Do you mind driving?"

"Of course not. Are you all right?"

"Two glasses of wine is two more than I'm accustomed to." It wasn't a complete lie. Only a little one.

The only sound in the car came from cricketsong and wind blowing through the window. Savannah put her head back, closed her eyes, and conjured before her conscience could do the conjuring for her. She was getting good at it, especially where Ade was concerned. Kiss after kiss, sex-scenario after sex-scenario. All of them ended in her bedroom. Her body ached. She almost groaned but the crunch of tires on gravel opened her eyes. Ade parked behind the house. Savannah tried vainly to calm her pounding heart. Fear welled alongside the desire and, despite Ade's nearness, so did the headache. She waited for him to come around to her side of the car. Auntie Bea would approve of his chivalry, and her graciousness. Soon enough, she'd get to see it firsthand.

Ade opened the door for her. No pang of perceived chauvinism. Not even when he offered his hand. Savannah headed for the back steps, but he tugged her gently back. "Let's sit on the front porch a few minutes and listen to the crickets."

Had he glimpsed inside her head and found one of her scenarios? Or had he been doing some conjuring of his own? Savannah let him lead her. He sat first, opening his arm to her, and she settled in against him. There they sat for long, silent moments, just listening to summer sounds.

"Will you see me differently now?" So soft, his voice.

Savannah picked up her head. "Why would I?"

He smiled sadly. "You will. Perhaps not this night, but in the days to come. I will do something foolish and you will think back to our conversation and…"

She touched a finger to his lips. "This is something foolish," she said. "Just be who you are. That's all I ever want you to be."

"The man I was does not deserve this kindness."

"Maybe he doesn't. But you do." She settled into him again. "You can't make up for your past in a few weeks, but you have a lot of years ahead of you to make good. You will. I'm sure of it."

Savannah gasped, covered it with a cough. Her own words echoed in her head. Eleven years. Had she made good? Had she lived her life to honor her lost children? To make up for not being smart enough, selfless enough to give up her family, her name, her career? Would it have made a difference? Or would Doc have found them anyway?

Doc. Gun. Hands. Fingers. Bang. Could she ever make up for that?

"You are far too good for me, Savannah Callowell."

"Don't say that."

Ade ran the backs of his fingers along her jaw.

Savannah leaned into his touch. She closed her eyes. *I had two little girls, once.* Simple words. Why could she not say them? A tear rolled down her cheek. Ade's caressing fingers caught it, wiped it away. He pulled her back into his arms, pressed her head gently to his shoulder.

I had two little girls, once. Sally and Ginger. They were twins. They were my whole world.

The fingers that had caressed her face now rubbed circles on her shoulder. Savannah's body eased. She kept her eyes closed. Imagined her girls going from six to seven, from seven to seventeen. Love bloomed up from her belly. Would they have been studious? Artsy? Rebellious? Would they have always been the best of friends? Or grown apart as life tugged them along different paths? All the possibilities they never got the chance to become whirled through her head.

His fingers move down her side, make slow circles there, through the summer-thin cloth of her dress. A comforting gesture turned arousing.

Savannah does not quell it. She shifts so she can look into his eyes, to there find what she hopes to. Desire. Caution, but desire. Savannah touches his cheek, smooths the hair from his face. She kisses him. Lightly, at first. Ade pulls her gently onto his lap, kisses the lingering sorrow from her lips. Savannah tastes it—slightly bitter, slightly sweet. He unbuttons her dress and eases it from her shoulder. The feel of his hands on her elicits a soft sigh. Kissing, caressing, his fingers pinch. Savannah gasps. The pain almost feels good. Almost. He pinches again, harder.

"Ade, what—" She scrambles off his lap, but his grip is too strong. "Doc."

"Surprised, Savvy?"

"Let go of me."

"Never, darlin'. You're mine, and the more you try to be his, the harder I'm going to hang on. Make it easier on yourself, and get. Him. Out!"

The last word reverberates between her ears and Savannah is running, somehow running even if her legs are like wet sandbags. The thickness travels up, spreads into her head and blooms like a dandelion ready to scatter into the wind.

"He can't catch you! He can't if you don't let him!"

Voices in unison. Three, not two. Disembodied and sweet. Savannah runs harder, faster. From her shoulders, wings sprout. One black. One white. And carry her aloft.

* * * *

"Savannah. It's okay. I'm here. No one is going to harm you." Ade rocked her back and forth, rubbing her back and soothing while she thrashed.

Savannah elbowed him in the jaw, bolted upright. If not for his quick reflexes, she'd have knocked him square in the nose. She blinked. Looked at him. Behind her. And deflated into sobs so heartbreaking, he felt his own heart fill with them.

"*Corazón. Mi corazón.*" Ade smoothed his hand down her back. "*Estoy aquí. Shh...estoy aquí.*"

After a few moments, her tears eased and she was silent. Still, Ade didn't let her go.

"I was dreaming," she said, her voice muffled by his embrace.

"I suspected as much." *About your husband? Your murdered children?* "Do you want to tell me about it?"

She shuddered. "Not now. Okay?"

"Of course it's okay. Come." He rose to his feet, offered her his hands. "Let us go inside. I will make you a cup of tea. We will watch something on the television. A comedy. Or a documentary. Get your mind in a better place."

Ade didn't let go of her hand once Savannah was on her feet. He held it gently, led her inside and to the deep couch in her parlor where once they had fallen asleep together. "Wait here."

"Ade?"

He turned back. Savannah opened her arms and he went to her.

"I'm sorry if I hurt you," she whispered into his collarbone. "So, so sorry."

"It is all right, *corazón.*"

Savannah kissed him, and let him go.

Ade hesitated but he left her. In the kitchen, he searched the cabinets for teabags and teacups while the water heated. *You don't have to tell me. I already know your past, corazón. When I was still that despicable man, I Googled you.*

Had the moment presented itself? Twice in one night?

He dashed about haphazardly, trying to out-maneuver his thoughts. The teakettle squealed. Pouring water into the cups, he breathed the steam deeply into his lungs, held it. He'd missed his chance to confess his prying. To tell her now was about absolving himself of sins he hadn't meant to perpetuate. She would tell him. In her time. Exhaling that cleansing breath, he headed back to the parlor.

"I know you are there, Adelmo Gallegos." Anita's deep, smug voice came from the next room. The sound sent shivers up his back, froze him mid-stride. "Did you really think you could hide forever?" Tinny and slightly computerized. An answering machine, of all things. "Every ignored text and voicemail just made finding you more of a challenge. You know how a challenge turns me on, *guapo.* It wasn't hard, really, but I'm getting bored of this game. Come back to Boston and let's put all this nonsense behind us. Unless, of course, you are too cozy there on the farm in Bitterly with your daddy and uncle. Hmm? Cozy in the little house with Dr. Savannah Callowell, formerly of Backstorm, Georgia where her husband killed himself after murdering their little girls? You always did know how to find the most interesting woman in—"

The machine snapped off. Ade stared at his own finger on the button. He hadn't even felt himself move.

Savannah didn't look at him. "I saw the light blinking and...I...thought it was Auntie Bea."

Dull. Mechanical. So far away. If he touched her now, she would shatter like crystal on granite. He reached for her. "Savannah."

She stepped away, put her hand up between them. "I was going to tell you. In Georgia, but...and now...I can't, Ade. I just..."

She walked away, her gait clumsy, her fingers pressed to her brow.

Ade's belly flipped. His heart flipped with it. Wrong or right no longer existed. No calculated risk. No best-case scenario. There was only truth. "Savannah, wait."

She did not.

He called after her. "*Mi corazón*, I knew. I already knew."

She paused. Turned.

"Please, Savannah. I love you."

Her hand moved from her brow to her belly, clutching the material of her sundress into a bunch. Tears rolled. She didn't brush them away.

Ade's skin itched and burned but he held her gaze. Then she was fleeing.

He didn't chase her up the stairs. Ade deflated. He flopped cross-legged to the ground, put his head in his hands and tugged at his hair.

Anita Durst. Even at a distance, she could level his life. What a fool he had been. She'd known when he was in Ecuador. He let himself believe the lack of texts and calls meant he'd evaded her. Insidious. She'd succeeded in lowering his guard. Ade wracked his brain trying to remember if he'd said anything to anyone. He had cut off all contact with everyone but...

Carl? It had to be. But he'd only received messages, not answered them. On his cell phone. The one Anita had given him. The one with her name as primary on the plan.

He'd destroyed it too late. Whoever she had paid to track him through his cell beat him to the punch. How long before she showed up on his doorstep? On Savannah's doorstep.

Anger trembled his hands. She would not get the opportunity to hurt Savannah again. Rising to his feet, he dug his ancient cell phone from his pocket. He punched in her number, surprised he knew it, and headed outside.

Chapter 14

beckoning, soft and shadowy

I was seventeen...seventeen and really dumb. I thought I was smart. A smart ass is more like it. I can curse, I decided, so don't go getting your panties in a bunch.

He said he loved me. He said we were going to blow this pop stand and go out to California where I'd be a star. He was going to be my manager. He said he had contacts, friends in the biz. I believed him because I wanted it to be true. I thought I my life was so bad, having to choose between Bitterly and college. College. More school. I couldn't do it. But wasting my life in Bitterly wasn't cutting the mustard either. I packed my bags, snuck out of the house, and met him at his place.

He was so old. Thirty, I think. I never knew exactly. Sure, he was good looking, but what the heck? I know I decided I can curse, but I don't want to say h-e-double-hockey-sticks in the state I'm in. You never know who's listening, you know? And that's just too close for comfort.

Anyway, I was just a kid, but I should've known there was something wrong with an old guy who squats in a rundown house outside of town and makes promises to dopey young girls. Thing is, I got cold feet once I was there. He'd been trying to get me out to his place for weeks. I thought I was so cool. I knew what he wanted. I wasn't that much of a dope. I thought I'd go through with it, but I couldn't. He got mad, hit me over the head with a hammer, and got what he wanted anyway. I'm pretty sure he didn't know if I was dead already, but I can tell you, I wasn't. That's why they call me the Drowned Girl, because after he bashed me and had his way, he rolled me up in a carpet and tossed me into the river.

Drowning was the least bad part of that whole thing, I'll tell you.

I figured you should know all that, considering we're in this together now. She heard us, I think. Don't you? I never tried to do that before, in a dream. Not sure I could do it again. I bet you do, though. You've done it before, I can tell.

Poor Savvy. Something happened with Ricky Ricardo that's making her cry. I missed that part, somehow. He likes it when she cries, Anger-ball, I mean. I know who he is, and that you know too. It's why you protect them both. I know you won't talk to me. Maybe you can't. But I'm pretty sure you know what I'm saying.

We're stuck in this Nowheresville because people did bad things to us. I don't know about you, but I'm done with that. I'm getting out. Somehow.

* * * *

"...too far, this time, Anita. You already cost me my career. What else do you want?"

Savannah hadn't meant to listen, but her window was open, and she couldn't help it. The porch where he stood, whisper-shouting into his phone, was directly under her window. Her open window. That she hadn't closed.

"You are full of shit." Anger had thickened his accent. The expletive sounded more like *sheet*. That accent she found so sexy. So endearing. And then he was gone, the crunch of kicked-up gravel his only good-bye. Back to Boston. Yes, to confront the woman causing so much chaos in his life. Would he return? Did she even want him to?

He'd known. All along. About Doc and Ginger and Sally. Or thought he did. His heartfelt confession, the nightmare, the message on the answering machine, it was all too much. It still was the next day, after a night-fearing slumber. Savannah lived in a perpetual state of queasiness. Work was her only solace, and she dove into it with a vengeance. That Edgardo and Raul asked nothing about Ade's absence told her they already knew.

My father never told you what I have been doing in the United States all these years? You did not Google me?

Ade's words echoed from their first meeting. Savannah vaguely remembered brushing it off, and now understood it had come too close to discomfort to consider. What a fool she had been. The Internet made all information available to anyone with a computer and enough curiosity to key in a few words.

Several days of struggling against the urge later, Savannah slipped into her cool, dark office after the workday was done. Her fingers hesitated over the keyboard. She typed her own name into the search box, clicking quickly out of it the moment it loaded. Fingers shaking, she refreshed the page, scrolled through the hits. Aside from one article on the clinic in East Perry written four years ago, and *Savvy Gardening*, they all had to do with the murder/suicide that chased her from Georgia.

Ade read these.

And so did Benny, Savannah was suddenly certain. And probably Johanna. And many others curious about the woman—at the time, the only black woman in Bitterly—who bought the Larson farm. Tears welled. Savannah swiped them away. New locations were popping into her head. Maine? Florida? Idaho, maybe. She would change her name this time, choose a place where she wouldn't stand out in a crowd. And that made her angry. What the hell kind of world was it when the color of her skin made her a curiosity? More tears rolled, because that could be true for anyone, no matter their skin color, depending upon where they went.

Thoughts and thoughts led to more thoughts pelting her. Injustice and curiosity. Pity and strength, and mourning and murder. The dull ache ever in her head swelled, blurred her vision. She wanted it all to stop. She wanted to finally be free of the headaches and the past, free of the one memory hers and hers alone—Hands up. Fingers trembling. Bang— because she had told no one. Not even the authorities.

"There is only one way to be free."

Savannah spun at the words. The wheels of her chair squealed. She squinted into the afternoon's fallen shadows. No one. But the voice—had it been in her head?—wasn't hers.

Slumping back in her chair, she blew out a deep breath. Drew in another. Let it go. If Benny and Johanna and half the town knew her story, she had been oblivious to it. No one brought it up, not even after her alter ego, Dr. Callowell, became common knowledge. Conversation didn't hush the moment she walked into a gathering. The pity she worked so hard to avoid never came.

Tap-tap-tapping the mouse, she clicked through a few of the articles now almost a dozen years old. She spotted the one she kept in the Box. She read none. But the pictures. Savannah lingered over those.

Doc in his uniform, smiling the smile he took with him to the desert, but didn't bring home.

Sally, two front teeth missing and her hair in the same spikey fashion Savannah had worn for years after.

Ginger, her freckled nose crinkled and her shoulders scrunched, caught in the moment the photographer called out, "Say cheeseburger."

Savannah didn't weep, even if her belly tumbled over and over itself. Her babies. Her girls. Doc. Oh, Doc. She breathed deeply, eyes closed and conjuring the wings dear, deluded Carmen assured her sprouted like shadow and cloud from her shoulder blades, until the pounding in her head eased. Taking comfort from the notion, letting it go as the fantasy it was, Savannah clicked out of the search engine.

Her desktop background, a screen shot of *Savvy Gardening*, appeared. Savannah looked at the image of herself. Really looked at it. The woman on the screen smiled, her dimples as deep as Sally's had been. She remembered the day Benny took it with her cell phone, an unchoreographed moment while they broke up soil two springs ago. The young people who worked for her had been tossing little dirt bombs at each other. One of them had just hit Savannah's white shirt.

She laughed softly. A white shirt? While breaking up dirt on a farm? Savannah couldn't remember if had been a choice or happenstance, but she did remember the happiness of working her own land with people she cared about. She remembered anticipating the planting, the sprouting, the weeding and feeding and watering. She remembered Edgardo and Raul, watching the kids' antics and shaking their heads like indulgent uncles.

The curser arrow hovered over the Google icon. She clicked. Up popped the search screen. Savannah bit her lip, her fingers poised on the keyboard.

Dr. Adelmo Gallegos. She hit *enter*.

Up popped at least as many hits as her own name had garnered. University staff pages. Links to dozens of lecture series. Several scientific articles complete with images. Ade in a white coat, hands in a bin of black earth. Looking into a microscope. Standing before a rapt class, tie undone and arms in the air. Savannah's heart pattered. She clicked on the image option. The page loaded.

Ade dressed in a tuxedo, a curvy brunette on his arm.

Ade with a statuesque redhead, not just in one image, but several.

Apparently, he liked blondes. Short, tall, lean and athletic, curvy and soft, long hair, short hair, curly or straight, they dominated the images a dozen to one. Image after image going back to the late nineties. Woman after woman. Ade, always dressed impeccably and sporting that expensive smile. The pattering of Savannah's heart became a thud. Leaning forward, she typed into the search engine: Dr. Adelmo Gallegos and Anita Durst.

It came up before she even clicked the *enter* key. Dr. Anita Durst of the Boston Dursts. If Savannah had an opposite in the world, it was she. Tall and leggy, fair as a princess in a German fairytale, svelte as an athlete. Electric-blue eyes. And blonde. Gorgeously, ethereally blonde.

Savannah clicked on the image. It led to a society page, newspaper article covering a university winter gala of the year prior. Anita, dressed all in baby blue, and white fur—politically correct faux, of course—her arm tucked regally into Ade's. That she was several inches taller didn't matter. Ade was larger than life, radiating all the charm and sex and charisma Savannah recognized, yet without any of the tenderness she had come to know. The eyes in the image were cool, the eyes of a man aware everyone was watching him.

She read the society page about the number one couple in the city of Boston, the couple on everyone's *who's who* list. Speculation about a summer elopement appeared in not just that article, but several others Savannah found. Aside from that, nothing. No scandal. No big break-up newsflash that might have sent Ade into hiding. After a small mention in the commencement program the May just past, new information about Adelmo Gallegos stopped.

Savannah folded her arms on the edge of her desk and rested her head upon them. She knew nothing about Anita Durst, and yet she knew everything she needed to know. The woman, her family, had kept it all out of the society pages for one reason, so Ade could come back.

Three days, and no word. Not a call. Not a text. Savannah refused to ask Edgardo or Raul.

She lifted her head, stared at the screen. She clicked through the images and finally found one of Ade by himself. Kneeling on some bank, along some waterway, sleeves rolled up, elbow-deep in muck, he was looking over his shoulder at a young man. Spontaneous. Smiling. Handsome despite the dirt and disheveled clothes, the hair sticking up in all directions. This was the Ade she knew. This was the Ade she loved. She had no idea who the other man was, the cool one, the man with all those women on his arm.

She checked the date on the picture. Almost a dozen years ago. When the picture was taken, Ade had still been a man of ideals, a man who got dirty out in the field with his students. She scrolled back and back in time, even found a picture of him as a twenty-two-year-old college graduate.

Savannah grabbed the pic. And another. And another. She put them all in a file that started with the college graduate and ended with Anita Durst on his arm. Click. Click. Click. The slideshow showed her the gradual changes from student to teacher, and the more abrupt ones moving on from there. She saw the hardness grow, and his light go out. Had he known it was happening?

Pausing on the crossroads' picture, Savannah gasped. While he slopped in the mud that day, she had been in ineffectual hiding. Soon after, she would be fighting for her life. Their lives, hers and Ade's, had shifted at the same time, in such different ways.

"I came out of the darkness and into the light," she told the computer screen. "You left the light for darkness."

Tears stung. She let them roll without brushing them away. Her tragedy had been sudden and horrific. She had risen from it a stronger woman. A smarter one. For the first time since leaving Georgia, Savannah understood she had stalled shortly thereafter. The determination to honor her daughters in a life fully lived became mired in hiding who she had been, what she had endured. Hiding it from no one, as it turned out. Only obsessively trying to.

And yet, she and Ade were again at a similar crossroads. If all he said was true, he had been forced out of his false-Eden, but willingly and eagerly followed the path leading out of it. Savannah had only to step back onto the path as he whizzed by, let herself get caught up in his momentum until they were in stride.

Please, Savannah. I love you.

His words trembled through her, tingling every inch of skin. Right clicking on the pic of muddy Ade, Savannah saved it as her desktop background. She clicked out of the search engine, closed all the windows, but left the computer on. She still needed to record ledger entries. Later. Right now, she wanted to find Edgardo and Raul. She had a few questions, and until Ade came back to the farm, they were the only ones with answers.

* * * *

Did you see that? Did you see? He backed down, and Ricky Ricardo isn't even around. She did it. Savvy did. Wow.

Maybe that's how I get out of here. I have to stand up to what happened to me. But, how? Savvy's got her ghoul right there to stand against, but I haven't seen mine in...well, ever. Not since, you know. Then again, Savvy doesn't know he's there. We do, but she doesn't. Hmmm, maybe my ghoul is around here someplace. Maybe I have to figure out where.

And maybe I'm just too scared to even try.

* * * *

The city's twisting, illogical layout confounded Ade when he had first arrived in the Athens of America. He fell in love with the place despite this. It wasn't long before he mastered the T, Boston Commons and the surrounding landmarks. It took longer to become familiar with all the beautiful intricacies and nuances hidden within the touristy haunts. The pubs and restaurants that didn't appear in guides. The world of art and music outside of famed halls and museums. The intellect never bound by ivy walls. Of science beyond institutions. New York's grandeur and energy wowed, and it overwhelmed. Ade had spent two full semesters in Manhattan and never fell as hard for it as he did for Boston.

After nearly a week searching for Anita in all the places they'd once frequented, Ade had to accept that it wasn't home anymore. It wasn't that place he loved more than anywhere else in the world. What had been the goal of his life became the scene of its destruction. But it was more than that. Beantown still glowed in all those ways the academic in him loved. What it suddenly and so surprisingly lacked had nothing to do with the city itself.

Anita had given up the apartment, supposedly because he and she were moving to the grand Durst estate in Cambridge the moment he returned from visiting his sick mother in Ecuador. The doorman's sputtering reaction to seeing him walk into the lobby had gotten that much information, at least. Anita's success in keeping their split out of the society pages seemed tight enough. Not so within that society itself.

Former students he ran across in his search for Anita were as surprised to see him as the doorman had been. Colleagues, however, only pretended. Ade was too good at the game to be fooled by it. He could not suppress the mean-spirited chuckle, inward as it was. People were talking, they simply were doing so quietly. A different Ade would manipulate this to his advantage. Curry favors. Spin gossip. The new and, in his opinion, improved version of himself had no patience for it.

"She's playing with you, man," Carl said, when at last Ade had no choice but to go to the one person he could, if not trust, at least guilt into giving up Anita's whereabouts. "After months of refusing her calls, she's refusing yours. Go back to wherever you were. She'll find you when she's ready."

"I don't want her there. I don't want her infecting my life there. I have left this world behind, Carl. I found happiness. I found who I was, who I forgot how to be. Please. I need to see her, to end this."

"Look," Carl finally said, "I feel for you, Ade. I do. I don't like all the shenanigans that go on around here. I don't like the power her family has over this whole institution, but I told you before. I'm just an old history prof who doesn't have it in him to start again. I'll pass on your message, because she's going to know you were here, and she's going to come after me for information. Other than that"—he held up a finger, crossed to the open door and closed it—"all I can say is, she hasn't missed a board meeting since she took her father's position on the board. Next one is this afternoon. Four o'clock. And I'm going to be perfectly honest with you. If she gets to me before then, I'm going to tell her I told you."

"Will you at least tell me if she gets to you?"

"How?" Carl asked. "After all I just said, you're not giving me your new cell number. You'll know. She won't show up. Or she will. Sorry, Ade. It's the best I can do."

Parked in the staff lot where Anita Durst, thirty-eight and a perpetual student, had her own parking space, Ade kept watch for her customized, baby blue Porsche. Even if Carl did inform her he'd be waiting for her, Anita wouldn't even see the ancient rust-bucket that had taken the place of the Audi he'd given back to her. The Dursts did not see poverty, they threw money at it.

A quarter to four and still no sign of her. Ade groaned, reached for the key. She was giving him no choice. He would have to go out to Cambridge and...

The passenger door flew open. Ade nearly banged his head on the roof.

"This is a new look for you, *guapo*. I like it. *Muy macho.*"

Anita climbed nimbly into the cab beside him. Ade did a quick scan of the lot. No baby-blue Porsche. She'd gotten to Carl, but there she was anyway. The roundness of her middle detracted nothing from her grace, or her beauty. If anything, she was even more exquisite than before becoming pregnant. Straightening, he gathered his old self around the new one, and faced her. "Carl told you I'd be here."

"He's been reluctantly helpful," she answered. "Don't be angry with him. He did try to resist me. As you can attest, that's fairly impossible to do."

His jaw clenched. "You are looking well."

"I am, aren't I? Who'd have thought it?"

"And you are feeling well?"

"Never better. Why? Do you care?"

"I am making small talk, Anita. Now I am not. Leave me alone. Leave my father and uncle and most especially, Savannah alone. She has endured—"

"Oh, spare me your lover's sob story." Anita waved her hand in the air. "I didn't do anything to her but leave a message on her answering machine."

He wouldn't give her the satisfaction of knowing exactly what she had done. "She is not my lover. She is my employer."

"You live in her house."

"Until my father and uncle return to Ecuador and I move into the trailer."

Anita tsked. "A room in an old farmhouse, a trailer, this…vehicle. My goodness. Dr. Adelmo Gallegos, King of Academia. How far you've fallen."

"Your opinion means nothing to me," Ade said. "Neither does any of this. I don't expect you to understand. I don't care if you ever do. I am here for one reason only."

"Your baby."

"That"—he gestured to her belly—"is not mine. If it were, I would not have left."

She flashed those perfectly capped teeth her daddy bought her when she debuted, batted her eyes. "You'd have done the chivalrous thing, and married me?"

"The child is not mine, Anita. You and I both know that."

"Because there were others?" Anita laughed. "Darling, you know how birth control works. I used it with them. I didn't with you. We have been over this before."

"And I have told you before, I don't believe you. Your baby cannot be mine. I am—" Give her his ultimate sorrow to use at will? Share with her what he had shared with no one but Savannah. The wound pricked open when Anita claimed he'd fathered her child seeped through the ineffectual bandage of Ade's imagining. Sterile. One hundred percent conclusive. He'd had every test. Twenty long years ago. But what if? "I want a paternity test."

"Is that so?" Her bought smile never reached her eyes. Ever. She caressed her belly. "I'm sure you know by now that those toys I had scattered about the city have already been paid off and cut loose. I'm also sure you've heard that you are in Ecuador with your sick mother, and I am patiently awaiting your return. I am one hundred percent certain this baby is yours, but if a paternity test will end this nonsense and bring you home, Ade, you got it."

"Good. I am sure the Durst influence is such that you can get us an appointment first thing in the morning."

"Tomorrow?" Anita chuckled low in her throat. "I could get a doctor to do it now if I wanted. You should know by now there is nothing a Durst wants that a Durst does not receive. But no, I'm not going tomorrow or any time before this baby is born. I'm not having a needle stuck in me. Not even for you. We have our whole lives ahead of us. I can wait a little while longer for your mother to recover from her terrible illness. And you can wait until he's born." She reached for the door handle. "This truck really is disgusting, Ade. If you expect me to—"

"He?"

Her lips curled, more sneer than smile. "It's a boy. Didn't you know?"

Ade shook his head.

"Did you listen to any of my messages?"

"They're all the same."

"Not all of them. Yes, Ade. A son. You are having a son. Does that make a difference?"

It just makes it more real.

"You really are old world, aren't you?" She climbed down from the truck. "Poor Ade. Things are just not going your way. I'm having a C-section on September 19th. Mark your calendar. If you want a paternity test, show up and get it. Until then, enjoy your time with your tragic not-lover in Bitterly. My gift to you, to make up for all the lovers, sorry, not-lovers I had. Even though you had plenty too. Once this baby is born, we are a family. I know you, Ade. You might not like it, but I know you. You'll be back."

Anita blew him a kiss, and slammed the door. He watched her walk away, blonde hair snapping behind her like whips. She was so certain. A boy. A son.

His son.

He turned the ignition, revved the engine. Slamming the truck into gear, he jammed on the gas and tore out of the parking lot. Ade wouldn't slash wide that scarred-over wound and feed it the smallest bit of hope that, by some miracle, he had fathered a child. Anita's certainty would soon be dashed and she'd be left trying to figure out which of her exiled lovers had done the deed. It was only a month. One month in the grand scheme of things wasn't so bad. He'd go back to the farm, apologize to Savannah for what Anita had done, for not telling her sooner that he knew of her past, and hope, despite karma, everything turned out okay.

Chapter 15

o'er the cloven Gulf of time

Life on Savvy's continued on its normal track. High schoolers tended the fields under her foremen's watchful eyes. Benny worked the farm stand, Irene occasionally strapped to her chest. Vegetables grew, livestock thrived, and both locals and out-of-towners, always beautifying their country gardens, searched her rows for exotic new plantings. Savannah worked alongside them all. And though the headache always ready to break over her like an egg didn't do so, the dread of it skulked.

And Ade wasn't around to help soothe her.

She busied herself unpacking a box of herbal creams and soaps in a small but effective effort to quell the urge to call him. He would be back. Or he wouldn't. She would deal with whatever happened. It's what Savannah Callowell had done all her life. Deal with it. Make the best of it. Move on. At least the time apart had given her the distance she needed to parse out all he had confessed. That he never told her he knew of her past had felt like betrayal at first. A more rational piece of her mind understood.

Hello, new employer Savannah. I'm sorry to hear that your husband murdered your children and then killed himself, but it's a pleasure to meet you.

Yes, he had familiarized himself with her for purely self-interested intentions. It only became harder as the manipulative man who arrived in Bitterly became the Ade she fell in love with. If her life taught her anything, it was not to squander happiness on misplaced grudges, pretense, or pride. It taught her that people changed, for the worse and for the better. It taught her to live in the present, because the past was unalterable, and the future, as she most recently discovered, could be written in whatever way she was strong enough to write it.

"Hold the door!" Benny backed through the swinging door carrying a nursery tray of annuals. Savannah leapt to her feet and held it wide, letting in Julietta Coco-Bowen. She carried a baby in each arm and looked about ready to drop one of them. Savannah hurried to take Irene from her, bounced the child on her hip.

"She's a lot bigger than Julian." Julietta blew her white-blonde hair out of her eyes. "And squirmier."

Benny deposited the tray on the counter and hurried back. "Here, let me take her."

"I got her." Savannah clutched the baby closer. "It isn't often she'll actually come to me."

"You sure? Dan got an emergency call about some sprinkler system he installed and my parents are in New York, visiting—"

"When do I ever bother about Irene being here, sugar? Don't be silly. Take care of Julietta's order."

"There are two beauty-berry-bushes out front," Benny said over her shoulder. "I'm just going to grab a couple gallon containers of the delphinium before the rain starts. It's black as the plague out there. You sure you have her?"

"Positive. Go."

Irene watched her mother leave the store, tiny lip quivering. Savannah bounced her, made cooing noises, but the child whimpered anyway.

"Babies," Julietta groaned. "I don't get them. At all."

"Even after having your own little boy?"

"Especially after. Kids, I get. I like kids. I love them. But babies? They're a mystery to me. Thank goodness Efan is so good with Julian. I'd be afraid for him otherwise."

"You're a wonderful mother, sugar."

Julietta shrugged. "I'm good at a lot of things, but mothering an infant isn't one of them. Doesn't mean I don't love the little wriggler. He just confounds me. I never know what's wrong with him when he cries."

"I've never even heard him cry. I don't think I've ever even seen him awake."

"Oh, he's awake plenty. When the rest of the world is sleeping."

Savannah patted Irene's bottom. Dug deep into her newfound strength. Could she say it aloud? Julietta would be a safe first. She wouldn't startle and demure but offer a bluntly honest reaction without even trying. The welling in Savannah's belly came less like nausea than it was like joy. "I remember those days."

Julietta blinked those uncanny eyes. "You do? Wait. I don't get it."

"I had two daughters." The words blew out of her mouth on a whisper. Had she said them? Truly? Savannah's heart leapt. Joy and fear freed her voice. "I had two daughters. Twins. Ginger and Sally."

"Twins? Really? Do they live in Georgia?"

"No. They"—she held Irene just a little closer—"died a long time ago."

Julietta cocked her head, brow furrowed. "Wow. I'm sorry to hear that, Savvy. I had no idea."

"Most don't. It's not something I ever talk about."

"Why?"

"I…I used to know. Now I'm not so sure."

"You didn't want people feeling sorry for you." Julietta nodded curtly. Surely. "I know how you feel. Try being the freakiest in the Coco Freak Show."

"You're not a freak, and neither are your sisters."

"I guess you're right. Everyone has escaped mental patients for parents, and watched their father die."

Savannah tried to hide her wince in a hug for Irene. Saying her daughters' names aloud, acknowledging their lives and their deaths, that was one thing. The rest? She shuddered. Enough. She had said enough. More than she had in all the years since Doc pushed needles into their tiny veins and pumped them full of opiates.

Benny came backwards through the double, swinging doors of the farmstand, carrying the delphinium and, thankfully, robbing Julietta's attention. She set the flowers on the counter. "Asleep?" Benny laughed softly. "How'd you manage that, Savvy? It isn't even naptime."

Savannah looked down at the baby resting quietly against her chest. Sweet breath tickled her chin. The peace only a sleeping child could instill washed through her.

"I didn't even realize she stopped fussing."

"Maybe you should come to my house at four in the morning." Julietta leaned in and kissed Savannah's cheek. "I'm sorry, Savvy, about your girls. I know how bad it can be, keeping that kind of thing locked up inside for too long."

Benny's lips pressed together. Her eyes darted everywhere but at Savannah who pretended not to notice her friend squirming. "I'll ring up Julietta's order," she said. "You put Irene down in back."

Savannah put the sleeping baby onto the cot in her office. She brushed back baby curls. Irene suckled in her sleep. Savannah's heart swelled. Tears stung. She hurried back to the storefront. Benny was already loading up Julietta's car. Savannah grabbed a jar of the calendula diaper cream from the shelf and ran outside.

Julietta was carefully, lovingly putting her son in his car seat. The child didn't wake but to wriggle more deeply into slumber.

"For you," Savannah whispered. "Actually, for Julian. Thank you, Julietta."

"For?"

"For being who you are."

Julietta nodded, her eyes straying to her sleeping son. "I don't know what I'd do if I lost him," she said. "I don't know if I'd be much help, but you know where to find me if you, you know, want to talk or something."

"Thanks."

Thunder rumbled, a far-off purr. The inky sky crackled. No rain fell. Benny came to stand beside her, slipped an arm around her waist and pulled Savannah in close. Together, they watched Julietta get in her car and drive away.

"How long have you known?"

"Not long," Benny answered. "After Dan and I got married. Before Irene was born."

"Did you Google me?"

"Only after I asked Johanna."

"Did she know?"

"Some. Enough to leave it rest. People love you Savannah."

"Then wouldn't that make them leave me my secrets?"

"Secrets?" Benny turned her to face her. "You have no secrets, Savvy. You wear your grief like a medal for everyone to see. Some are going to wonder about how you earned it. Out of love. Out of curiosity. In Bitterly, it's never been out of malice."

"I never thought it was. It's just that...I left Georgia because there, I was always the woman whose husband killed her daughters and then himself. I lived when they died. I couldn't get beyond what happened because it was there, in everyone's eyes, no matter where I went."

"Believe me, I know that feeling," Benny said. "Not to say Henny's death was anything like—"

"Loss is loss."

"I suppose. But that's not my point. My point is, no one wants to be that person. Well...maybe there are some who do, but you and I don't.

And now I'm not, because I actually did move on with my life. I found Benedetta Marie Grady again, and that allowed me to become Dan's wife and Irene's mother instead of always being Henny's widow."

Savannah dropped her gaze. "I can't ever stop being their mother."

"Of course you can't." Benny put a gentle finger under Savannah's chin, lifted her face. "You once told me I was a victim, and you were a survivor. Do you remember that?"

She remembered it clearly. It was the mantra of her life, and one she strove to live by. *You live for the future*, Benny had answered. *I live in the past.*

"I guess."

"Savvy." Benny hugged her about the shoulders, leaned her cheek to Savannah's. "I can't even imagine the horror, the sorrow. Irene cries and my whole world turns darker, because she's not happy. You came to Bitterly, you live life to honor your girls, but your past followed you in ways you don't want to believe. I get it. Even after all I've experienced, I'm still skeptical."

"What did you experience," Savannah asked. "You never told me."

"Are you really going to try changing the subject right now?"

Savannah laughed softly. "I hear you. I do. And I know you're right." She bit her lip. First things first. "Ade knew about everything before we ever met…"

* * * *

They spent the rest of the afternoon unpacking boxes. Slowly. Savannah told Benny about Ade's confession, though not the confession itself. Dan showed up to gather his daughter just as she started to stir. After kissing him good-bye and shoving him out the door, Benny confided in Savannah, concerning the events of the previous summer. "I know you don't believe in this stuff," she interjected over and again.

Savannah listened, silently amazed by how real it all was to her friend. She tried to keep an open mind, even got little chills when Benny told her about the handprints in concrete she couldn't have known about without her ghostly friend's prompting. What they did not speak of was Ginger, Sally and Doc. Benny knew everything—almost—and strangely, it made Savannah feel better. Unbound.

"Carmen won't come back though," Benny said, breaking down the last box for the recycling bin. "Whatever she sensed here scared the daylights out of her. She says she's not used to that kind of energy."

"And you think it's real."

Benny shrugged. "I know there are spirits here. And more than one. They're everywhere, Savannah, if you're open to it."

"And you are?"

"I don't seem to have a choice." Benny grabbed a bit of stray packing. Her shirt rode up, exposing a tattoo on her lower back that Savannah hadn't seen before—letters, curled and swirled and difficult to read.

"What are you looking at?" Benny tugged her jeans higher. "Plumber's crack? Do I have a plumber's crack thing going on?"

"I was just looking at your new tattoo."

Benny turned, pulled up her shirt. "Isn't it great? It's a quote I've always loved. It's totally me, don't you think?"

Round about what is lies a whole mysterious world of what might be.

"Henry Wadsworth Longfellow." Savannah's recall was sharp, a reason she did so well in med school. The quote and the quoted flashed behind her eyes, just as she'd seen it on the *Spirit Reckonings* site. Coincidence? Maybe, but Savannah didn't believe in those any more than she did in ghosts.

"You know it?"

"I've seen it before," Savannah said. So Benny was Spirit Reckoning. How had she not guessed? Storing the knowledge away, Savannah slipped her arm around her friend's waist. "Thanks, Benny, for the girl talk."

"It's not girl talk. It's bad-ass-woman talk. And I'm only repaying the favor. You've always been there for me, from day one."

Benny. The Coco sisters. There was, after all, a reason why she'd bonded with these women as she bonded with no one else in Bitterly. Not sisters in sorrow, but sisters in survival. For the first time since moving to Bitterly, Savannah saw herself, and her circumstances, clearly.

The sound of tires on gravel split them apart. It was already past closing.

"You go," Savannah said. "I'll take the last customer and close up."

"Okay, thanks."

Savannah took her place behind the counter.

Benny halted abruptly at the swinging door. "Oh. Hi, Ade." she hurried past him without looking back.

Savannah couldn't move, even if she wanted to rush into his arms, to feel his go around her and hold her close, to hear him call her *corazón* and whisper words of love.

Ade stood as frozen to his spot as she was to hers, his hand still holding open the door. His hair stuck up in all directions, like it did in the photo now her desktop background. His clothes looked slept in. His face was tired. His voice cracked. "I'm sorry, Savannah."

His words severed the roots holding them both in their places. She went to him, he to her, and they met in the middle of the empty farmstand. Arms grasped. Fingers touched. Lips kissed.

As afternoon turned.

As crickets chirped.

As the breeze picked up and the rain finally burst and the headache always lurking lifted away.

Chapter 16

words, once whispered

"I should not have done what I did…"

Ade held her closer, savoring the feel of her body, the warmth despite August's lingering humidity. They had talked the rest of the afternoon, through dinner preparation, over food, and finally took it out to the front porch.

"I was being cautious, and suspicious. That is what I learned to be. Can you forgive me?"

"There's nothing really to forgive," she said. "As it turns out, most of the people I know and love have done the same. It was silly of me to think keeping it to myself kept it a secret." She shifted in his arms so she was facing him. "I won't lie. It did hurt, especially hearing it blurted out like that, like it's no big deal. She wanted to hurt me, and she doesn't even know me."

"She was trying to hurt me. You didn't matter at all. That is Anita. She doesn't care about anyone."

"Not even you?"

Ade shrugged. "I fit into her plan. I don't know if she is capable of love, and it makes me feel very sorry for the child she is carrying." A lump rose to his throat. He did feel for the child, any child, born to Anita Durst. But if the baby was somehow, impossibly his?

"You got very quiet." Savannah touched his face.

Ade met her gaze. "She is absolutely positive the baby is mine. It is the only reason she consented to a DNA test. I know it cannot be, but…"

"But part of you has a tiny bit of hope that it is?"

He nodded.

"What would you do?"

"I honestly don't know, Savannah. The thought of a lifetime connected to her in any way fills me with such dread. Revulsion. But a child would connect us forever."

"Then you'd go back to Boston?"

No quivering lip. No misty eyes. A straightforward question that deserved an answer. "No," he said. "I could never go back."

"I sense another 'but' coming."

He managed to smile. "But I could not leave my child to her and her family, no matter what. I am left hoping for both, Savannah. I'm afraid to hope. I'm afraid for that hope to become real. This, I believe, is what the popular saying, 'Karma is a bitch,' actually means."

Savannah bit her bottom lip. The lip he wanted to kiss and kiss and kiss. How was it possible to be so enamored of a lip that all other thoughts left his head?

"I asked your father and uncle about you, about your childhood, while you were away."

Ade dragged his eyes from her mouth. "You did, did you?"

"I needed to know where you started, what kind of kid you were. I know they love me, Ade. I know they'd never lie to me, even where you are concerned."

"And what did they tell you?"

"Many things." She laughed. "But the most important was that you're finding your way back to who they've always known you were. They are very proud of your accomplishments, but it saddened them to see your ideals become corrupted."

"And I thought I was fooling them."

"No you didn't." She shoved him lightly. "You fooled yourself."

She settled back into his arm, rested her head on his shoulder. There they sat for a long while. The storm had left behind a dewy dusk of a rain-washed earth and insects singing their way out of hiding. Ade appreciated the comforting song. All that needed saying about both of their pasts and presents had been said, except for three small words he'd blurted without meaning to, but meant with all his heart. He kissed her temple, lingered there while the words tumbled in his head. "There is an elephant in the room."

"I don't see one. Or a room."

He laughed softly, lips again pressed to her temple. The words wouldn't cooperate, and if Savannah knew what elephant he referred to, she wasn't helping him out.

"I want to show you something." Rising from the wicker couch, Savannah held her hand out to him. Ade took it and let her lead him. Into the house. Up the stairs. To her bedroom. His heart thumped and his groin twitched, but instinct told him this was not seduction. Savannah sat him on the edge of her bed. She opened a trunk set under the windows, and from it pulled a box. Sitting beside him, she rested her palms flat to the lid.

"I have never shared what's inside here with anyone," she said. "Not even Auntie Bea or Benny or Margit."

She lifted the lid, set it aside, pulled out items one by one and placed them tenderly on the bed between them.

"They were Sally's and Ginger's. Little things I kept. And this." She touched the newspaper clipping. "You've probably read it. I kept it because it was the most clinical, least sensational. Just the facts."

Ade picked it up. He scanned the print. Yes, he had read it. And several similar.

"What none of them say"—she took the clipping back from him—"is the whole truth."

"I don't understand."

Savannah stared at the clipping, squinted. Her fingers moved to her temple, first one hand, then the other. The clipping floated to the floor. Ade knew the look. He feared it. Taking her into his arms, he pulled her close. "Enough," he said. "Enough for tonight."

She didn't speak for a long time. Body tense, eyes closed, she took deep breaths until she was soothed. Lifting her head, she met his gaze in the room lit only by the moon rising and sunlight fading from evening to night. "I wanted to show you these things, Ade. Words are nice but they're filler for the real stuff. You gave me your past, your fears, your deepest insecurities. I could do no less and still claim to love you."

He wanted the words. Badly. But he didn't ask for them. Ade only pulled her close again and kissed her tenderly. Passionately.

Savannah pressed a hand to his chest. "There's more to tell you."

"I know," he said. "But not this moment. When you are ready. We have nothing but time, *corazón*."

She nodded almost shyly, lifted her face and closed her eyes. Ade obliged, surprisingly content with kisses even if his body wanted more.

Savannah smiled against his lips. "I dreamt this."

"You did?"

"I did." She pulled away just enough. "Dream after naughty dream. I was so embarrassed every time I saw you after one of them. You never noticed?"

"Now that you say it…"

"No!" She laughed, covering, her face with both hands. "I give you permission to lie to me without consequence if it means sparing me the humiliation."

Ade moved them, pulled her in, kissed her tenderly once, twice. "I want you in a way I have not wanted a woman since I was a young man with no experience. This is a tremendous thing for me. I thought I would never feel tenderness, Savannah. I did not think myself capable. I want you, but this time, when the time is right, not fortuitous."

"And the time is not right," Savannah said. "Not until you know if Anita's baby is also your baby."

"No, Savannah. And yes." He squeezed her hands. "Whether or not the child is mine has no bearing on how I feel about you, but it could change how you feel about me."

"Don't say that."

"You don't know the Dursts. Your life is complicated enough. You might not want me in it if it means dealing with them." Ade smoothed the backs of his fingers along her cheek. "She will dredge up your past and make a circus of it if it pleases her. She will attempt to drag you through every horrifying detail and twist it to make you—"

Savannah pushed off the bed. Arms wrapped around herself, she stood at the window looking out. Her hand started for her temple, and stopped. She faced him. "I can't let her, anyone, dictate my life," she said. "I am only now just realizing how I've let my past dictate my future. I thought I was living it by my own terms, but what I've been doing is denying it all, to an extent. That, and only that, is the reason I want to take this slower, Ade. I want to climb into bed with you right now and stay there for days, but it would be better to wait, for so many reasons. It's not just sex for me. If it were, you wouldn't have gone to bed alone after our first dinner together that night you arrived."

"Really?"

She nodded solemnly. Ade attempted to quell the idiotic grin trying to make an appearance.

"And you are becoming a new man," she continued. "A new man who doesn't jump into things. A new man who savors the moment. I want to savor this moment too, all these moments. Does that make any sense?"

Standing beside her at the window, Ade took Savannah into his arms. He swayed back and forth, a slow dance to cricketsong. "There is something sexy about waiting, is there not?"

She swayed with him, kissed his throat. "There is." His jaw. "Have I told you"—his earlobe—"that when you're around, my headache goes away?"

"No." Ade shuddered, cleared his throat.

Her hands moved up his chest, and down, stopping at the buttons of his jeans before moving up to his chest again. "Right now, I have no headache at all. Carmen said—"

"Carmen?" he asked. "The older woman who visited with Benny?"

"Yes."

"What did she say?"

"Never mind." She waved it away, a weary smile on her lips. "It's silly. Too silly to even mention. I am wiped out. Maybe we should say good-night. We have a long day in the fields tomorrow."

"I'm feeling a bit drained myself."

She pulled out of his arms, offered him a teasing handshake. "Good-night, Ade."

Ade took her hand and kissed it. "Good-night, Savannah. Sleep sweet."

"Sleep sweet."

Closing the door behind himself, Ade blew a breath through his lips, pushed fingers through his hair. He crossed the hall to the bathroom, brushed his teeth, inspected the growth of facial hair and decided to let it go, anything to keep his mind off Savannah in her own room, probably undressing, waiting for him to finish in the bathroom they shared. His mind wandered and his body responded. In his own room, he stripped down to nothing. Sliding between the cool sheets only heightened his arousal. Desire knew nothing of pretty words and noble actions and earnest promises. Ade groaned. And so did the door that opened with a rush of air. He came up on his elbows.

"Savannah?"

"Screw waiting," she said, and dove into his arms.

* * * *

Well, now…uh…I wasn't expecting that. Oh, Savvy, you have no idea how lucky you are. Come along now, you two. This is nothing you need to be seeing. Your mom is safe with Ricky Ricardo. Let's go keep an eye on your daddy, though, just in case.

* * * *

Spent and sweating in Ade's arms, head resting on his chest, Savannah listened to the beat of his heart. She listened to heartbeats all the time.

Mothers'. Babies'. None of them sounded like his. Ade's thumped like a symphony in her ear, against her cheek, the most beautiful sound she had ever heard, and she was glad she hadn't let him go to bed alone.

Whatever the future had in store, they had at least this night of confessions and promises and love. Like the keepsakes in the Box, she would be able to take it out and revisit it, live it over and over again. It was more than she ever expected to have.

She will dredge up your past and make a circus of it...

His words had nearly undone her, had almost made her deny what she wanted not just for herself, but for Ade. Listening to him prepare for bed, the water running and the pipes creaking, Savannah's mind had reeled and her body rebelled. She loved him. He loved her. No one, nothing, should have the power to keep them apart.

Lying against his chest, fingers soothing circles into his just-enough chest hair, she felt slumber take him in the gentle rise and fall of his chest. Savannah considered slipping quietly from his bed and going to her own room. Briefly. Instead, she settled more comfortably beside him, closed her eyes and, smiling, let slumber take her too.

Chapter 17

friends long dead

"You must come, Savannah. Quickly." Ade tugged her from the row of beans she was picking, insistently when she lagged.

"Is something wrong? Is it Edgardo? Raul?"

"No, no. Nothing is wrong. I have found something exciting. Please, *corazón*, just let me show you."

"Finish this row before you leave," she called over her shoulder as Ade hauled on her arm. The kids among the beans shouted or waved back. Savannah picked up her pace so Ade wasn't hauling her as much as leading her. "What's got you all excited, sugar? Did you find something up in the field?"

"Not in the field. On the way back." He climbed into the coot, barely waiting for her to sit all the way before taking off. The machine didn't go very fast, but Ade's enthusiasm made it seem like Mr. Toad's Wild Ride. Savannah grabbed the back of her seat and held on tight. She laughed over bumps, her heart as light as the sunshine dappling through the trees. Sharing their days, sharing meals, sharing a bed had changed everything and nothing between them. Each day she told herself if this was all she got, she was already more than grateful, and each day made that a little bit more of a lie, because grateful as she was, Savannah wanted more.

Ade slammed the coot into park and leapt over the side. Savannah barely got a leg over before he was there, holding out his hand.

"You're vibrating, sugar," she drawled. "The suspense is killing me."

"Only a moment more. Come."

Hand in hand, they left the dirt road and struck out into the woods. Ade had already hacked through the underbrush, so the going was fairly easy as well as short-lived. The coot on the road was still visible through the trees. He halted.

"There."

At first, Savannah saw nothing but more green and bramble. Then, "Peaches!"

Stunted, bug-eaten, they were nonetheless peaches even to her untrained eye. Ade led her forward. He plucked a slightly shriveled thing from its branch. "Taste."

"Are you certain it's safe?"

"This is as organic a peach as you will ever get, *corazón*. It has been growing untouched here for, if I guess correctly, close to one hundred years."

Eyeing it skeptically, Savannah bit into the fruit. Her eyes rolled. "It's like honey straight from the hive. Peach honey. And so…so…"

"Juicy?"

"That too. It's soft without being mushy. I'm from Georgia, and I've never tasted a more delicious peach. Is it one of those extinct varieties you told me about?"

"Not extinct," he answered. "But rare. Very few growers bother with this kind of fruit. It's a clingstone, most assuredly. See how the flesh holds on to the pit?"

"Oh, yeah. Is that what they mean by 'yellow cling' peaches? They're clingpits?"

"Clingstone," he corrected. "When the flesh clings to the pit they're clingstones. When the flesh separates from the pit, they're freestones. There are also semi-freestones, but you can figure that out, I'm certain. But this, Savannah, this peach is precious. The age of the tree, the location of it, the size and texture of the fruit tells me many things that lead me to assumptions requiring more research to see if my guess is correct. But come. There is more."

"More?"

He took her hand, led her further into the wood. Savannah tried not to be too distracted by the feel of his hand in hers, the sweat of their palms mingling, and how that mingling sweat brought to mind other mingling sweat through coolly humid nights unable to get enough of one another.

Focus, Savannah. Focus. This means a lot to him.

"Wow." She saw the old foundation before he pointed it out to her. Stones set in a rectangle, the remnants of a cellar door, a chimney and hearth, bits and pieces of a house left barely standing. All of it charred in places evidencing the fire that must have taken it. "I wonder if this is the original homestead."

"I would imagine so," Ade said. "If not the original, then a subsequent one. If we can date the house, we can date the peach tree, maybe even find records to tell us for certain what old variety it is. I would not be surprised to find more of them hiding in the forest. If there are, we could potentially resurrect the orchard, maybe even rebuild the old homestead. We could—"

"We?" Savannah held on to his hand all the tighter while the woozy sensation ebbed. Ade's blurred image sharpened into focus.

"My enthusiasm ran away with me," he said. "I shouldn't make assumptions."

"I just..." Savannah moved a step closer, took his other hand. "I haven't thought about our future beyond the DNA test."

"I have. I do. Most of my thoughts are nothing but."

"But if the baby..."

"I don't care, Savannah. If you will have me with or without Anita Durst making our lives miserable, there is no place I want to be but here in Bitterly, on this farm with you."

"It's a little soon to be pledging your life to me and my farm, sugar."

"Is it?" Ade took her into his arms. "Says who?"

"Says...I don't know. Sensibility?"

"I disagree. Do I make you happy?"

"Is that a real question?"

He smiled and held her closer. "Denying happiness is not sensible. It is wasteful. It is...blasphemous."

"Well, fiddle-dee-dee. Those are strong words. And how do you know we will still make one another happy in five years?"

"You would have us wait five years? Just to be safe?"

"Maybe not five years, but it has only been a few weeks."

"Five days? Five weeks? And it has been nearly two months. So what is your point?"

"It's so soon. Still so new."

"Again, your point being? That something so new cannot be trusted? That one must wait for something to go wrong? Please, tell me, *corazón*, what has caution gotten either of us?"

Determined, like a pit bull with a rabbit in its jaws. And earnest as one of those hands-in-the-air faithful Savannah used to look askance at back in the days Auntie Bea took her to church. The waiting headache throbbed once, and subsided as it always did when he was near. Always warning, reminding her. There was one secret left to tell.

She took a step back, but kept his hand. "Let's explore a little."

"Yes," he said. "Let's."

And though he squeezed her hand and led the way, Savannah couldn't mistake his disappointment any more than she could the sunshine threading through the canopy.

Bits of broken glass, pottery or china, a man's shoe, charred beams moldering for years, remnants of lives lived and left to ruin after the fire. All these things and more lived in the dirt and leaf mold of decades.

"It's getting dark," Savannah said, looking up from the old hearth shovel Ade had found. "We should head back."

"Perhaps tomorrow, we can go into town and do some research at the library."

"I'll have to see how much got done today. If we don't get those beans in, they're going to start spotting."

"Yes, of course. And we have the whole winter to research. We should gather some of those peaches. Taytay and Tío will be pleased to know I found something"—he startled slightly, brushed dirt from her chin—"worthwhile in all my searching."

"And we—" She cleared the thickness suddenly tightening her throat. "We should mark the tree. So we don't forget where it is."

Ade's hand slowly dropped, grasped hers. They headed back through the wood to the coot where they placed their artifacts into the bed. Savannah looked over them, scarcely able to believe such things had been left behind. Had the family lost someone in the fire, making it too difficult to return to the scene? Maybe it simply happened at a time they were too busy to salvage anything, and then never did. Could it have been arson? Scenario after scenario, and any one of them viable, tumbled through her head. She would find out. She and Ade. Over the long winter months with nothing but time on their hands.

Ade grabbed the fluorescent marker tape out of the coot bed. "I will gather some peaches and mark the tree. Why don't you get started turning this beast around."

"Ah, so you discovered its shortcomings, have you?"

He walked backwards, laughing. "It does prefer to go in straight lines, does it not?"

By the time Savannah got the coot turned on the narrow road, dusk was falling. Ade came trotting out of the woods, glancing over his shoulder.

"I think we might have disturbed the structure of the old place," he said. "I'm hearing a lot of crashing noises. We should have the building inspector look at it before going in again."

"We probably should have thought about that to begin with." She shrugged. "I got caught up in it, I guess. I'll call Town Hall tomorrow."

Ade hopped into the coot beside her. Savannah drove the dusty, forest road, basking in the sensation of his eyes on her. He didn't look away any time she turned her eyes to him, but smiled the sort of smile that turned her belly upside-down, and set her lusty bits afire. A flash of that same look of bewildered, seductive joy on Doc's face threatened to spoil it all.

I loved you. I did. And then...now I love him. Savannah's jaw clenched. The ache twinging in her temples flared again. *I can't allow the past to define my future.*

Over and over she pushed those words through her head, words given to her by Auntie Bea during one of the numerous, recent phone calls. A mantra. A chant. A prayer. Whatever it was, it worked. Headaches bloomed into happiness instead, spread through her blood and bones. Each time, it became easier. Each time, it became more true.

* * * *

My stomach hurts. But I don't have a stomach. I don't have anything. I'm nothing. In Nowheresville. And this is where it all began. Ended, I guess. This is where it E.N.D.E.D.

How did I get here? Where I never-ever-ever wanted to be again. I just wanted to see where Savvy and Ricky Ricardo were going. I'm tired of hanging around the farm. Was it so wrong to want to wander a bit? I didn't realize...I had no idea Savvy lived so near the shack. She owns it, for goodness sake. Is that really what drew me to her to begin with? Was there some psycho draw that pulled me in without me even knowing it? I don't know. I don't know. I don't know!

But here I am, only there's no shack now. Just a burned out foundation where his place used to be. Did he burn it down to hide the evidence? Maybe Pop did. Or Mom. If I could do more than hurl stuff around, I'd finish the job. I'd dig a hole to hell and push it in. Dammit! I said hell. Now I swore and said it twice. Who cares? I'm doomed anyway. I have been since the minute I laid eyes on that...that...

No more swearing. No more hurling. I have to be as brave as Savvy. I have no idea what happened after the cold water filled my lungs. And I don't know if anyone ever solved my murder. All I know is I'm the Drowned Girl, and hardly anyone knows my story beyond the rock. No name. No date. No story bearing any resemblance to mine. People don't want to remember the bad things, even if they remember them best. Maybe that's why no one seems to get that I'm the one who puts stuff in their shoes at the Hunter's Moon. It's all connected, and they have no idea.

Chapter 18

familiar voices, deep

"There are a lot of people in the yard," Ade shouted over the roar of the engine.

Savannah sat forward in her seat. He was right. A lot of people. Too many for after closing hours. A hole opened in the pit of her stomach. "Can you see who it is?"

"Taytay and Tío," he said. "And Benny. I think…is that Margit?"

The wheel jerked but Savannah didn't lose control. "It is." Oh, no. No, no, no. "Something's happened."

The last yards to the house vanished in a roar and dust. Margit was coming forward while the others stayed back. Not just Edgardo and Raul, Benny and Margit, but Johanna and Charlie and Dan. Savannah slammed the coot to a halt, switched off the ignition and hopped out before she could gain her bearings. "What's wrong? Is someone hurt? Margit, what are you doing here?"

Margit took her into her arms, held her close. "It's Bea, Savvy. She's gone."

* * * *

Ade gave the space beside Savannah to her oldest and dearest friend who took her inside, made her tea, and sat with her while she cried. Taytay and Tío made sure the last of the beans were brought in. Ade directed the high school kids when the foremen's English didn't cut it. By the time they finished for the day, Johanna and Benny had put together a feast. Dan and Charlie were waiting in the yard.

"Get your dad and uncle to come in and eat," Charlie said. "You know my wife. She way overdid it. It's a Coco thing."

"I will try." Ade brushed off his jeans. "They are stubborn hermits."

"Tell them Savvy asked them to," Dan suggested. "They'll come."

And they did, after cleaning up in the doublewide. Everyone gathered in the rarely-used dining room, ate from the abundance Johanna prepared. Everyone but Savannah. Once the food was cleared away, Johanna kissed Margit, who had to leave first thing in the morning, before turning to Savannah and hugging her close. "You okay?"

Savannah nodded, murmured something Ade couldn't hear. The magical afternoon had turned so quickly. Was life ever such? Had he ever noticed before?

"Emma's got a lasagna going," Johanna said. "Either she or I'll bring it by tomorrow."

"It's not necessary," Savannah began, but her lip trembled and she said no more.

Ade walked Johanna and Charlie to the door, stepped out onto the porch with them.

"She'll be okay." Johanna hugged him around the waist. "She's been through worse."

"I know." Hesitant arms encircled her, his eyes all the while on Charlie, who only smiled and squeezed his shoulder.

"You call if you need us," Johanna said, stepping back and letting him go. "We're only a few minutes away."

"Thank you."

They said their good-nights. Ade stood on the porch until they drove away, waving as they did. Good people. Good friends. Again, so soon. He laughed softly despite the sorrow emanating from the house. He went inside.

"I'm going up," Savannah said. "I'm exhausted."

"I'll come with you." Margit started to rise, but Savannah pushed her gently back into her chair.

"Finish your wine. I could do with a few minutes alone. Okay?"

"Of course it's okay. You shout if you need me, hear?"

Savannah nodded, her gaze moving to Ade. He took her into his arms, kissed her tenderly despite his father's glare. "*Corazón.* Sleep sweet. I will see you in the morning."

Savannah kissed him again, lingered there against his lips, breathing him in as if she could. And then she let him go, headed up to bed. Alone.

He watched her. They all did, even Taytay and Tío, who had been mostly silent all evening.

"It's a shame the family didn't let her know before it was too late to get there." Benny was first to speak. "Heartless."

"To be fair," Margit said, "no one has seen her in years. Savvy was close to Bea, not to anyone else, and no one knew Savvy had been calling her auntie regularly the last few weeks. She's just not on their radar anymore."

"And that's what makes it worse," Benny added. "She can't even be angry with them. Only with…her…self. Did anyone just feel that?"

"Oh, no. Here she goes again," Dan drawled. He put an arm across his wife's chair. "Cold? Or was it the spider-web thing this time?"

"Spider webs. Don't tease me or I'll never tell you anything again."

"Sorry, love." He kissed her cheek. "Honest."

"What are you two talking about?" Margit asked.

"I'm sensitive to…things," Benny said. "There's something in this house. A not-so-nice something, and something else. I felt the not-so-nice something once, and it was…not so nice. This is different." She got to her feet. "It's nothing. I don't know how to explain it anyway. Dan, if you'll take care of the last of these dishes, I'll get Irene ready. We should head out too."

Dan cleared dishes. Margit helped him despite his protests. There was little left to do, Johanna and Charlie having done most of it already. Left alone with his father and uncle, Ade was all too aware of their continued silence.

"I am going to bed," his father finally said in their native tongue. "We will start on the zucchini tomorrow. They're getting seedy. Raul, are you coming?"

"In a moment, Eg." He lifted his cup. "When I finish my coffee."

"You should not drink coffee before bed. You know it keeps you awake."

"And you should not be such a hen, old man. Go to bed. I will be along soon."

Edgardo shook his head, glared at his son, and left them. Ade grimaced. No one was eavesdropping, but he spoke to his uncle in their native language anyway. "He is still angry with me."

"You promised him, Ade."

"I did not break my promise. I fell in love."

"You sleep in her bed and there was no marriage vow made. My brother has gotten conventional in his old age."

"Taytay needs to mind his own business."

"You know that does not happen in our family." Tío reached across the table, patted his hand. "In time, he will see your heart is true."

Ade blew a breath through his lips. "It's my own fault. My past does not speak well for me."

"Your past is the past. You love Savannah, and she loves you. Any fool can see that. My brother is not just any fool. He is a big one. And a stubborn one. But you are his son and he is very proud of that. He'll come around."

Tipping back his cup, Raul drained it.

Ade could almost taste his uncle's coffee by the smell of it. Thick and black and deeply roasted. "How do you sleep after that? That has to be the equivalent of three regular cups."

Raul winked. "It's decaf. Your father might be a fool but I am not. Don't tell him, okay? Provoking him is one of the few pleasures of living with him." Raul rounded to Ade's side of the table, kissed his cheek. "You are a good boy, Ade. Be patient with your father. He loves Savvy like she is his own daughter."

Ade sat alone at the dining room table, absorbing the peace of the house. Dan and Margit, talking softly in the kitchen, said good-night to Raul as he passed through. The screen door slapped closed. Benny crooned to her baby in the living room. Irene must have woken when her mother picked her up. Perhaps Benny was nursing her. The peace combined with the sounds of a summer night to fill him up and soothe his soul. Ade smiled, amazed that such domesticity could stir his heart into contented thumping. It was akin to but not the same as the way his heart used to race during a heated debate. Gentler, but no less intense.

He waited for Benny and Dan to leave, walked them to their car and waved them off as if he were indeed the man of the house. Margit left the kitchen light on for him, but had already gone up to bed. Ade switched off the light, stood alone in the dark house. He tried to feel whatever it was Benny did—cold or spider webs or even just a sense of not being alone after all. Lita always told him there was more to the world than what was readily seen. It took a special kind of person to not only understand it, but to be truly aware. He had been such a person once. Maybe even that, he could regain.

Heaving a weary sigh, Ade started for the stairs. He trudged up, his legs strangely and suddenly leaden. The higher he climbed, the harder it became to take that next step. By the time he reached the top, he could barely cross to the bathroom to get ready for bed. Brushing his teeth was a chore. Had he worked so hard that day? Whatever it was, Ade could not wait to go to sleep.

He grasped the doorknob to his bedroom. It wouldn't turn. Ade tried again. He tugged. Harder. It finally gave way, nearly sending him toppling backwards.

Standing in the doorway looking at his hand on the knob, behind him, back to the knob, Ade shuddered, shook off the chill. Exhaustion, physical and emotional, did strange things to a body. He closed the door behind him and began to undress.

"Did the door stick?"

He nearly ripped a button from his shirt. "I did not see you there, *corazón.*" He crossed to the futon that served as his bed, sat on the edge. "Yes, the door was stuck."

"It did that to me too," she said.

"I will lubricate it in the morning."

"I think I have some WD40 out in the barn."

"I saw some. It looked old."

"Probably is. You'd have to ask your dad or uncle."

"Why are we discussing lubricants when you are obviously naked in my bed?"

Savannah didn't smile. In the glow of moonlight coming through the windows, her earnest eyes glistened. "My head hurts. I thought the Box would help but it didn't."

Ade stripped off his clothes, left them on the floor as his fastidious nature never allowed. Slipping between the sheets, he caught the sweet scent of her. It aroused him, but it stirred something deeper within, and despite his body's ache, he only held her in his arms.

Savannah snuggled in beside him, her head on his shoulder. She breathed in deeply, and out.

"Better?" he asked.

"Yes."

"Curious, how that happens."

"It's psychological, I'm sure. But who cares. It works. And I love being in your arms."

"Then that works for both of us, because holding you is all I want to do for the rest of my life."

Savannah came up on her elbow. "Do you really mean that, Ade? Or is that just something romantic you said without thinking?"

Ade mulled it over. "I said it without thinking," he admitted. "But it is nonetheless true."

"How do you know?"

"Because I have never wanted to hold anyone forever before. I could not imagine my future with any one person. I imagine it with you all the time."

"Like this afternoon, at the old foundation."

"Exactly like that," he said. "I said that without thinking, too, but what you don't understand, *corazón*, is that I might have said such things to other women before, but I was wholly aware I said them, because I did so with a purpose. With you, there is no ulterior motive, only spontaneous wanting."

"Wanting?"

"Yes. Wanting. I want you. I want a life with you. I want things I never wanted before."

"Then you meant it when you told me you love me."

Ade's heart stuttered. He wiggled his hand out from under the sheets to touch her cheek, her lips. "I was beginning to fear you hadn't heard me," he said. "It was better than fearing you did not return the sentiment."

"Can you doubt that I do?"

"No. You showed me your daughters' things. You shared your past. That is love."

Savannah snuggled into him again. "I'm not going to Georgia for the funeral," she said. "I should have gone before Auntie Bea died. Now that she's gone, there's no point. There's nothing for me there."

"You have family..."

"No, I really don't. I have people who raised me, not people who love me. The only one who did is gone."

Warm tears pooled on his skin where her cheek rested. Ade held her closer, kissed the top of her head. He moved slow circles along her shoulder, arm, the curve of her waist.

"I wanted her to meet you," she whispered. "I wanted you to meet her."

"I would have liked to hear her call me a Spaniard."

"I really screwed up, Ade. She loved me best and longest, and I couldn't get past my own issues to go see her."

Shifting so they were face to face, sharing a pillow, Ade's heart and body warred. She was so beautiful. And so sad. So desirable. And she needed him. To soothe her headache, and her grief.

"I was raised Catholic," he began, "but Lita's mountain version. A devout woman who had crucifixes on every wall, a Virgin Mary on every flat surface, but had no idea she was a raging heathen."

Savannah laughed softly this time.

His heart leapt. "There are worlds within worlds, outside of worlds, she told me, where we live alternate lives, die different deaths. Maybe she was right, *corazón*. Maybe in another version of you and me, I did meet your aunt. Just not in this one."

"But this is the one we have."

"Right now," he said. "But, according to Lita, when all the possibilities of who we are or might be are no longer in this world, we meet one another, and become whole."

"Round about what is"—Savannah tilted her head, grinning—"lies a whole mysterious world of what might be."

"A psychological romance of possibilities and things that do not happen." He quoted, and kissed the tip of her nose. "Longfellow, correct?"

"Yes. I didn't know there was more to it."

"It is one of my favorite quotes."

"Benny's too. She has the first half of it tattooed across her lower back. It's also quoted on her blog, *Spirit Reckonings*."

"Benny has a blog?"

"Apparently a spiritual one. Maybe it's more paranormal."

"I imagine it's a bit of both." Ade shifted closer. Their bodies pressed together. Skin to skin. Her legs entangled with his, the top of one foot caressing his calf.

Savannah closed her eyes, leaned in, kissed his lips so tenderly. "I love you," she said. "Much as it scares me, it makes me happier than I've been in a very long time."

"We have both traveled long and painful roads to get to this moment, *corazón*. I have much to regret, and yet how can I? All of who I was brought me here. To you."

She stiffened in his arms, and only then did Ade realize his horrific mistake.

"I…that does not mean…you have a…your past…" He closed his eyes to the tears in hers, took a deep breath. "Your sorrow was visited upon you, Savannah. You have done nothing to regret."

"Haven't I?"

"How can you even wonder?" He kissed her cheeks, mouth, anything his lips could find without letting go of her. "What you endured…my darling, you can't—"

Savannah kissed the words from his mouth. She rolled on top of him, straddled his hips. Her warmth nearly undid him. Her need pushed him closer to that edge beckoning in flashes of electric hunger. Ade forced himself back from the edge. Her curves were a silhouette his hands had to touch, his fingers demanded he caress. Savannah needed him to make it last, to tame the demons she still held inside. That he could do. He'd done it before for reasons less than noble. He could do it now even if his body burned for release.

* * * *

She watched him sleep a long time. On his back. Naked on the sheets mostly discarded in a tangle at the foot of the bed. The even rise and fall of his just-hairy-enough chest. Mouth slightly open. His eyes twitching dreams. What did Adelmo Gallegos dream? New dreams, she hoped. Dreams that involved her. No matter her past or his, no matter the baby that might be but probably wasn't his, Savannah couldn't imagine her present without him in it. As if he had always been part of it, like Edgardo and Raul, Benny and Dan. How did such a thing happen after so many years determinedly alone? In so short a time?

She wanted to touch him, to run her hands along every rise and contour of his lean body. Doc had not been the one and only lover in her life, but until Ade, he was the only man she had seen so completely. So vulnerable.

Hand hovering just an inch or so above Ade, she let it float the length of him. Already, she knew its shape. She knew the scar on his abdomen earned after the appendix within burst. His pelvis, his hips, thighs— Savannah never fancied herself a woman enamored of the male form. As a doctor of women, her appreciation for the female body as a work of great beauty could never be compared to the more utilitarian body of a man.

Doc's body had been beautiful, though. Tall and burly, fair and freckled. And hairy. Doc had been so hairy. Savannah loved every tickly inch of him. Adored every scar, every lump and bump. Big hands. Big heart. A Great Dane who thought he was a lapdog was her favorite tease. Whatever he became in the desert couldn't take away the joy he had once brought to all who knew him. Even after all he'd done, the horror he had inflicted, Savannah didn't hate him. For all he had done, neither could she admit how much she would always love him, always miss him, always wish she could go back in time and talk him out of enlisting after September 11th changed everything. It had been the patriotic thing to do. And sensible. The military would pay off the med-school loans already incurred if he enlisted as a field doctor, then continue his specialty training after the conflict was done and they all came home. It would be over in no time. Field doctors didn't see action. They were the heroes patching up soldiers who did. Savannah had been all for it, even if it meant not seeing him for long stretches. She was still in med-school herself, and was hardly ever home. They'd been too busy to miss one another.

One tour became another. And another. Each time he came home on leave, Doc had changed a little more. It wasn't until he was home for good, after the girls were born, that he hit her for the first time.

Just a slap. He hadn't meant it.

He promised to go to the army-appointed therapist she'd been begging him to see. But he didn't.

He swore he'd never do it again. But he did.

Savannah breathed in deep, let it out long, returned to the present and the man sleeping under her hovering hand. This man who made love to her like she had never been made love to before. The things he did. The way he touched her. Savannah's whole body shuddered its own memory of what his fingers and tongue could do, not to mention the glory between his legs.

She blushed at her own thoughts. The past wouldn't take away her future. Beyond all sense and reason, Ade had come into her life and changed it for the better. She truly and with all her heart believed she'd done the same for him. They could be happy. They would be, once the matter of Anita's baby was resolved.

Savannah was as unsure of her hopes for the outcome as Ade was. To have a child to raise, even part time—

She caught her breath. Her hovering hand jerked. She'd done it. She imagined her future with Ade, a future more distant than the immediate. Raising a child together meant a life together. A solid, real, enduring life together. Could they? Letting the feeling come, she found it a happy one. More than happy. Joyful. Even if she had one secret left to share. The one that could change it all.

Chapter 19

speak to those who lie asleep

It's dark out here. A different kind of dark than at the farm. I'm never scared there. Or in town. Only here.

I want to leave this place, but I feel stuck. Like my feet are chained to the ground. If I had feet. Didn't I have the thought once, about getting stuck to the place where I died, and wondering if there was a piece of me here? I'm pretty sure I did. And I was right. A piece of me is stuck here, because I don't have feet and something is holding me to this spot. I can almost feel his hands on me, the hammer, the flash of pain when my skull cracked and my brains leaked out. And I can feel...that. What Ricky Ricardo and Savvy do. Only it's not like that at all, aside from the mechanics.

It's me, but it's not me. She's here, that dope who fell for lines I never would have. She's living it over and over again. The swack. The rape. Getting wrapped up in the carpet. All this time. Over and over. I'm afraid. I don't want to see her. I don't want to remember in such detail. I'm ashamed to admit it, but I'd leave her here to keep reliving those terrible hours if it meant sparing myself, but she has a hold on me. Either I break it, or I become her.

I can't become her.

I guess that means I have to find her, get her out of here. I guess that means I have to face him, or the piece of him that rapes and kills me over and over again in this house. I guess this is it. Do or die.

I crack myself to bits sometimes. I wish this was one of those times.

* * * *

"Does everyone have a basket?"

A chorus of yesses rose up in the morning air. It had come to her as she woke, on the futon beside Ade, that her vegetables knew nothing of headaches and losing foremen, of falling in love or dying aunties. They needed harvesting, and things were already getting out of hand. It had taken a week to organize and get the word out, but Savvy's first annual overstock harvest was already a success. A good portion of Bitterly arrived, paid their twenty bucks, and stood ready to pick their own fresh produce. If only Margit had been able to stay, but she was already almost a week back in Georgia. At least she promised to be back for Halloween, and planned on bringing a certain Yale doctor with her.

"Remember, only this field. Stay out of the pumpkins or you're not going to have any for Halloween. Raul, Ade, Edgardo and I are here if you need help. And feel free to ask my amazing young field hands for assistance. That's what they're here for. Okay, is everyone ready?"

Another cheer.

"Have at it."

The citizens of Bitterly—both seasonal and full time—walked carefully among the rows of zucchini and tomatoes, beans and cukes, swiss chard, kale, broccoli rabe, and peppers of all kinds, choosing whatever vegetables called to them. Men and women, young and old, chatted as they harvested, laughed when their skills proved less than sufficient. The newly hired students seemed taken by their roles as teachers, and proved both helpful and knowledgeable. Savannah couldn't be prouder of them, of her staff, of herself.

She spotted Charlie McCallan, an easy target with his abundance of red hair, and made her way to him. Johanna and several of their children picked zucchini alongside him.

"Where are Finn and Valentine?" Savannah asked about their two youngest.

"Caleb is watching them for now," Johanna answered. "Tabitha is in town. They're playing house. It's adorable."

"Tabitha?" Savannah grimaced. "Oh, yes. Nina and Gunner's daughter. How's that working out?"

"A little touchy. She's an angry kid. Understandably. Nina and Gunner thought being up here in the country might do her some good. I'm afraid she's viewing it as they wanted to get rid of her. She likes Caleb, though."

"Who doesn't?" Savannah laughed. "He's just like his dad."

"I heard that." Charlie looked up from picking, a smile as always on his face. "He's a good kid. More ambitious than I ever was, though."

"Says the man running for mayor," his wife teased. "We have a babysitter for later, so he and Tabitha can come to the barbeque. Is that okay?"

"Of course. It's going to be fun. I hope the kids don't get freaked out that the beef I'm putting on the grill was born and raised on the farm."

"They're Bitterly kids," Charlie assured her. "They know the realities of farm life."

"Besides," Johanna added, "you don't have to tell them."

"True enough, sugar."

Savannah walked among the rows, stopped to chat with most everyone who looked up from their tasks as she did so. Benny and Dan, Irene strapped to one or the other of them, didn't pick as much as they helped out. Heart swelling, tears threatening, Savannah looked out over the field of people she'd known for so long, who probably knew her better than she had any idea. It didn't matter. They had accepted her from day one.

"You look happy, *corazón*." Ade's arms slipped around her waist from behind. His chin rested upon her shoulder. Savannah reached backwards, pushed her fingers through his hair and drew him ever closer. He kissed her shoulder. "This was a wonderful idea."

"I'm going to make it a yearly thing," she said. "It's the perfect time of year, just before all the fall vegetables start coming ready to harvest, but when the summer stuff is starting to slump. Summer's nearly over. It'll be fall before we know it."

Ade jerked, but his arms didn't fall away.

"September 19th is coming up real fast, huh, sugar."

He kissed her shoulder again.

Savannah turned to face him. "Whatever happens, we'll handle it."

"Of course we will. I have no doubt."

"But you still don't know what to hope for."

He shook his head.

"Then either way will bring a bit of happiness."

"It is not me I fear for," he said, "but you. No matter if the baby is mine or not, she will try to hurt me through you."

Savannah opened her mouth to deny her ability to do so, but closed it again. The need to tell him that one thing she still had not, gathered in her throat, pushed at her tongue and teeth and lips. It swelled in her head, threatened to bloom. Ade's hand on her arm steadied her.

"Your head?"

"A little," she lied.

"Come. Sit in the shade. I will get you something to drink."

"There's so much to do. I'll be fine."

"It will all get done, and what doesn't, doesn't matter. Please, *corazón*."

Savannah went to the shade tree where they had set up every mismatched lawn chair in the barn. Big coolers of water and lemonade stood at the ready, manned by some of her high schoolers handing out paper cups. She sat in one of the chairs, waited for Ade to bring her a drink, and tried to clear her head.

"There." He handed her a cup of lemonade. "Nice and cold."

She sipped.

"Better?" he asked.

"No. But I will be. Thanks, sugar."

"Good." He opened his mouth, closed it again. A smile played at his lips.

"What?"

"Sugar," he said. "It is your pet name for everyone."

"Habit, is more like it."

"Even more reason for you to choose another name for me."

"A new name? You mean like darling?"

"Too common." He nudged her with his knee. "What else do you have?"

"Baby?"

"Infantile. Next?"

Savannah sipped her lemonade, eyed him up, down and sideways. "Love machine?"

Ade's laughter turned heads. He lowered his voice. "Something you can say in public."

"I don't know," she said. "What made you call me *corazón* that first time?"

"It just came out," he confessed. "You are my heart, plain and simple."

"You're mine."

"Too late. I already staked my claim."

"Villain." She slapped his arm playfully. "I'll have to think about it. I sailed through med-school with better-than-passing grades, but creative, I am not."

"I'm sure you will come up with something. Until then"—he slapped his thighs, got to his feet—"rest. I will be in charge a while."

"It might take longer than that," she called after him, but Ade only waved over his shoulder.

Savannah leaned back in her chair. Ade was right. He deserved something better than her fallback, sugar. Everyone was sugar. Except Doc, whose name was actually Martin. She had nicknamed him the first day they met, after he tried to impress her with his degree.

The headache eased, but didn't give up. That the pain became worse when she thought of Doc, the girls, or anything even slightly related to them was too obvious to deny. So, too, was the fact that Ade's presence somehow soothed it. Carmen's notion of her late husband's broken soul trying to do her harm nudged at her. If she could only believe, maybe…

Savannah nudged it back. That road led to places she would not travel. Doc was gone. Sally and Ginger might always be in her heart, but they were not wings. They were not little guardians protecting her. They were objects in the Box brought out and cherished when she needed comfort more than she could bear. Tactile. Solid. Little bits of their lives to hold in her hands, smell. Kiss. That was as far as she would go with the whimsical. It was all in her head. Literally. It was no broken soul causing her pain, but the festering of a secret she had kept, even from Auntie Bea.

Hands up. Fingers trembling. Bang.

Tears welled. Savannah wiped them away before they could fall. This was a festive day, one she'd been looking forward to all week. No tears. No headache. No memories. No secret. Not now.

Ade stood with Charlie and Dan at the end of a tomato row, laughing. Savannah's heart bumped. She forced back the past, imaged instead the future. A year from now, two. Charlie and Dan had been friends since childhood, but they would pull Ade into their brotherhood just like they had Julietta's husband Efan, Emma's Mike, and Nina's Gunner. Savannah wasn't a Coco sister, but it wouldn't matter. Families formed in all kinds of ways. These people, this place, was the family she never had, and the one that had been taken from her. She had never realized.

Savannah finished her lemonade. Instead of heading for the cluster of men, she found the women. Though they'd arrived separately and started on different rows, Benny, Johanna, Julietta, and Emma had come together. Bending to the vines, she joined their conversation, their laughter, their harvesting. The basket of beans filled, Savannah's heart did too, and the headache lifted away without her even noticing.

Chapter 20

backward to forgotten things

I don't remember screaming out loud. I screamed and I screamed inside, but no sound made it out of my mouth. I think he broke the connection when he bashed me in the head.

That's what I'm hearing now. Screaming. My silent screaming. This place is so weird.

* * * *

The fields were picked clean before dusk. Sweaty and weary, Savannah stood in the gravel parking lot with Ade, watching the last car drive off in a cloud of dust. The day had gone well, and the night was only just beginning.

Already manning the oil-drum grill he'd built himself, Dan Greene was waving a piece of cardboard over the glowing coals when Savannah and Ade got back to the yard behind the house. Their friends sat tipping back beers, drinking wine or the last of the lemonade. Even Edgardo and Raul, who rarely socialized, sat among all the others, chatting the best they could in the English they'd mastered, she suspected, far better than they ever let on.

"Who is that?" Ade pointed to the motorcycle pulling around to the back of the house. The passenger, a young woman, slid off the back and pulled off the helmet Connecticut law said she didn't have to wear. A mass of long, black hair tumbled out. The driver put the kickstand down and likewise removed his helmet.

"Caleb?" Savannah shook her head. "Johanna said he and Tabitha would be coming. This isn't going to be pretty."

"What do you mean?" Ade asked. Savannah only had to point to Charlie, already bearing down on his son as if he'd run over a kitten. On purpose. In front of its mother. She grabbed Ade's hand and started for the gathering converging around father and son.

"...irresponsible and heartless thing to do, especially with Benny here," Charlie growled.

"Leave me out of this." Benny put up her hands. "I drove a scooter for years. Motorcycles don't bother me."

"You have a car," Charlie blurted. "What do you need this thing for?"

"I don't have a car anymore," Caleb answered. "I traded it in."

"And what'll you do when it rains? Snows? It's not like this is..." Charlie's rage-red face paled. "Are you moving to Florida? Like Will?"

Caleb's defensive stance melted. "Dad, no. I'm not moving to Florida. I just wanted a bike. Can we talk about this without an audience please?"

"You should have thought of that before showing up on a motorcycle." Johanna shook her head. "I have no idea how my sister and Gunner feel about Tabitha riding on the back of one."

"I never rode in a car until I was twelve." Tabitha's deep, accented voice took an edge off the tension. "Always on the back of a motorcycle, and most of the time with two others hanging on me. Is fine."

"I didn't mean to make a scene here or anything." Caleb put a hand on his father's shoulder. "I'm sorry, dad. I knew you'd be upset, sorry Benny, because of Uncle Henny. But I've been saving up a long time. I took the safety course and got my license all on my own. I'm eighteen. This is my decision to make."

"As long as you live in—"

"Don't." Johanna held up her hand. "Don't say it, Charlie, or you risk becoming every dad-stereotype ever known."

Charlie pushed fingers through his hair, blew a breath through his lips. "We'll talk more at home," he said. "It's been a long day. Let's just enjoy the barbeque Savvy went through such trouble to put together."

Everyone but Caleb started away, already resuming a more festive mood, if slightly forced. Savannah kissed Ade's cheek and motioned him to follow the others. Caleb didn't keep her waiting long.

"I'm sorry, Savvy. I didn't think dad would freak out like that."

"You hoped he wouldn't, sugar. But you knew exactly what you were doing."

He blushed. "Not very subtle, I guess."

"Just be responsible," Savannah said. "Most bike accidents are caused by car motorists. You have to be more diligent about knowing everything that's happening around you."

"I know." He grinned. "I did my research. This wasn't a whim, done on impulse."

"Forgive me, sugar, but a motorcycle is always a whim, especially when you live in a state where you can't drive it a good portion of the year. Own that, and don't try to make it seem like there's a practical reason for your purchase."

"There's the gas money."

"Cute." She shoved him toward the trees where tables and chairs were still set up. "Go. Eat. There's tons of food."

Caleb trotted across the yard and right to Tabitha, who leaned into him and whispered something that made him smile.

Ade was instantly behind her again, nuzzling the nape of her neck. She turned to him. Forehead to forehead, arms around one another, neither of them moved but to sway. Savannah closed her eyes, savoring the hard thrum of her heart. The way it jounced about in her chest. In her yard, on her farm, surrounded by friends more like family, held by this man she loved, contentment filled her, overflowed and surrounded her. Astounded her. It buzzed like thoughts in her brain, words on her tongue.

She lifted her face. Dusk cast Ade's in shadow. The sobriety of his gaze steadied her.

"I'm happy, Ade." She breathed the words more than spoke them. Savannah licked her lips. "Happy in a way I've never been before. It's not just because of you. I'm not that much of a romantic. But it is you. And it's me. Even if September 19th comes and you end up back in Boston, you've been part of something huge in my life. I'll never be the same, and that's such an amazingly good thing."

His fingers feathered down her cheek, across her chin to the other. "I'm not going anywhere."

"Neither of us knows that for sure. I just wanted to thank you, no matter how this turns out, for being the exact person I needed at just the right time."

"It is no less than what you are to me." He held her closer. "Call it fate. Call it chance. Whatever aligned to bring you into my life, *corazón*, will not be thwarted by Anita Durst."

Savannah bit her bottom lip. "I don't believe in fate or chance."

"No? Magic, then."

"Not magic either." This was the moment. It would never be more perfect. She steeled her resolve. "I believe that we get back what we put out, even if it takes a long time." Pain, quick and warning, sliced through her head. "Do good, good comes back to you." Another stab. "But so does the bad."

Ade's fingers caressed her jaw, her throat. "What is it, *corazón*?"

Pain throbbed. Tears formed. Savannah held his gaze and tried to find her courage there. She had to do it, had to tell him even if it meant watching the love in his eyes turn to horror.

"You two going to stare into one another's eyes all night or can we eat?" Dan waved his spatula in the air. Ade turned his head and in that moment, Savannah's resolve washed out of her body, through the soles of her feet and into the ground. Deep into the ground. Reason took its place. This wasn't the perfect time. It was exactly the wrong time, with all their friends as witness. She had to tell him. She would tell him. After everyone else had gone.

"We're coming," Savannah called, and grabbed Ade's hand. "There'd better be some burgers left."

"Are you all right?" Ade asked, tugging back a little on her hand. "You looked troubled a moment ago."

"I'm fine," she answered. "I thought my headache was coming back." She stood on tiptoes to kiss his lips. "Let's get some food before there's nothing left but hot dogs."

* * * *

It's colder now. Funny, how I don't normally get things like hot and cold, wet or dry. I'm not sure what this place is. It's not the burned out house. It's not the woods. It's someplace…else.

She's still screaming, but it's louder now. I'm getting close. So close. Too close. I wish I had a hand to hold. I wish…no wishing. It's just me, myself and I. Like it was then. Now. Whatever it is. I'm getting out this time. Not alive, of course, but…

* * * *

Edgardo and Raul said their good-nights before Mike and Efan got the bonfire going in the fire pit. Gathered around it, tucked into one another like puppies in a pile, the lot of them chatted, roasted marshmallows and ate s'mores until even Dan's stomach was sick. Aside from Caleb and Tabitha, they were adults, one and all. Even Benny had—wonder of wonders—left Irene with her mother instead of bringing her along. Savannah couldn't remember a time she'd been with these friends without their plethora of children. It felt strange, but nice. Very nice.

"We should probably head home." Johanna groaned to her feet. "My boobs are like rocks. Time to nurse Finn."

"Ugh, mine too," Benny said. "I keep waiting for Irene to get tired of nursing but, no, she has no intention of detaching."

"I think that was a little too much information for some of our company." Emma gestured to Caleb.

Tabitha's barely concealed grin erupted. "Men love tits until an infant is involved." She snorted, bouncing her own, ample pair in cupped hands. "Then it becomes embarrassing."

Quick glances passed among the adults. Caleb still had not looked up.

"Well, mine aren't faring any better." Julietta got to her feet, hauled her husband to his. "This has been great, but we should get home, too."

Emma and Mike, with no infant home waiting to be nursed, got up as well. Only Caleb and Tabitha remained beside the fire, she looking quizzically at his bowed head. The adults ambled to the cars parked closer to the barn.

"There's a story there," Emma said. "Not a good one."

"I imagine not." Efan rubbed his chin. "She was on her own a long time."

"All her life, as far as we know," Johanna said. "Nina and Gunner have their hands full, that's for sure. But Caleb seems to be good for her. He likes her. And she seems to trust him."

"He might be getting more friendship than he anticipated. Ouch!" Dan jumped away from his wife. "What'd you pinch me for? I only said what everyone's thinking. Tell her, Charlie. Mike."

"I notice you're asking the men." Benny pinched him again.

"I was thinking it." Johanna raised her hand. "But Caleb's a smart kid. He won't give anything he's not willing to. He's a better influence on her than she's a bad one on him."

"You can still say that," Charlie asked, "even after the motorcycle?"

Johanna blew out a deep breath. "I have to say, that one took me by surprise. But I stand behind what I said. Caleb's a smart kid. I trust his judgment on the bike and on Tabitha. If they share more than friendship, it could be worse."

"They're cousins." Emma grimaced. "That's gross, Jo."

"They're cousins like Savannah is our sister. Come on, Em. Don't be such a prude. It's not like you and Mike haven't been going at it since you were, what? Fourteen?"

"Fifteen," Mike drawled.

"Michael!"

He scooped his wife up into his arms and started for their car. "I can still make her blush," he called over his shoulder. "Let's see if I can still make her eyes roll."

He tossed her into the passenger seat and dove in on top of her. Emma squealed and laughed and all went suddenly silent.

"That's it for me." Dan threw his hands up. "When did this group get so kinky?"

Everyone got into cars and pulled away amid honks, waves and shouted good-nights. Even Emma and Mike drove off, disheveled and grinning. Still beside the dying fire, Caleb and Tabitha spoke softly. Savannah kept her distance. Ade's hand slipped into hers.

"A good night," he said. "And a great day."

"It was pretty great." She twirled into his arms, her back resting against his chest and her eyes on the sky. "So beautiful. All those stars."

"You should see the stars in the mountains of Ecuador. You have never seen so many."

"Maybe I will one day."

He nuzzled the spot between shoulder and neck. "You will." Kisses feathered her skin. "Perhaps for *Navidad*." Down her shoulder. His hands pushed into the waistband of her shorts, pressed her to him. Savannah's reached back, pushing her fingers through his hair. Ade bit her. Tenderly. "*Te adoro, corazón. Te quiero hasta la luna y más allá.*"

"Excuse, please." Tabitha's deep voice startled them apart. "I am very sorry."

Savannah straightened her clothes. "It's okay. Ade and I were just— what did you need?"

"Your bathroom?" Tabitha shrugged. "It is a bouncy ride on the back of Caleb's motorbike."

"Oh, of course. Sure. Ade, would you put the fire out? Caleb'll help."

Leading Tabitha into the house gave Savannah the opportunity to cool down, gather her composure. The young woman hadn't seemed flustered, interrupting what she had. What little Savannah knew of her past suggested she'd been witness to many of life's intimate offerings, both good and bad.

"Here you go." Savannah flicked on the light for her, and headed back to the kitchen. Someone had already cleaned up, washed dishes, stored the leftover food. Standing center in her kitchen, she could find nothing left for her to do. Thank goodness. She didn't have the energy for anything more than taking a shower and climbing into bed. Unless Ade was interested in continuing what had been interrupted.

"Thank you." Tabitha came into kitchen, still drying her hands on the front of her jeans, her eyes everywhere at once. "And for the barbeque, too."

"My pleasure, sugar. You're welcome here any time."

The young woman's nose wrinkled, as if smelling something unpleasant. She made a shooing motion with her hands, before her, behind and to each side. "*Mamioro*," she muttered. "You should do something about that."

"Do something about what?"

Tabitha grimaced again. "There is a spirit here. One that brings illness. You should call in a priest."

Savannah's scalp prickled. "I—uh—will do that. Thank you, Tabitha."

Tabitha's grimace shifted to disdain. "Suit yourself," she said. "If you end up with brain cancer, don't say you weren't warned. Good-night, Savannah. And thank you again."

Politely rude. Young and world-weary. Wise and reckless. Savannah couldn't quite put her finger on what Tabitha was. Different, that was certain. Smart. Superstitious, apparently. Yet, brain cancer? Of all the ailments she could have blurted...

Fingers pressed to temples, Savannah soothed the phantom headache, for once, not truly blooming. Outside, Ade called good-night to Caleb and Tabitha. The motorcycle revved and rumbled away. Savannah watched without truly seeing from the doorway, her thoughts still tumbling Tabitha and Ade, the day and the night, weariness and desire round and around. Then Ade was pulling her into his arms, into a kiss, and backing her into the kitchen.

"Let us go to bed," he said against her throat. Savannah's head cleared of all but him. He left a trail of kisses from her chin to the top button of her shirt. She stopped him there.

"I'm disgusting." She laughed softly. "I've been sweating like a pig all day."

"Pigs do not sweat, *corazón*." He started again at her chin. "And I was always told women do not sweat, they glisten."

Savannah let him get her blouse open but stopped him at the button of her cut-offs. "Then I glistened like a dewdrop all day. I need a shower." She held out her hand. "Join me?"

Ade took it, grinning that grin, the one that first turned her knees to Jell-O. Half smile. Half smirk. All charisma meant to light her up from the inside. Maybe it had been calculated once. Maybe, but maybe not. For now, it was all hers.

Chapter 21

sudden unremembered wings

My mom used to bake these cupcakes. Pink, but not strawberry. I'm not sure what flavor they were, really. And the pink didn't come from food coloring. Man-o-man, did I love those cupcakes, especially when she put red sprinkles on them. The sugar kind, not jimmies. It made them look like jewels. All the kids wanted to come to my birthday parties because of mom's cupcakes. She never shared her secret with anyone, no matter how much they begged, but she said she'd tell me in time for my first child's first birthday.

I think this place is memory, if that makes any sense. I keep tasting mom's cupcakes, hearing my pesty brother taunting me with the dead frog he chased me with that one time, smelling cut grass. A moment ago, it was the Christmas I was ten, when I got my first new bicycle and not a hand-me-down from Cousin Kim. The moment before that, I was sitting in my fifth-grade classroom that smelled of chalk, and the pencil sharpener that hung on the wall next to my desk. I'm not seeing all this stuff but... experiencing them somehow. I'm not sure if it's something preparing me for what's coming, or me stalling.

I think I'm stalling.

And still she screams. I scream. There is only one way to make her stop. I'm so scared. Mommy, I'm sorry. Daddy. What you must have gone through. At least I died and, until recently, it was over for me. But you lived this, imagining what happened to me, every day of your lives, didn't you? Is that what this is? Your hell on earth? Maybe. I don't know. I'm sorry. So sorry.

Breathe, Tilly. Just bre—well, you know what I mean. Let go of the cupcakes and Christmas and the pencil sharpener. Let go of all the pranks you've played in Bitterly. Let go of everything but that moment. That terrible, terrible moment. You can do this.

* * * *

No moonlight. No dawn. Just those eternal moments when neither sun nor moon held court in the sky. The light-between-light cast lavender shadows in the corners of the room, across Savannah's sleeping face. So peaceful. So beautiful. So loved. Ade's heart did that swelling-thing he still wasn't used to, even though it happened the first time he saw her coming down the back porch steps. Alien and wonderful. Uncomfortable and fulfilling. Frightening and freeing. How could love be of such disparate parts, and yet make so complete a whole?

Ade tickled fingers along the contours of her body, on top of the sheets. She stirred but didn't wake. Letting go the breath he'd been holding, he rested his palm on her hip. Already he'd memorized every curve of her body. Despite the rigors of their lovemaking, Ade roused all over again. His libido had never failed him, even if biology had.

Until Savannah, infertility was a perk to his lifestyle. And until Anita, he never realized how that old wound had not scarred over so much as scabbed. It hadn't taken much to prick it open, to make him hope and fear and hope again.

The churning in his chest changed course, became a sinking feeling in his gut. What would he do if the baby Anita carried was, impossibly, his? Could he sacrifice what he had with Savannah for the child? Could he sacrifice the child to the Dursts, who would use and misuse him to their own gain?

The answer to both questions was a resounding no! But the second echoed longer within the confines of his brain. His child. His son. Ade wanted it to be true. Because Savannah had opened his heart to love. There had to be a way, should the child turn out to be his. There had to be. How hard would it be to play along with Anita's wishes, then snatch the boy and whisk both him and Savannah off to the mountains of Ecuador where no one would ever find any of them?

Ade almost laughed at his own, desperate idiocy. It came out more like a stifled sob. Savannah stirred again. Her eyes opened to slits, a smile curled her lips, but she fell back into slumber while he again held his breath. Tears, as alien as love, stung behind Ade's eyes. He pressed them away, pretended they had never welled.

"Te quiero hasta la luna y más allá," he whispered. *"La luna ye más allá, corazón."*

He would find a way to have it all. Somehow. Adelmo Gallegos always did.

* * * *

Golly. There it is. The moment. Moments. And I feel…detached. Like that isn't me. I know it is, but I don't really feel anything. Disgust, sure, but not fear. Not pain. Maybe that's why we're both still here. She has to relive this so that I don't have to. And the girl at the rock drowns over and over, glad to be finished with living. However many versions of dead-me there are, this one is the worst. No wonder she's holding me here.

What a mess. All that blood. And there he is, doing what he did. Gross. The only sex I ever got besides those back-seat necking sessions at the drive-in over in East Perry. Ain't that a peach? I let Tommy Fitzgerald get to second base once. And Greg Smalls. And…what was his name? Oh, right. Victor Larson, who my parents thought I was smitten with. I was, obviously. Until this…this…I can't call him a man. Monster. That's what he is. Look at him going to town on a girl already half-dead.

I'm stalling. Stalling, stalling, stalling. I'm not alone after all. She and I are in this together, and that's the only way out for both of us. And the Drowned Girl. All for one and one for all.

He doesn't see me. He's not even here. Just his shadow. Her memory. Keeps her. Trapped. She won't let go. It's all that she is. This. Moment. Is not death. Pain. Fear. Anguish. Humiliation. Grief. Eternally. Death came later. Let this go.

Let it go.

Let it go.

Let it…

* * * *

"…go!"

Savannah startled awake, the dream already fading. Two girls. Twins? Fleeing. Something. In the woods. Heading for the river. The metallic scent of blood, a swift kick of pain. Twins. Flight. Fear. Blood. Unwanted memory reared up in her half-slumbering brain. The dream was nothing Savannah wished to hold on to, so she let it go.

Lips brushed hers. Savannah blinked all the way awake. Ade, propped on his elbow, gazed down on her. Dawn touched his face, shadowed the contours she knew so well. Little more than two months knowing him, loving him, she could not imagine life without him. How this love happened was as complete a mystery as any, but it was real. It was hers.

Almost.

Savannah's insides clenched. Fading dream and too-clear memory chased about in her head, leading her to Ade, his honesty, her secret still between them. He had given her all he was, good and bad. He trusted her with the truth. Until she did the same for him, none of this was real. It couldn't last. She had to tell him before September 19th took him to Boston, away from her, possibly for good. There was never going to be a perfect time, but there would be none more so than this one, in the dawn light, Ade's gentle gaze upon her, her body still caught in the rhythm that carried them both through the night. Touching his face, fingers trembling, she quelled the urge to lift her lips to his. "I need to tell you something." Her voice sounded harsh against the silence of morning.

Ade only smiled. "Anything, *corazón*."

Pain stabbed between her eyes, spread to her temples.

"It's about what happened in Georgia."

"I already know—"

"—what the media reported." Vision blurred. Pain bloomed from head to neck. Savannah gasped. "No one knows the whole truth. No one but me. I want you to know." Her body ached now, pulsing pain in waves through every nerve, muscle, bone.

It's all in your head. A psychosomatic symptom caused by this truth you've been holding all these years. Let it go. Let it go!

Ade gathered her into his arms, caressing circles on her back. Between her shoulders. Where Carmen said she had wings.

"It all happened the way you read about," she said, caught her breath, buried her face in the crook of Ade's throat. "Except Doc didn't kill himself."

His arms twitched, the caresses faltered, but he didn't let go. The pain between her eyes sliced open her mind, spilling out the memory suddenly there, completely inescapable. Doc. Fighting for the gun. The explosive pain of bullets. Her leg. Her side.

"Some reports said he got the gun from me and shot himself." The Savannah of her mind's eye fought, bloody and wheezing. "Other reports say the gun went off and he was on the wrong side of it." The gun flew out of both their hands, spun circles on the ground. "The truth is…the truth is—" Savannah's throat constricted, so tight she could barely breathe. She held tighter to Ade. Bodies pressed together, skin to skin, she held him as tightly as he held her. "The gun went flying. I picked it up. Took aim and—" The pain silenced her.

Ade's comfort came from far away, unable to reach her.

"and—" Not a word, only a sound came out, more like a groan.

Still far away, Ade pulled back, touched her face, spoke words of concern Savannah didn't quite understand. She felt...fury. The kind that had sent a marble bowl flying, a ceiling fan spinning. It burrowed into her. So deeply into her.

It. Is. In. Your. Head. Let it go. For them. And for you.

Warmth, like warm water, pooled in Savannah's belly. *Let it go.* It spread. Chest, arms, legs. *Let it go.* It loosened her throat. Love welled unbidden, from somewhere well hidden, and in that instant, she felt her wings for what they were.

The vision behind her eyes wavered, became dual images, superimposed one over the other. Savannah saw herself as memory always showed her—gun in hand, aiming, shooting as Doc's hands went up. She also saw herself trembling, fingers bloody and slipping on the trigger, Doc lunging for her. Murderous. Desperate.

She gasped breath back into her lungs, lifted her face from the safe and the dark. Dawn lit Ade's features. Concerned. Loving. Frightened. Savannah swallowed the constriction in her throat. Closed her eyes and again saw those two images, frozen in that moment before her finger found purchase on the trigger, and pulled.

Eleven years. Memory showed her scrambling for the gun, taking aim, firing. Even in the hospital, between delirium and slumber, she remembered with such clarity there was no question about its veracity. Self defense. No one would ever claim otherwise. She had always known, or thought she did, the truth. She had killed him. She had shot Doc. Aimed for the heart when a knee shot would have taken him down. A killer. A murderer. No better than he.

Savannah's heart stuttered, like being clenched in a fist. She inhaled deeply, unwilling to allow the pain to rise. She grasped for the second image never conjured before this moment in Ade's arms, at dawn, in this confessing light. She remembered. She remembered. Scrambling. Grasping. Trembling. Slipping. Weeping. Pleading. Doc's hands going up. Surrender. Relief slumping her shoulders. The gun barrel dipping. The lunge. The shot. The blood.

"The truth is," she said, not a hitch in her voice. "I shot Doc. I killed my husband. We fought for the gun." The false memory faded, bringing the true one into sharper focus. "I got it. I begged him to stay back. I told him I loved him." No wishing. No misplaced, misremembered guilt. Truth. "He put up his hands. The moment my guard went down, he lunged for me. I pulled the trigger, and that's how he died."

Ade didn't speak. He only held her tenderly. Savannah kept her eyes closed, replayed the true memory. Like a dream escaping daylight, the false memory fell away in chunks she had no desire to reclaim. Eleven years, she told herself she shot him dead when she'd had it in her power to incapacitate him instead. How had she ever believed herself capable of such cold calculation? It was laughable and sad at the same time. Headaches and nightmares suddenly made sense. It wasn't guilt wracking her brains, but a memory fighting to be remembered.

Savannah almost laughed at herself. The notion was as ludicrous as Carmen's. Memory wasn't sentient, and there was no such thing as ghosts. The warmth that filled her moments ago, helping to free the locked-away truth, wasn't her daughters giving her strength. They were gone, just like Doc was gone. There was only Ade, only herself. Only their love.

That, she would believe in.

* * * *

I didn't know I could cry in this state. I don't think I knew I could feel so much, either. All this time spent bored and lonely, I guess it dulled my other emotions. Unless...oh, right.

It's because I took back those pieces of myself, isn't it? Bloody Girl in the farmhouse, Drowned Girl at the rock. Maybe that's what happens when someone dies so violently. The only way to keep from becoming a soul broken beyond healing is to split up, let different pieces of you carry the worst away. I was the lucky one. I got to remember life, got to roam about Bitterly and cause mischief now and then. That's why it was up to me to pull myself back together. Like Savvy. She didn't need me. She didn't need her little girls. She defeated anger-ball all on her own. Though, I think Ricky Ricardo had something to do with it. Now he holds her while she cries and I can't help crying myself. Love really does conquer all, when it's true. Maybe that's naïve, but what the heck. I'm only seventeen, right?

Being smart wasn't my thing when I was alive. Obviously. Too square. It took being dead to figure out life. There might be a few more pieces of me wandering around, but I think they're more like shadows, like the monster in Bloody Girl's haunting. I feel...whole. I remember the pain and the fear, the relief of drowning. Really remember now, and not just sideways, sort of. Humpty Dumpty got put back together again. Not sure how I feel about it yet. Not great. I think maybe that means it's time to move on.

Now if only someone would tell me how.

Chapter 22

across my mind

The lone peach tree in the wood near the old, burned out foundation seemed to be the only one. Ade deduced that it had been a family tree, not part of an orchard. He and Savannah took a rainy day to do some research on the Internet, and at the Bitterly Library. The house had been abandoned for a bigger, more modern home after James Larson Jr. returned from Germany after World War II. He married shortly thereafter, bringing his wife into the new home already occupied by both his parents, his brother, his brother's wife and their young son, Victor. It was in all the society pages, including the birth of James's first child a scandalous six months after the wedding.

Sometime in 1952, Wyatt Barnes took up residence in the old Larson place. Tall, dark and handsome as a movie star, polite until he was drunk and full of boasting, Barnes had been a buddy of James' during the war, and needed a place to stay. He'd been drifting for years, in and out of trouble with the law. Only his status as a veteran kept him out of jail on more than one occasion, facts the Larson family didn't learn until much later, after it was too late.

It wasn't long before even James couldn't stand to be in his company. Wyatt became more of a loner, taking odd jobs now and then. He mostly kept to the house and tended a small garden—as far as anyone knew.

Then a girl went missing in October of 1953.

She'd been blonde and blue-eyed with a spattering of freckles across her nose. Hometown pretty and coming-of-age wild. The picture above her obituary showed her squinting into the camera, a mischievous grin on her bow of a mouth. Matilda Tully, known to her friends as Tilly. The headlines dubbed her the Drowned Girl, after she was found wrapped in a carpet and wedged under the lip of a giant boulder in the river. Her father, a man with a temper by all accounts, and frustrated with his wayward daughter, had been arrested and accused of the crime. Had it not been for James Larson checking in on his old war buddy, Mr. Tully might well have gone to jail for his daughter's murder. In the old farmstead, James found a girl's shoe wedged haphazardly under a floorboard, and his friend gone without a trace.

Only articles written for larger papers mentioned the blood and brain matter James also found. That had been kept out of the local papers. James himself, a man of means with children of his own, wrote an article for the Danbury News Times that got picked up by the Associated Press, offering a substantial reward to anyone with information leading to the arrest of Wyatt Barnes. A year to the day after the young woman's murder, the old farmstead was set ablaze. Arson. No one was ever apprehended, and neither was Wyatt Barnes.

Ade read through the articles and archives with a scientist's curiosity, looking for facts and keeping his emotions in check. Not so with Savannah, who seemed to take the whole thing quite personally.

"It all happened long ago, *corazón,*" he soothed, but Savannah cried anyway.

"On my property. Oh, that poor girl. And her family."

Her affinity, and fragility since her early morning confession, didn't escape him. Tears shed for this murdered girl were tears shed for her daughters, for herself. Even for Doc. Savannah was an intelligent woman. She would work through it and out of it on her own. It had already begun. There was a freedom about her, since her confession. Freedom and happiness that touched everyone around her. Benny noticed it. Taytay and Tío. Everyone and anyone who came to the farm. She was sunshine, and the world was a field of flowers she cast her rays upon. Best of all, her headaches were gone.

September 19th loomed. Anita had not tried to contact him, despite the fact that he'd given her his new phone number, in case she had the baby prior to her surgery date. Both he and Savannah counted down the days, together, on a calendar hanging on the kitchen wall. Each day they put an X through increased the weight on Ade's psyche. With only three days left umarked, he felt as old as Taytay and Tío.

Emerging from the farmhouse, ready for a day of work, Ade waved to his father stepping out of the trailer.

"Buenos dias, Taytay."

"I have not gotten my wedding invitation yet," Taytay launched right into his favorite subject.

Not confiding in his father and uncle had been difficult, but necessary. He was confused enough, without adding their reactions to the mix.

"It must have gotten lost in the mail," Ade said. "I'll have another one made out and sent right away."

"Before I go home, eh?" Taytay clapped his shoulder, winking. His blustered disapproval was weakening against the force of Savannah's continued happiness. Conventional or not, his father knew love when he saw it.

It was Wednesday, and Savannah had already left for the clinic in East Perry. Ade's plan was to go up to the old foundation and finish clearing the last of the brush away. When he first found the place, his ambition had been to restore it, as well as the yard he was discovering underneath the bramble. Alongside the peach tree were beds of tulips and daffodils, copses of forsythia and lilac. A domesticated bit turned wild again. Preserved and waiting. It had been a home, once. A happy home by all accounts, before it became the site of a murder. His ambition dug in deeper after discovering this sorrowful fact. He wanted to rescue the site from that terrible moment, free it to be what it had been before, and could be again. The land had preserved its domesticated bits for a purpose. Adelmo Gallegos knew how to listen to this ecological call, and he did so with a vengeance.

Neither did the more personal symbolism escape him.

Dusk was tipping into evening by the time he pulled the coot into the barn and switched off the ignition. Voices in the yard sent him to the bonfire pit rather than to the house. Benny and Savannah stood close, arms loosely around one another's waists. Softly as they spoke, he nonetheless heard the solemnity of their words.

"Is something wrong, ladies?" he asked.

Both turned their heads. Arms dropped away. Savannah dabbed her eyes with the corner of her shirt.

Benny sniffed. "Nothing's wrong. I just gave Savannah some sage to cleanse the house with."

"And that makes both of you weepy?"

"Well, I grew it myself. It's like my baby or something." Benny pursed her lips. "I notice you didn't ask what sage has to do with cleaning."

"I know what smudging is." Ade shook his head. "My Lita was *layqa*. The local witch, if you like. I know what sage is used for. It is an ancient practice worldwide, and a wonderful idea."

"You don't think it's hippie bullshit?"

He laughed. "There is actual science behind that hippie bullshit. Negative ions and serotonin boosting. All very fascinating. But if you prefer hippie bullshit…"

"Funny. Very funny." Benny turned to Savannah. "I told you he's a keeper. If you don't marry him, I will."

"You're already married, Ben," Savannah said. "Happily."

"Then that makes it even more imperative for you to keep me from making a terrible mistake." She kissed first Savannah's cheek, then Ade's. "See you both at my place this weekend?"

"Me, not Ade," Savannah answered. "He has to leave for a few days."

"Oh, that sucks. All right then, just you. It's going to be a blast."

"I've never canned before, tomatoes or otherwise. I hope it's not too hard."

"Emma has done it tons of times," Benny said. "That reminds me. I'm going to bring a few bushels over to my house now, save a trip."

"I will help you," Ade offered.

Benny waved him off. "I'll grab a few of the kids. They're always hanging around. Smoking." She grinned. "But thanks."

Ade took Savannah into his arms. Benny's footsteps on the gravel drive faded, and were gone. Evening sounds descended. Peace.

"You're home late," Savannah said. "Tired?"

"Exhausted. When did you get home?"

"About five minutes before you did. I heard the coot coming as I got out of the car."

"Late night for both of us, then."

"And about to get later." Savannah tugged at his hand, led him into the house. "Call for takeout. The Chinese place on the Green delivers. I'll be down in a minute."

He wanted a shower, but Chinese food sounded good, as long as it wasn't the place Taytay and Tío patronized like it was their mama's kitchen. Making the call, he kicked off his work boots and replaced them with his clogs.

Savannah returned, wearing the long, loose-fitting dress he loved for the way it made her look like an Earth Goddess, and the ease with which it was removed. In her hands, a familiar box. She held it out to him. "I want you to help me."

He took it.

Savannah crossed her arms close to her body. Tears welled, rolled down her cheeks. She wiped them away quickly. "It's time to put them to rest. Benny gave me the words. I need you there so I don't chicken out."

Ade followed Savannah outside, back to the fire pit already crackling.

"I asked your dad to start it for me," she said, "before you got here."

"How much does he know? About everything?"

"I suspect as much as you did before, anyway. Everyone knows. I was a fool. There is no disappearing anymore, not like Wyatt Barnes did. Maybe that's a good thing. Hiding is exhausting, and in the end, destructive."

The Adelmo Gallegos who came to Bitterly would have taken her words as a dig, but they were not aimed at him, even if they applied. Ade took them to heart, in complete agreement.

Savannah lifted the lid, conscripted it to the fire. It was only cardboard, after all. Heavy, but still paper. Old paper. It burned quickly. She took out the booties first. "Time to fly, my sugarbeets," she said. "The ties that bind are gone and the gateway is open. Go in peace, in my love. We'll meet again."

The fast-food-meal toys, the valentines and drawings and the bits of ribbon that had once tied back their hair all went into the flames. Rising to her feet, she tossed in the one clipping she kept. Together, they watched it burn until the last curl turned to ash, then into the fire went the box.

Powerful. Unconquerable. Standing over the fire, her face bathed in its glow, Savannah's true beauty burned as brilliant as all the stars and starlight. She wasn't an Earth Goddess now, but a force of air and fire rising up to streak across the sky. This was the image forever embedding itself into Ade's mind. When he was old and remembered only the past, he would be able to pull this image out and feel every skin-prickling charge stampeding across his skin. If life were kind, he would be able to simply reach out and take her hand, kiss it, and smile a secret smile.

Savannah turned suddenly and put her arms around him, rested her cheek to his. "Thank you."

"I only held the box."

"You're here. That's what matters." She stared into his eyes, hers narrowed in thought, not adoration. Ade loved this look just as much. Her every expression was honest.

"I'm not the kind of woman who needs a man to be her knight in shining armor," she said. "I've never been romantic, or whimsical. I never was, anyway. Since you arrived on the farm, I find I'm a little of both, and that bothers me."

"Why does it bother you, *corazón*?"

"Because it means I've been living a lie. All my life. I never believed in love conquering all, or that my daughters' spirits stayed with me."

"And now you do?"

"Kind of." She shrugged. "But it's more than that. I am the commander of my own life. I make my own destiny. Or so I thought. You got here and everything turned upside down, because something about you drew me out of myself, even when you were just pretending to be nice."

"That didn't last long. My old ways did not stand a chance against you."

"And you were ready to change," Savannah said. "That's my point. Remember what I said, about you being the exact person I needed to come into my life, just when you did?"

"Yes. And you are that for me as well."

"See? How does that happen? How did we both just *poof* into each other's lives just at that moment we needed to? Falling for you helped me let go of the past. I honestly don't think I ever would have done it without you. It feels...orchestrated. My heart is wrestling with my brain these days. I'm trying to find logical reasons for things happening to me, and all I can come up with is love. For you. For them. It's confusing and wonderful and completely frustrating. But I guess I'm stuck with being a whimsical romantic. And it's all your fault."

"I would love to take the blame." He kissed her. "With all my heart, but there is another way of looking at it that might appease your logical brain, and you've already said it yourself, in a way."

"I did?"

"I was ready to change," he said. "And so were you. You were able to fall in love with me because you were ready to let go of the past. There have been dozens of men to come and go from your life, *corazón*. You were not ready for any of them to have an effect on you. When I arrived, you were."

Savannah studied him, brow furrowed adorably. "I'm not buying it," she said. "Not completely."

"You can't say I didn't try. I, for one, believe in the power of love, and that love doesn't end when life does. I forgot, for a little while. I remembered because of you."

"And because Anita destroyed your life in Boston."

Cold water in the face, dripping down his spine, trickling down his legs to pool at his feet. Ade tried not to shudder, but he did. "That too," he said. "I'd like to think I'd have come to my senses before I was too far gone."

"I'm sorry." Savannah took his face in her hands and kissed him. She smoothed the hair from his face. "I kind of hit you over the head with that, didn't I?"

"A little bit, yes."

"It's never far from my mind." Now a tear did fall. "I'm going to miss you."

"It will only be for a few days. I will call."

"I don't want you to call," she said. "Go to Boston. Do what you need to do and come home. And if you don't come back...if you don't come back..."

"I will be back, Savannah."

Tires on gravel. Headlights blinding, the delivery boy pulled up the drive.

"I'll get the food," she said. "You go set the table."

"Savannah, I—"

"No, really. I'm sorry, love. I should not have brought it up. We only have a couple of days left. Let's not waste them talking about things we can't resolve, okay?"

"Okay," he said as she hurried away.

In the kitchen, Ade took out plates and cups. He dug chopsticks, still in their paper wrappers, out of the silverware drawer. *Love*, she had said. Not sugar. Not Ade. *Love*. Something else to store away in the folds of his brain, to take out when he was old and withered.

"My mouth is already watering." She came through the screen door carrying the food. "What did you order that smells so dang good?"

Ade took the box from her, set it on the table with one hand and pulled her into his arms with the other. He kissed her long and he kissed her hard. He lifted the all-too-easy dress from her body. Carrying her to the couch, he gave her no opportunity to protest, even if she would, which she did not. He made love to her as if it were the first time, the last time, the only time. While the food cooled. While the crickets sang. And another memory embedded itself alongside all the others he would cherish the rest of his life.

* * * *

I know I shouldn't watch. It's indecent. But they don't know I'm here. I need something to wash my own experience out of my head, right? Something beautiful and loving and satisfying. I really hate remembering so clearly. I was right, what I thought. The only way to stop now is to move on. It's pulling me toward...something. Something better than Nowheresville.

Well, I've stuck around this long already, I'll stick around just a little longer. I want to see how things work out with Savvy and Ricky Ricardo. It's almost the Hunter's Moon. That I feel too, like it's part of me. And maybe, just maybe, I have a bit more mischief up my sleeve.

Chapter 23

dazzling shapes

"You could have been in the delivery room."

He'd gotten the call as he was preparing to leave for Boston on the morning of September 19th. Anita was already in the hospital. In labor. The baby, apparently, had a mind of his own, and he wanted to be delivered rather than extricated. Already, a Durst.

Anita sat upright in bed, beautiful even after delivering a baby. More so, if possible, for the lack of makeup and uncoiffed hair. Summer tanned and always fit, it was hard to believe she'd just pushed the perfectly formed, seven-pound bundle in Ade's arms into the world.

"By the time I got here," he answered, "he was already born."

"Four hours, start to finish." She winked. "Not bad for a first timer. If I'd known how easy it was going to be, I'd never have planned the C-section."

"Surgery requires a much longer recovery time. You're lucky your son had a better idea."

"Our son," Anita corrected him. "Gideon."

"Gideon? That's his name?"

"He looks like a Gideon, don't you think?"

Ade gazed down at the perfect little boy. His heart swelled. "Gideon is a good name."

"His surname is Durst for the time being," Anita said. "We can have that changed later."

"If there is need."

"Come on, Ade." Anita sneered. That, at least, had not changed. "You're already in love with him. I know I am. Don't deny it. He's your son."

*I want him to be. You have no idea, you treacherous...*But even in thought he couldn't continue. She had been treacherous. Greedy. Self-serving. Cold. Calculating. But Ade wasn't the only one who love had changed. It wasn't simply the fact that she naturally delivered her baby after a C-section had been planned, or the lack of primping before he entered the room. There was a depth to Anita he would never have recognized before leaving Boston, before falling in love with Savannah. But he recognized it, was certain of it. And still Ade gazed down upon the infant, wishing for this impossibility to be real. "After the DNA test results come back. Not a moment before."

Anita sat higher in the bed, adjusted her non-issue dressing gown. "About that."

"You can't deny me a DNA test. I've already been to the lab and given—"

"Settle down, *guapo*—"

"Don't call me that."

"You used to like it." Anita shrugged stiffly. "They already took a swab from Gideon, too. But..."

"But what? Don't play games with me, Anita. I'm done with them."

"So I see." She deflated with a deep, slightly artificial sigh. "Listen, you know me, Ade. I'm not going down without a fight. We can make this easy, or we can make this hard. Without a sample of my DNA, which I am not legally bound to give, the test results are harder, take longer. I will give that sample if you stay here in Boston for one week. With me and Gideon. After that, I'll let them swab me or do whatever it is they do, and you'll have your results in a couple of days. What's a week or so in the grand scheme of things?"

Ade rose to his feet. He placed the baby into the bassinette beside Anita's bed and went to the window. Her certainty felt less confident than it had the last time he saw her. Had the baby been born with dark hair or even a single feature belonging even marginally to Ade, she might have simply given him the DNA sample. Gideon's dusting of blond hair and already-dimpled cheeks were all his mother's. Ade was no fool. She asked for the week in no doubt that he would fall in love with the child, with her, with Boston and his old, prosperous life all over again. Of this, Ade only feared the first. And yet the week she asked for would give him the opportunity to see if he could sacrifice his heart for the child, or the child for his heart, should Gideon turn out to be his son. "All right, Anita. One week."

"Thank you, Ade."

The catch in her voice turned him to face her. Vulnerable. Truly vulnerable. Anita smiled and pressed the nurse's station button. "I'm ready to go home," she said. "Please send someone in to assist me."

"What are you doing?"

"Do you really think I'm staying here when I have a nursing staff at home waiting for me? I only had Gideon here because I thought he was going to be a C-section. Now help me up. We'll be home within the hour."

* * * *

Savannah tapped out of the call, slipped her smartphone into the pocket of her jeans. She would not cry. She would not feel sorry for herself. It was only a week longer than anticipated. Maybe two. He hadn't even needed to call and let her know. She'd told him not to. But he did, and he apologized, and he assured her he'd be home as soon as the week was up.

If only his voice had not caught. If only she'd not heard the sorrow in it.

"Was that Ade?" Benny came up into the kitchen of the old Weller house, a box of tomatoes in her arms.

Savannah took it and set it onto the counter. "He's going to be gone longer than anticipated. Anita refused the DNA test."

"She didn't."

"Yes, she did."

"Then she knows the baby isn't his. She's trying to suck him back in."

"I'm sure she is, sugar, but that doesn't mean Ade's not the father. I can't really blame her for trying."

"I guess, but—"

"What butt? Chicken butt," Savannah snapped Auntie Bea's old southern saw. "Let's just get the rest of the tomatoes and bring them up to the house. The others will be here any minute."

They made several trips back and forth from Savannah's old pickup, carrying bushel baskets of tomatoes. Before they finished, Johanna arrived with Nina and Tabitha in tow, as well as Finn and Valentine.

"Where are the twins?" Benny asked as they greeted one another.

"Charlie and Gunner will bring Tony and Millie along later," she answered. "They're all working in the bakery with Caleb today."

"Caleb will be crazy person before he closes the store." Tabitha chuckled. "I tell you this. Is true. He is terrorist of his bakery."

"Terror—oh." Johanna laughed. "Territorial, I think you mean."

Tabitha shrugged. "What it is, I don't know. But he is it. They make him crazy. Especially the twins. They fight, aye!"

"Not going to argue with you on that one." Johanna handed a sleeping Finn to Savannah. "Take him, will you? I have to pee."

Bouncing the baby in her arms, Savannah watched Benny, Nina and Tabitha hand bushel-baskets and boxes up the steps. Emmaline arrived with Julietta, Emma joining the haul line. The job was done before Johanna came back from the bathroom.

"Alrighty then," Emma called over the noise. "Tabitha, take the kids to the playroom. Your ten bucks an hour starts now."

"You said fifteen."

"Did I? Jules? Benny? Johanna?"

"For watching all these babies, she should get twenty." Julietta handed over baby Julian who was, for the first time Savannah could remember, awake.

"Deal." Tabitha beamed. She spit in her hand and held it out to Julietta, who did the same and took it without wincing.

"Come, Valentini." Tabitha held her hand out to the toddler. "You be my helper-girl."

"Audrey's sleeping, Benny called after her. "I'll bring her up when she wakes."

Johanna was already busy washing tomatoes, so Savannah followed Tabitha to the playroom with Finn in her arms. She put him gently onto the blanket on the floor without waking him. "How are you going to watch all of them?"

"Is a room already baby-safe, no? I have watched more for less, in an overgrown parking lot they called a park in Greece. Only Americans would have such a room in their house."

"Not all Americans. I didn't have one. This used to be Dan's apartment, before he and Benny got married. They just converted it. I think they plan on having a few more."

"You have children?"

Savannah's heart pinched just a little. "I did. Two little girls. Twins. They died a long time ago."

"I am very sorry, Savvy. That must have been very sad for you."

"It was." She squeezed the girl's shoulder, tried to smile reassuringly. "If you need anything, sugar, just shout."

Starting back to the kitchen where the noise was already more laughter than cooking, her stitching heart eased. It would never not hurt, but it was getting easier to talk about them, getting easier to open up in general. She'd even told Benny about Ade and Anita on the day he left, after her friend found her crying at her desk. By the end of the workday, Johanna had shown up and the three of them had tea and a good cry over life events they'd endured. No one was without their tragedy, Savannah was learning. It was what one did after that mattered most.

Johanna and Emmaline, Julietta and Nina and Benny, all stood with their backs to her as she entered the kitchen. They already had an assembly line going. Washing, coring, slicing tomatoes, putting them into the pot to blanch before skinning them and putting them into jars. Later, Emma was going to teach them all how to make fresh tomato sauce. By the time the men got there, the house would smell like D'Angelo's. Better, because they'd done it all themselves.

Wrapping her arms about herself, Savannah stayed in the doorway and watched, just for a moment. These women. These friends. Their husbands and children. She thought she loved them before, when secrets kept her at arm's length. What she felt now bubbled up like pop-candy in soda, left her feeling light and giddy inside. She'd lost her parents, her daughters, her home, watched the man she loved become a monster. She lost Auntie Bea. She could well lose Ade too.

But you'll be just fine, sugarbeet. Auntie Bea's voice came as clear as if she were sitting upon Savannah's shoulder, as she always would. Auntie Bea, and all her beloved dead. "Move over." She hip-checked Benny and picked up a knife. "Show me what to do."

"Quarters for the small ones," Benny said. "For the big ones, eighths."

She was better than fine. Savannah was truly happy. She had always said she was in charge of her own destiny. Now she believed it. Her future would be what she made it, and Savannah Callowell was going to make it a good one.

* * * *

September ended. After that first call, Savannah didn't answer her phone when she saw Ade's number come up, instead listening to his voice-mail messages in bed at night, when missing him was the worst. The phone calls came fewer and farther between, his messages shorter. He told her he loved her, that he understood why she wasn't answering his calls, and that he loved her even more for it. After a week in Boston, Anita had consented to the DNA test, the results of which were due back on October 3rd at the latest.

It was October 2nd. He had not called in four days. Savannah picked up her phone countless times, her finger poised to tap in his number, but she always slid it back into her pocket. She had set him free, with all the love in her heart. He had to come back on his own, or not at all.

Out in the pumpkin field with Edgardo and Raul, inspecting the damage done by squash-bugs, Savannah barely heard what either of them were saying. Something about boards between the rows and dusting the plants with fossils. Savannah okayed their plan, hoping it was something Ade would approve of, and then teared up at the thought that maybe it wouldn't matter at all if he would object or not.

"Is okay, Savvy." Edgardo patted her shoulder. "Ade come back. He love you."

"Don't mind me." She sniffed. "Now, tell me about more about the fossils you want to dust the pumpkins with."

"Not fossils." Raul laughed. "Di-o-tom-a-ceous earth. You know this word?"

"Oh, diatomaceous earth. Yes. I do. And how's that going to help?"

"Bugs no like it. Bad." Raul stuck out his tongue. "Make them run away."

"But it won't hurt the plants or anything."

"Only the bugs. We try, yes?"

"Yes. Let's do it. Can you get the stuff you need at—"

The familiar sound of the coot chugging along took the words from Savannah's mouth. Aside from herself, Edgardo and Raul, there was only one person who knew how to drive it. She saw the dust it kicked up before she saw the vehicle itself, or the man driving it.

Savannah wouldn't run, but she couldn't keep her feet from moving toward him. Her heart pounded painfully. Joyfully. Ade waved, cut the engine and hopped out, still dressed in clothes meant for a Boston museum, not her farm. He didn't come toward her. Savannah stopped in her tracks.

"I've missed you," he said first.

"I missed you too." She took a step closer. "Just tell me, Ade. Just tell me and get it over with."

Ade crossed his arms over his chest. Leaning against the coot, he squinted in the sunlight. "There is so much to tell. I'm not sure where to start. I discovered many things in Boston."

"Like?"

"Like even Anita Durst is capable of change. I always admired her mind, her beauty, even her cunning. I suppose I should not say having a child actually changed her, but it did…alter her."

"That's…good?"

"It is good. For Gideon's sake."

"Gideon? That's the baby's name?"

"Gideon Durst, yes." Ade pushed off the coot, closed the ground between them. He took her hands in his and kissed them. "Before I say anything more, I must tell you the most important thing I learned, and the only reason I agreed to stay in Boston to begin with."

"All right. I'm listening."

"I had to see if I could, Savannah. Forgive me, but I did not know if I could sacrifice my child for my heart. I had to find out, before any results came back, and I came to the conclusion that no, I could not."

"I...I see."

"No, *corazón*, you don't. I could not sacrifice my child for my heart, but neither could I sacrifice my heart for him." He pulled her into his arms. "What sort of example would that be to set? To teach him that love was not worth fighting for. That it was ever all right to sacrifice it. I told this to Anita, before she provided her DNA. I made sure she understood, no matter the results, I would not stay."

"Then, Gideon is—"

"Not mine."

Savannah caught her breath. Her head lightened. "Oh, love. I'm so sorry."

"It was devastating," Ade said, "but not unexpected. And perhaps I had a selfish reason for staying in Boston all this time. I got to see what it felt like, for a little while, to be a father."

"And now you know."

"And now I know."

Savannah took him into her arms. She swayed back and forth. "I wanted it to be true, for you," she said, "even if it meant losing you."

"*Corazón.*" He kissed her. "It has been so difficult, being without you, even if it was the only way to get to the truth in my own heart. The results are, after all, for the best. Anita and I can go our separate ways. She will be a good mother. Not the kind that bakes cookies and bandages skinned knees, but Gideon will be loved. Ferociously."

"How did she react to the results?"

"Not well," he said. "At first. She was so certain, and she wanted her happily-enough-ever-after. Anita is used to getting what she wants. But then, the strangest thing happened."

"Oh?"

"She let me go. She gave me back my things, unfroze my bank account, and even offered me a position at the university. Not the same offer she made when she was coaxing me back, but a respectable one."

"Wow. And you..."

"Turned it down, of course. My place is here. With you. If you still want me."

Savannah pinched him.

"Ouch!"

"Was that a real question, Dr. Adelmo Gallegos."

"You forgot my middle name. It's not nearly as intimidating without the middle name."

"I don't know your middle name."

"Raul."

"Dr. Adelmo Raul Gallegos."

"And the confirmation name."

Savannah sighed. "And that is?"

"Cristobal."

"All right Dr. Adelmo Raul Crisotbal Gallegos." Savannah draped her arms around his neck. "What do we do now?"

Ade kissed her nose, each cheek, her lips. "We harvest the pumpkins, give Taytay and Tío a grand sendoff, and settle in for a long winter, just you, me, and the sheep."

"And the tomatoes."

"Tomatoes?"

"Jars and jars of tomatoes." Savannah laughed softly. The contentment found before he left settled around her again, dug in roots. She slipped out of his arms, took his hand and hauled. "Come on. I'll show you, when we get home."

* * * *

Benny had still been in the farmstand when Ade arrived. It was she who told him where to find Savannah. Of course, by the time he and she, Taytay and Tío got back to the house on the coot, Benny had already called the sisters Coco in anticipation of celebrating his return.

"I had no doubts whatsoever," Benny whispered, hugging him tight. "I knew you'd be back."

"Yes, I know. You are sensitive to such things."

"Are you going to tease me too?"

"No," he said. "I am going to thank you for having faith in me."

"No need for—"

"Make way! This cake is heavy." Johanna backed through the door, pushing them out of the way to set the massive cake onto the counter. "Tony is going to kill me. This cake was supposed to go to D'Angelo's. I told him I dropped it. Don't squeal on me. This just seemed like a better occasion to reveal my newest creation."

"What is it?" Ade swiped a finger through the icing near the bottom, stuck it in his mouth before Johanna could slap it away. "Coffee? No, chocolate?"

"Mocha," Johanna corrected. "Mocha frosting, chocolate cake soaked in espresso, and chocolate filling. Mochalicious Dreams. What do you think?"

"I think the name is as hokey as all your others," Benny cut in. "But it sounds amazing."

The Coco sisters arrived one after another, carrying supper offerings. Even Nina was there, having promised Tabitha the weekend in Bitterly that had absolutely, positively nothing whatsoever to do with Caleb's first weekend home since school started. The husbands and children stayed outside where it was still light enough to toss a football. After setting up tables and chairs, of course. Soon, Emma and Johanna were shooing everyone still lingering out of Savannah's kitchen, including Savannah herself.

"I'm going to fetch your father and uncle," Savannah said as she darted past him. Ade grasped her hand, halting her. Such chaos. Such glorious chaos. And he had a lifetime of it to look forward to. He hoped. "I love you."

"To the moon and back, love." Savannah threw herself into his arms, kissed him, and darted away. Skipped, was more like it.

Ade's heart swelled. During the time he'd spent with Anita and Gideon, he was forced to realize just what he was sacrificing. The life he'd worked for. A beautiful, intelligent, powerful woman who could give him the world. Gideon might not be his blood, but he could love him, be his father.

Anita had shown him just enough of what he could have to entice, always implying how easy it would be to slip into that life, to play the part she'd set up for him. Because love had changed them both, they could even be happy.

But they were lies. Every one of them. The man he'd become in Bitterly couldn't survive life within those lies, most especially the one that suggested he could ever be happy without Savannah. He'd said a final good-bye to Anita and Gideon, to Boston, the place of his dreaming. The farther behind he left it all, the less any of it seemed to matter. That was the way of such things. They were tenacious because their bonds were so flimsy.

"Hey." A nudge, and a kind hand on his shoulder. Benny smiled down on him. "You okay?"

"I'm fine. Why?"

"I've never seen you cry before."

"I'm not crying."

"Then what's that?" She pointed to his cheek. Ade lifted a hand, wiped the trickle of wetness away.

Benny smiled. "See?"

Ade let go a long breath, wiped his cheeks dry. "It has been an emotional day. And it's good to be home."

"Always." Benny wiped her own tear from her cheek, her wedding rings glinting in the setting sunshine. Ade took her hand, turned it this way and that, dotting his shirt and hers with crystalline light. "I never noticed your rings before. They're quite remarkable."

"My husband might seem like a meat and potatoes, handyman kind of guy, but he has a poet's soul. They're fire opals, because I set fire to his life. The engagement ring came after the wedding band. We kind of did it backwards. Baby first, then wedding, then engagement."

"Beautiful. Where did he get them?"

"Here in town, I think. There's a jeweler on the green who specializes in estate…hey." Benny grabbed his arm, hauled him farther away from the crowd. "What are you thinking?"

Ade grinned. "Exactly what you think I am. Will you help me?"

"Absolutely." Benny bounced on the balls of her feet, clapping like a little girl with a huge secret. "When can we go? Tomorrow? Can we go tomorrow? Oh, wait. I think they're closed tomorrow."

"Before my father and uncle leave," he said. "Let them go home happy, and with news for my mother."

"That gives us time. We'll have to be sneaky."

"What makes me think you'll have a plan before supper is on?"

Benny hooked her arm through his, squeezed it. "Because I already do."

* * * *

A crash of thunder woke Savannah in the early hours of the morning. Blinking away slumber and dreams, she came up on her elbows. Ade slept peacefully beside her, flat on his stomach and arms splayed. She could barely see his face for the hair flopped over it. Wild. That's how he looked. Wild and handsome and extraordinarily hers.

She settled back into her pillows, lifting her left hand to the scant morning light. She didn't need sunshine to see the ring on her finger, to marvel at the fiery heart of the solitaire ruby set in gold. It blazed even by moonlight. She imagined using it as a torch should all the light go out of the world.

"*Mi diosa fuego*," Ade had said, slipping it onto her finger during dinner at D'Angelo's the night prior. "I am forever yours. Will you be forever mine?"

The whole restaurant had waited, breath held. How did they all know? How did anyone know anything in Bitterly? Because secrets simply didn't stay silent, and Benny had been involved. Savannah learned this only after she'd said yes and the cheering died down. After Johanna emerged from the back with a cake, trailed by her sisters, their husbands, Edgardo and Raul. After the impromptu that wasn't exactly impromptu engagement party erupted, and after all went home. Benny had hugged her then, tears streaming down her cheeks.

"I hope you don't mind. It's just all so…so magical. Isn't it?"

"It is, Benny. Of course I don't mind. Thank you."

At home that night, she and Ade planned. Not a wedding, there was time for that, but a future. The homestead in the woods. The renovations to be made. What they would do with the farmhouse once they'd moved up there. And then they'd made slow and passionate love, their own celebration of the forever they promised. Savannah's body lit with the memory of it all. She snuggled closer to him, kissed his shoulder.

Another rumble of thunder. Wind whistled through the window screen. The cold had come early. Only halfway through the October and already they could only keep the window open a crack. Rain pelted the glass, came in through the bit that was open. Savannah got carefully out of bed to close it, stopping short with her hands on the sash.

A teenaged girl stood in her yard, looking up. She was tall and blonde and strangely dry, despite the sudden downpour. No car she might have just stepped out of. Unfamiliar. She was certainly not one of Savannah's hires. Leaning back to throw open the window, to call out to the girl to come in out of the rain, Savannah startled still when the girl waved once, and vanished.

She hurried quietly down the stairs. She found no one at the kitchen door. No one in the yard where the girl had been. No one walking away down the drive. Savannah opened the door to get a better look, and saw the shoes.

Her clogs, the ones Ade brought her from Boston, sat in the rain on the stoop. She bent to retrieve them. They were full of pebbles. In one clog a white feather. In the other, a black one.

Bringing them inside, Savannah was careful not to spill the pebbles. Eleven years in Bitterly, she knew about the tradition of putting shoes outside on the night of the Hunter's Moon, but Savannah had not put her clogs on the stoop. Not last night or any other. But the feathers…

She grabbed a mason jar, once filled with summer tomatoes, from the drying rack on the counter. The pebbles were water-washed and smooth, most likely from the river. The white feather was like down. The black one, sleek. Savannah put them into the jar, pressed them against the sides, and poured the pebbles carefully in around them. Taking the jar into the parlor, she tried to keep her hands from trembling. She wasn't frightened or sad or even skeptical. Savannah was hopeful. She set the jar onto the mantel, and took a step back.

Closing her eyes, she breathed in. And out. Wings. Guardians. Broken souls. Who was she to say such things were impossible? Maybe some autumnal spirit called out by the Hunter's Moon had truly filled her clogs with pebbles. Maybe her girls added the feathers. Maybe there was something as impossible as magic left in the world. Had someone told her last July the Fourth that she'd be blissfully in love, engaged and ethereally happy, she would have said that was impossible too. Yet here she was.

Arms wrapped around her waist, Savannah let joy tremble through her. She had no answers, and she was fine with that. From sorrow came joy, came sorrow again. That was life. Messy, chaotic and infinitely wonderful.

Turning away from the jar, Savannah started back for the stairs. The warmth of her bed and Ade's body beckoned. There were still a couple of dawn hours left to sleep away. Or not sleep at all. She didn't have to decide until she got there, but she was pretty certain she was wide awake.

Be sure not to miss book one in Terri-Lynne's Bitterly Suite Romance

SEEKING CAROLINA

A Bitterly Suite Romance

Her beloved grandmother's funeral has brought Johanna Coco home again to Bitterly, Connecticut—only to confront Charlie McCallan, the high school sweetheart who married another, despite his pretty promises. Now divorced and as devastatingly handsome as ever, Charlie seems like a man to lean on as she and her sisters grapple with their grief—as well as the mystery of the family's missing matriarch, Carolina. But Johanna's heart is haunted not only by her own demons, but the pain of Charlie's betrayal…

Now that Johanna is back, Charlie is determined to make things right. But first he needs to prove to her that the past is past—and they can overcome it, if she'll let him explain. It's no easy task when he's up against the ghosts lingering in her life, trying to convince her that happily-ever-after is not in the cards for any of the catastrophe-prone Coco sisters—least of all Johanna. But her fearless first love is ready to do whatever it takes, demons be damned.

A Lyrical Shine novel on sale now!

Learn more about Terri-Lynne DeFino at
http://www.kensingtonbooks.com/author.aspx/31624

Chapter 1

Snowflakes do not fall; they dance. Will-o'-the-wisps in Les Sylphides. White on black. The poet wind scatters them and they twirl amid the tombstones—stately guardians dressed in gray—and fall, at last, to sleep.

Disturbing that slumber is a sacrilege, I know, she cannot not bring herself to commit.

No matter the cold.

No matter the dark.

No matter she is trespassing after cemetery hours. She will stand perfectly still until she is another guardian among the stones.

* * * *

Rough hands chafed warmth back into Johanna's hands, her arms.

"Are you crazy?"

The masculine voice mumbled words she did not care to decipher. He was right. She was crazy. Crazy as a loon. Mad as a hatter, as a Cheshire Cat. Crazy as...

She closed her eyes, unwilling to finish the unkind, if accurate, thought. Trembling, drifting, all she wanted was to sleep.

"Oh, no you don't. Get up. Walk." He jammed a shoulder under her armpit and hefted her upright.

Johanna's feet moved of their own accord, half-dragged, but they moved. "Where am I?"

"Bitterly Cemetery," the man answered, "doing your best impression of a snowman...woman."

Oh. Right. Farts. She pushed feebly out of his arms. Her knees buckled, and she was grateful he hadn't let go. "I can walk on my own."

"I'm sure you can. Normally. Come on. I've got the heat blasting in the truck. Get warm, and I'll take you home."

Johanna let him help her. Bitterly, Connecticut was way too nice a town to allow miscreants. Everyone knew everyone and had most of their lives. This was no one to fear, even if he did frequent cemeteries after hours rescuing would-be popsicles from certain frostbite.

Her head began to clear. Memory edged around her trembling, the cold, her grief. The man scooted her into the truck, closed the door and came around the driver's side. "There's coffee in the thermos next to you."

"No, thanks."

His cell blipped and he turned a shoulder to answer it. Charlotte someone. She apparently wanted pizza.

Johanna tuned out, instead warming her hands in the hot air blasting from the heating vent. She thawed. Her trembling eased. Two days trying to get there in time, and she'd failed. Again. Was there no end to the ways she would fail her grandmother? Her sisters? She fought the tears rising up like rebels and failed at that too.

He handed her a crumpled tissue.

She snatched it from his hand, relieved it was only crumpled. "Thanks."

"No problem."

"I wasn't trying to freeze to death or anything. I was just paying my respects. I missed the funeral."

"I know."

"I'm sure the whole town knows." Johanna yanked off her hat, tried to smooth down static curls. "Well, the snow isn't my fault. The whole Northeast is covered. My car wouldn't make it and I couldn't rent an SUV and I'm damn sure not going to attempt these roads in anything else, so I had to take a train and then no one answered their cell phones. I had to walk from—"

"Jo."

She startled silent. Squinted. He pulled off his snowcap and a flop of auburn hair tumbled out. His beard lit a brighter copper than his hair. Eyelashes and brows arched over hazel eyes. A face she knew, despite the years. Johanna's heart stuttered. "Charlie McCallan? For real?"

"Took you long enough."

"You…you don't look…" She pulled at his beard. "You've grown up."

"It happens to boys when they turn into men." He laughed. "They get hairy."

He wore thick workman's overalls and a down jacket, but he was obviously and most certainly no longer the bony kid she'd once shoved into the lake.

She flexed thawing fingers. "It has been way too long, Charlie."

"I thought maybe you'd show up for the twentieth reunion."

"Twentieth?" Johanna slumped. "Really?"

"Last Thanksgiving. You should have come. Fifty-eight of the…what was our class? Ninety-something?" He shrugged. "Whatever it was, we had a good turn out."

"I don't remember getting the invite."

An eyebrow lifted, but Charlie only shifted into gear.

Tires crunched in the snow. The packing sound reminded Johanna of riding with Poppy in his ancient plow, making safe the streets of Bitterly through the long, snowy winters. Outside the warm cab, in this new winter, flurries drifted.

Charlie-freaking-McCallan. Of all people.

She had known him as unavoidably as she did everyone else in Bitterly—the ghost-white kid whose parents were caretakers of the town cemetery. They'd grown up together, largely circled in and out of friendship, until the summer they were seventeen.

The heat in the truck was becoming oppressive. Johanna unzipped her coat. "Working the graveyard shift? Pun very much intended."

"I don't really work the cemetery anymore. Mom and Dad retired, turned it over to the town. I fill in once in a while, doing maintenance."

"No one knows this place better than you." Johanna blew her nose. "And Gina? How's she?"

"In Florida with the yoga instructor she left me for."

Again her heart stuttered. Johanna loosened her scarf. Gina had been nice enough, pretty enough, and got pregnant senior year and ruined everything.

"And your…daughter, wasn't it? You had a few more, too."

"Charlotte," he answered. "She's good. I've got five kids. Two daughters and three sons."

"That's a lot of kids."

He chuckled, his eyes straying from the road to look her way. "It is. They also require a lot of pizza. Mind if I stop on our way past?"

"Oh, sure. No problem. Thanks, by the way, for…"

"No worries."

They drove in silence, the ineffectual wipers slapping a rhythm to go with the crunching tires. He pulled into town following the same trek

Johanna had made from the train station. She hadn't earlier noticed the faux-gaslights wrapped in pine and holly, the trees lining the Green, the candles in every window. Neither had she absorbed the olive oil boutique or the wine bar on either side of the pizza place that had once been the only restaurant in town. She'd been too furious that none of her sisters picked up her call. Her numerous calls.

Johanna sighed. The window fogged. Charlie was nice enough not to ask what was wrong. He could guess, and he'd probably be right. He pulled up in front of D'Angelo's Pizzeria, and left the truck running.

"I'll be right back."

She waved him away. The waft of cold air he let in made her shiver, but it felt good. Bracing. Clarifying. She opened the window and let the falling snow hit her face. Remembering. Johanna hated to remember. It was her number one reason for staying far away from Bitterly. The door opened and reason number two slipped into the truck, stretching nearly across her to set the pizzas down on the back seat. His jacket fell open. He was definitely not the skinny kid she'd pushed into the lake. He smelled good. Pizza and something musky.

"Sorry. They're hot."

She closed the window. "Does your father-in-law still make the pizza?"

"No. Gina's parents sold the place and moved to Florida about six years ago. But the pizza's still good."

"Smells it."

"You want to—"

"No, no. Thanks. I have to get home. My sisters will be waiting."

"Okay." He put the truck in drive, pulled carefully back onto the road. "It was good to see Nina. I see Emma and Julietta around town, but I don't think I've seen Nina, well, probably since I've seen you. Your grandfather's funeral, right?"

Eight years. Had it really been so long?

"I suppose so," she said. Eight years since she'd seen Gram and Emma in the flesh. She had nephews she'd never met. Cyberworld made staying in touch so easy. Video-chatting, instant messaging, texting. Nina lived in Manhattan. They met now and again for dinner or a show. Julietta had come down to Cape May a few times to help out with the bakery. But Gram…?

Tears again. She hated them, fell victim to them more often than she could count and they never did her any good. Ever.

"Hey, it's all right."

"No. It's not. But thanks."

Charlie fell silent.

Johanna blew her nose on the now-shredded and soggy tissue he'd given her for all the good it did. Covertly wiping her fingers on the inside of her coat pocket, she hoped his kindness held out and he'd pretend not to notice. "Town sure has changed a lot." She cleared the frog in her throat. "I never thought it would happen."

"It's all because of the expansion up at the ski slope. Slopes, now. Five different trails. Remember how rinky-dink it was? Bonfire in an old garbage can? Bales of hay as stops at the bottom of the hill?"

"And the tow rope that shredded our gloves." Johanna laughed. "I vaguely remember one of my sisters telling me about the changes."

Charlie paused at the red blinking light at the edge of town. "Now it's the Berkshire Lodge with ski lifts and instructors and a lodge where you can buy a seven-dollar hot cocoa. Tourists love it. After the expansion, the whole town started to surge. Remember the lake?"

How could I ever forget? "Yes."

"It's a country club now, one most residents in Bitterly can't afford to join. Pisses me off I can't bring my kids to swim there."

He drove out of town and into the farmland where the house Johanna and her sisters grew up in straddled the county line. Snow-humped fields and white woods preserved the country feel of her childhood, even while quaint road signs boasting names like Country Farm Lane and Flirtation Street indicated new developments set back from the road. There had been nothing out here when she and Nina first arrived at the house on County Line Road. She'd been just shy of four, and now remembered little of the children's home in Massachusetts, or adjusting to the doting grandparents she came quickly to love. But Johanna remembered New Hampshire. Mommy. Daddy. When there were so few memories to hold on to, it wasn't hard to hold them tight.

"Don't go into the driveway," she said as he was about to do so. "It doesn't look like it's been shoveled."

"My truck can make it."

"No." She grasped his arm, gave it a friendly squeeze. The windows in the house were dark, all but the one around back. The square of light on the snow peeked around the corner, a crooked finger beckoning. She imagined her sisters gathered at the table in the kitchen. Drinking tea. Or wine. Trying not to speak unkindly of their errant sister who missed Gram's funeral.

"Thank you, Charlie." Johanna looked for the door handle. "I don't know what I'd have done if you didn't show up."

Charlie reached across her, flicked the perfectly integrated handle she wouldn't have found in a thousand years of trying. The door swung open, letting the cold swirl in.

"Lucky for me I did."

"For you?"

He smiled. "You'd have come and gone before I ever knew you were in town. I'm glad I got to see you, Jo."

"Same…same here." Johanna stepped out into knee-deep snow. "I'll be in town a few days. Maybe I'll see you around."

"Kind of hard to avoid it, in Bitterly. Get inside before you freeze again."

Johanna scooped up a handful of snow and tossed it at him before slamming the door. He laughed and waved and pulled away. The light was still on in the interior of his truck, alighting on his hair like sunshine on a copper kettle. She watched until the curve in the road took his taillights from sight.

"It really is good to see you, Charlie," she said to the falling snow. Whether she was pushing him into the lake or he was chasing her with a dobsonfly, they'd been friends first. Johanna turned aside those thoughts, and to the house instead.

Home.

The word sent disparate shivers into her core. White with black shutters and a red door. The farmhouse porch, empty now but for the ring of firewood between the front windows, usually boasted a number of rocking chairs and porch swings. She and her sisters never complained about summer assigned reading. Afternoons spent on the porch, Gram's lemonade popsicles melting down their fingers, was one of their joys of summer.

Wrapping her scarf more closely around her neck, Johanna trudged down the driveway and around to the back of the house. She hugged the wall, peeking through the window from the shadows, her heart hammering. There they were, just as she imagined them, sitting around the table as they had so many times during those years they all lived happily there.

Nina, a Wagner dream of Valkyries—blond and bold and brutal, her hands wrapped around a teacup as if she would crush it, or hold it together.

Emmaline, who, like Johanna, had inherited dark curls and cocoa-brown eyes from their mother and, unlike Johanna, was spared her frenzy.

And Julietta.

Johanna's brimming eyes overflowed.

Awkward even when sitting still, as blond as Nina without any of her beauty, Julietta was a sprite straight out of a fairy story, all arms and legs and ears. Thick glasses accentuated the enormity of her pale eyes. Perpetually childlike, ridiculously brilliant, Julietta was the one. And they all loved her best.

Johanna wiped her eyes with her scarf, her nose with the back of her hand. She gave up trying to pretend she hadn't been crying, hadn't been frantic and furious and ready to succumb to the madness always looming like tomorrow's shadows. Stumbling to the back door that would be open because the lock had broken when she was fourteen and never been fixed, Johanna Coco went home.

* * * *

The truck slid to a stop at the bottom of the hill. Charlie rested his head to the steering wheel. He breathed deeply, inhaling the aromas of pizza and Johanna. Memory sparked. Summer after junior year. Her body pressed to his. The music, and the crowd, and the sand beneath their feet. She had turned and smiled that earth-shattering smile when he slipped his arms around her waist, pulled her against him so she wouldn't get crushed by the head-bangers moshing outside of the mosh pit. Charlie remembered her leaning into him, her hands holding him in place, the sweetness of her perfume ignited by sweat, and the seemingly inconsequential moment of contact that changed his world.

Headlights approached. He lifted his head. A plow-truck going up the hill stopped. Charlie rolled down his window as the other driver did the same.

"You stuck, Charlie?" Dan Greene, best pal since childhood, leaned an elbow out his window. "Need a tow?"

"Nah, just taking a few minutes peace. The kids are home waiting for their dinner."

"What are you doing way out here?"

Charlie thumbed over his shoulder. "I just dropped Johanna Coco off. I found her in the cemetery."

"At this hour?"

"You know those Coco girls."

"I sure do. Too bad she didn't make it to the funeral."

"She tried. This damn snow—"

"Don't you be cursing my livelihood. This damn snow is taking my sister's kids to the beach this summer. Kind of ironic, huh?"

Their laughter faded into the night. Charlie felt suddenly drained. Tight as he and Dan had always been, he didn't have the words to express his sudden chaos of thoughts. Tapping the side of his truck, he waved and let up on the break.

"Right. See you, Dan."

"See you, Charlie."

The scrape of Dan's plow on the road vanished as Charlie's window went up, trapping the scent of pizza lingering. Johanna's, like the woman herself, did not. Wild as the Coco girls had always been, Johanna was the wildest. She left after high school and seldom returned. For Charlie, that had been a good thing. He glommed every bit of news, every shred of gossip over the years. Her travels. Her pie-in-the-sky business ventures. Lover after temporary lover she brought home to Bitterly, never the same guy two visits running. Seeing her was always hard, harder when he and Gina stopped getting along. Last time, when she returned to Bitterly for her grandfather's funeral, the twins were newborns, Charlotte, Will, and Caleb were still in elementary school and he was still married, happily-enough. That was eight years ago, and now none of those things were true. Johanna was home, for however long, and Charlie was not going to let her escape Bitterly without hearing the words he tried to tell her that summer night on the beach and hadn't stopped thinking since.

Meet the Author

Terri-Lynne DeFino lives in a log cabin in Connecticut, but she's a Jersey girl at heart. Writer, mother, cat wrangler, and self-proclaimed sparkle queen, Terri began writing when she was seven. Though that first story remains locked away in her parents' attic, some of her works include Finder, A Time Never Lived, and Beyond the Gate. Visit her blog at Modestyisforsuckers.com, or contact her at terrilynnedefino@aol.com.

www.ingramcontent.com/pod-product-compliance
Lightning Source LLC
Chambersburg PA
CBHW031418250626
47155CB00004B/1541